Praise for Nancy Kopp's *Final Justice*

"Breakneck pacing and an attention to procedural detail distinguish Kopp's latest. . . . The novel's frenzied pace and constant action help keep the tension high."
—*Publishers Weekly*

"The heroine is a strong woman who doesn't let fear get in her way from doing the right thing . . . an extremely exciting novel [with] a clear social message." —*Midwest Book Review*

"Nancy Kopp's character, attorney Ann Monroe, is the new Perry Mason. May she live a long life."
—Laura Van Wormer

Praise for the previous novels of Nancy Kopp

"An exciting legal thriller . . . the characters are all top-rate." —Painted Rock Reviews

"An admirable portrayal of the moral decisions that many of us may someday have to face . . . a satisfying read . . . will leave you wanting more chapters." —*Mystery News*

"A taut and intriguing thriller that combines the desperation of a hunt for a serial killer with the courtroom dramatics of a high-profile lawsuit."
—*Romantic Times*

"Suspenseful. . . . What sets this book apart . . . is the strong development of the characters."
—*The Capital Times*

ALSO BY NANCY KOPP

Absent Witness
Final Justice

BLIND TRUST

NANCY KOPP

AN ONYX BOOK

ONYX
Published by New American Library, a division of
Penguin Putnam Inc., 375 Hudson Street,
New York, New York 10014, U.S.A.
Penguin Books Ltd, 80 Strand,
London WC2R 0RL, England
Penguin Books Australia Ltd, 250 Camberwell Road,
Camberwell, Victoria 3124, Australia
Penguin Books Canada Ltd, 10 Alcorn Avenue,
Toronto, Ontario, Canada M4V 3B2
Penguin Books (N.Z.) Ltd, Cnr Rosedale and Airborne Roads,
Albany, Auckland 1310, New Zealand

Penguin Books Ltd, Registered Offices:
Harmondsworth, Middlesex, England

First published by Onyx, an imprint of New American Library,
a division of Penguin Putnam Inc.

First Printing, April 2003
10 9 8 7 6 5 4 3 2 1

 REGISTERED TRADEMARK—MARCA REGISTRADA

Printed in the United States of America

PUBLISHER'S NOTE
This is a work of fiction. Names, characters, places, and incidents either
are the product of the author's imagination or are used fictitiously,
and any resemblance to actual persons, living or dead, business
establishments, events, or locales is entirely coincidental.

For Pat Grove
and
Georgia Weis

ACKNOWLEDGMENTS

Lorraine Gelly not only allowed me to name a character in this book after her (and volunteered her dog Pepper as well), she also came up with the snappy title. She was assisted in this endeavor by Lynne and Paul Darner. It is amazing how a leisurely train ride through the bucolic Wisconsin countryside can start the creative juices flowing.

My sincere thanks to all of the other folks who eagerly embraced the idea of being memorialized in print, especially Kathy Flood (whose namesake is probably my favorite character so far), Tom Cane, Mike Hoover and Coleen Kennedy from Wisconsin Court of Appeals District III; and Mike Laskis and Jill Bedner at Foley & Lardner, where I used to practice law. Your collective enthusiasm for this project helped make it a pleasure for me to write.

I invite all my readers to visit www.nancykopp.com for updates on my writing or e-mail me at nkmail@nancykopp.com.

PROLOGUE

Oak Greythorne held up the heavy tumbler and swirled the liquid inside, admiring the bourbon's fine amber color. Bringing the glass up to his nose, he inhaled deeply and felt a slight burning sensation in his nostrils. He greedily swallowed a large mouthful of the liquor and ran his tongue around his lips. God, that tasted good. It had been a while since he had taken a drink. He now realized how much he had missed it.

Greythorne had loved alcohol from the first time he had tasted it as a child. Even though fifty years had passed, he remembered the occasion distinctly. When he was in the third grade at the Latin School of Chicago, his grandfather had allowed him to finish the last few sips of a glass of sherry. The old man had been certain the child would be repulsed by the taste, but he had drunk the deep red liquid as if it had been cherry soda and gravely asked if he might have some more. His grandfather had laughed, pronounced the lad a man of the world and obliged. And so began a lifelong love affair with spirits.

Greythorne leaned back against the heavy, brocade sofa cushion, his mind wandering. The Latin School. That had been so long ago. Where had the time gone? Where had his life gone? At fifty-seven, he was no longer young. He could almost be called elderly, and he didn't like it a bit. His hourglass was running out. He swallowed some more bourbon.

There had been many good times and more bad ones for Oak Greythorne. Disparate images from the past floated through his mind. He saw himself as a student at the University of Chicago. That's when his alcoholic binges had begun in earnest, along with terrible mood swings. Now there were polite names for his numerous maladies—bipolar disorder, manic-depressive, panic attacks. But at that time his behavior had prompted only snickers and whispered comments, "crazy, psycho, loony." People thought Greythorne either did not hear the remarks or did not care what was being said about him. But they had been wrong. The more people made fun of him, the more he sank into depression and the more he tried to lose himself in the bottle.

After graduating from business school, Greythorne had finally sought medical help. A good therapist and prescription drugs had done wonders—for a while. But then he thought he was cured and stopped taking the drugs, and the downward spiral began again. He would eventually hit bottom and return to a medical regimen, but each time he would relapse and each time he would sink a bit lower.

In spite of his afflictions, Greythorne had managed

to build a successful business. But eight years ago he had suffered a complete mental breakdown and was hospitalized for three months. He had never fully recovered. He sold his beloved business and retreated into himself. His plush lakeside condo had turned into a virtual prison.

What a waste, Greythorne thought as he took another large swallow of bourbon. Everyone had always said he was a genius. Who could say what might have been if only he hadn't had to devote so much of his energy to fighting his personal demons?

He might have had a family. He'd been a handsome young man, tall, well built. Women had found him attractive—until they'd discovered his darker side. Then they'd all dumped him and moved on to more stable prospects. All except Janice.

Greythorne's eyes filled with tears as he recalled the great love of his life. Janice had wanted to stick by him, to help him, but he pushed her away, afraid that instead of her being able to lift him up he would pull her down with him into the abyss. What might his life have been like with Janice by his side? He would never know. He began to cry.

After a few moments the tears subsided, but then Greythorne's heart suddenly began to race wildly and he broke out in a cold sweat. Recognizing the familiar symptoms of a panic attack, he reached for the prescription bottle on the table next to the booze. Xanax. The best invention since bourbon. Greythorne opened the bottle and shook out two tablets. He popped them in his mouth and washed them down

3

with the last of the alcohol in his glass. Then he picked up the prescription bottle again and peered inside. His mind was hazy now. The bottle looked almost empty. Hadn't he just gotten a refill last week? What happened to the rest of the pills? Had he really taken so many?

Greythorne sat quietly for a time, waiting for the drug's calming effects to kick in. He did not know how much time had passed but his heart was still pounding madly and the feelings of doom were overwhelming. He remembered the doctor's warning about the possibility of an accidental overdose. He also vaguely remembered the admonition to never take Xanax with alcohol. Yet he was in desperate need of relief. He felt as if he were going to jump out of his skin. One more pill couldn't hurt, could it? His hand reached out for the bottle, then he stopped.

No, better not take more Xanax. Maybe a bit more alcohol would do the trick. He reached for the bourbon bottle, then hesitated.

He knew he shouldn't be drinking. He had been sober for months. He could just hear his AA sponsor chastising him. "Why didn't you call me? We could have gone to a meeting, talked things through."

"Bullshit!" Greythorne snorted. His sponsor was young enough to still be an idealist. What good was talking when you felt like your world was collapsing around you? At times like that, only liquor could ease the pain. So what if this was a major lapse? The hell with it. He would deal with his sponsor's wrath later. Tonight his own needs came first.

"I need a drink. Just one more drink, then I'll stop," Greythorne mumbled. He closed his eyes. His heart was still pounding. It felt like the walls were closing in. "Goddammit, I need a drink!" he howled.

"Here you are, Oak," a deep voice said. Was the voice real or imagined? Greythorne wondered. He couldn't tell. "You look a little stressed," the voice went on. "This will help you mellow out."

Greythorne opened one eye and through a thick haze he saw a full tumbler of bourbon being thrust into his right hand. He closed his hand around it and carefully guided the glass to his lips. He took a big gulp. Ahhh. That was heavenly. That was just what he needed.

"Take these, too," the voice said. Suddenly three more white tablets appeared in Greythorne's hand. He hesitated just for a second, then swallowed the pills and drained the rest of the liquor. Then he closed his eyes.

This was much better. He felt so much calmer now. His mind was going blank. All the bad thoughts were fading. Several minutes passed and his breathing slowed measurably. Then it slowed some more. Then it stopped completely.

"Nighty night, Oak," the voice said. "Rest in peace, you dumb bastard."

CHAPTER 1

"Emma, Louis Brisbane here." The authority in the caller's voice resonated over the phone. "Would you mind coming up to my office? There is a matter I would like to discuss with you."

"Of course," Emma Davis replied at once. "I'll be right there." As the thirty-year-old attorney hung up the phone, her chest felt constricted. Thoughts of doom rushed through her head.

"I must have screwed something up," Emma murmured, pushing her long, curly blond hair behind her ears. She quickly ran through the projects she had worked on in the ten weeks she had been at Franklin & Holland, one of Chicago's largest law firms. She had not handled any unusually complex matters, and she didn't think she had made any glaring errors. In fact, she had received nothing but praise from Tom Cane, her supervising attorney. So why was she being summoned to the office of one of the firm's senior partners? And not just any senior partner. A big, swinging-briefcase-type partner. A management committee member.

The management committee was comprised of six men who governed the entire firm, which included the four hundred lawyers in the main office in Chicago, as well as a dozen satellite offices around the country. Even decades after women began enrolling in law schools, Franklin & Holland remained an old boys club. There were, as yet, no old girls in the firm's top ranks.

A recent *Chicago Tribune* article estimated that Franklin & Holland partners had earned an average of $1.2 million the previous year. Management committee members were said to take home twice that amount. Why would one of these exalted leaders want to talk to lowly associate Emma Davis, who had just arrived after the Chicago giant merged with the Kansas City firm where Emma had worked since graduating from law school five years earlier? She didn't have a clue.

In any case, she couldn't sit there forever speculating on the reason for Brisbane's call. If she didn't hightail it up to his office pronto he was likely to have her fired for insubordination. She had heard that management committee types were prima donnas who expected everyone beneath them in the firm's pecking order to jump when they called. And Emma definitely ranked pretty damn low. She tried to pick up a legal pad and found her hands were shaking. Dammit! She'd better get a grip, or Brisbane would think she had a drinking problem on top of being a lousy attorney.

Have to calm down, Emma thought. She got up from her desk and stood behind her chair. Closing her eyes, she took a deep breath, then slowly let it out. She could feel her tension ease just a bit. She took several more breaths. She was ready to face whatever Brisbane wanted to throw at her. With a slight smile, Emma opened her eyes, caught a glimpse out of her thirty-fourth-floor window and immediately found herself fighting back a massive wave of nausea.

Damn! Since moving to Chicago, Emma thought she had made some progress in trying to overcome her lifelong fear of heights, but obviously she still had a way to go. Riding in elevators did not bother her—unless they were those glass capsules that crawled up the outside of buildings—nor did she mind flying. But get her anywhere near a window that was higher than ten stories and she would immediately feel the start of a panic attack.

So what the hell was she doing working in a Chicago Loop building that was roughly the height of Mount Everest? Emma chastised herself. She had thought it would be so cool to work in the big city. At least her little fifth-floor office in Kansas City had never caused an attack of vertigo. So much for the deep breathing routine, she thought, as she stumbled back to her desk. Now she was more of a basket case than ever.

Emma grabbed the legal pad and a pen and hurried out the door. She paused at her secretary's desk.

"I'm going up to see Louis Brisbane," she said, hoping that her voice was not shaking too badly. "I'll be back in a little while."

Lorraine Gelly looked up from her computer screen. "Why are you seeing Brisbane?" the redhaired, forty-something woman demanded. "Is there a problem?"

"Of course not," Emma replied, smoothing down the skirt of her powder blue suit. "Why would you think there might be a problem?"

"Because the last associate I worked for who was summoned to Brisbane's office was fired on the spot. By the time he came back down here, a security guard had packed up his personal belongings and IT had changed the password on his computer. Not that I'm implying that's what's going to happen to you," Lorraine said sweetly. "I just thought you'd want to know."

"Thank you, Lorraine," Emma said with a twinge of sarcasm. "You've made me feel so much better."

As she rode the elevator to the fortieth floor, Emma tried to psych herself up for her meeting. She had talked to Brisbane only twice before, once during her exhausting ten hours of interviews with countless firm members soon after she had asked to transfer to Chicago, and again during her first week on the job.

Emma hated to admit it, but there was something about Louis Brisbane that unnerved her. Although he was tall, dark, distinguished, and looked every inch the patrician lawyer, there was something almost sinister about him. Emma paused a moment and considered what that might be. His eyes. Yes, that was it. His eyes were dark and piercing. They looked as if they could see right through you. And more than that, they looked cruel. Brisbane was clearly not someone you'd want on your bad side. And he was not someone to keep waiting, Emma thought as the elevator opened onto the fortieth floor. She walked quickly down the hall toward Brisbane's office.

"Emma Davis to see Mr. Brisbane," she announced somewhat breathlessly to the great man's secretary.

J. Devereaux Braxton regarded Emma haughtily. "He has been expecting you," the perfectly coifed woman replied. "Go right in."

"Thank you," Emma said, trying hard to sound breezy and cheerful when in truth she felt nauseous. She took a deep breath, then marched into Brisbane's domain.

Brisbane swiveled around in his massive leather chair. "Emma, please come in."

Emma's first view of Brisbane's digs nearly knocked her off her feet. The man had a huge corner office with floor-to-ceiling windows on two sides, giving the effect that if you took a running leap, you could fly right out into space. I would die of fright if I had to work in here, Emma thought.

"Beautiful view, isn't it?" Brisbane said, mistaking Emma's wide-eyed look for excitement rather than stark terror.

"Lovely," Emma agreed, trying to avert her eyes.

"I was just watching some boats at the lakeshore.

11

Spring is such a splendid time of year in Chicago. Take a look yourself, if you'd like." Brisbane motioned toward a Meade telescope positioned at one of the windows.

"No, thank you," Emma said politely.

"Then please have a seat."

Emma dutifully parked herself in one of the dark leather chairs in front of Brisbane's desk and took a quick look around. She had been in other Franklin & Holland partners' offices and they were all lavishly furnished, but Brisbane's was simply magnificent. The parquet floor was accented by a series of thick Oriental rugs. The enormous desk was mahogany and in a corner was the most ornately carved file cabinet Emma had ever seen. I'm definitely not in Kansas anymore, she thought.

Brisbane took off his reading glasses and set them down in front of him. "How are you enjoying your start at Franklin and Holland?" he asked genially.

"Fine," Emma replied nervously.

"What cases are you working on?"

"The principal one is *Tift v. Forage King Industries*."

"That's a products liability action, isn't it?"

"Yes. At the moment I am researching successor liability issues because our client acquired the business from another company and it is not clear which of them actually manufactured the product in question."

"Who is the billing partner on the case?"

"Tom Cane."

"Oh, yes." Brisbane nodded. "Tom mentioned a couple of weeks ago how pleased he was with your work."

The constricted feeling in Emma's chest began to loosen a bit. Maybe she wasn't going to be called on the carpet after all.

"What else are you working on?" Brisbane asked.

"A number of other things. Just last week I was given a new environmental tort case."

"Are we keeping you busy enough?"

"I've been quite busy," Emma replied, not sure where the conversation was going.

"The reason I ask is that I have an assignment I'd like you to help me with—that is, if you can work it into your current schedule."

Emma was stunned. A management committee member was giving her an assignment? Of course she could work it in! "I'm sure I could find the time," she said brightly.

Brisbane smiled. "Excellent. What do you know about trusts and estates?"

Emma frowned, feeling the opportunity slipping away. "Just what I learned in law school, I'm afraid."

"Well, I need someone to help me with a T and E matter. An old school friend of mine, Oak Grey-thorne, died recently." Brisbane leaned back in his chair. "Oak was a rather tragic figure, brilliant but flawed. He was plagued by demons and prone to many excesses his entire life and, unfortunately, they finally killed him. He had no family and left his entire estate to a charitable trust. I would like your assistance in transferring the assets to the trust. Does this sound like something you'd be interested in?"

Emma searched for the right response. While she was thrilled that Brisbane had enough confidence in her abilities to offer her this plum assignment, she was concerned that her lack of experience in that particular field might cause him to realize he had made a mistake.

"I'm very flattered that you think I am capable of handling this, but I have never done any probate work before and I'm not sure I'd be able to do a competent job."

"Don't worry about that. I will be overseeing everything," Brisbane assured her. "I just need you to handle the legwork, so to speak. I have no doubt that you will do a wonderful job."

"Well, in that case, I would love to help you out," Emma said enthusiastically.

"Excellent," Brisbane said, smiling. "I'll have Devereaux bring the file down to you within a day or so, and I will put together a list of the tasks that need to be done. After you've had a chance to look that over, we'll talk again."

"Great!" Thinking the meeting was over, Emma stood up.

"One more thing," Brisbane said.

Emma sat right back down again.

Brisbane leaned forward and lowered his voice. "I'm sure I don't have to tell you that most associates would consider working with a senior partner to be quite a desirable assignment."

"Of course," Emma said.

"You probably understand better than I do that jealousy can sometimes erupt over associates' assignments and I'm sure you would agree that fits of jealous pique among young attorneys at a firm are counterproductive and should be avoided whenever possible."

Emma nodded, trapped in his gaze.

"So, if you don't mind, I think it would be best if you did not tell anyone else at the firm about this assignment."

"Certainly." Emma nodded again.

"Devereaux give you a special client code that you should use to enter your billing charges into the computer. Oh—and I think it would also be best if you would route any secretarial work to Devereaux rather than using your own secretary. It will just make everything smoother."

"Of course," Emma said.

"I'm glad we understand each other." Brisbane stood up and Emma did the same. He walked her to the door. "I'm so pleased that you are willing to find the time to help me with this project, Emma," he said. "If our collaboration on this matter runs as smoothly as I think it will, I am sure I'll be able to send other, more significant cases your way."

"Thank you, sir," Emma said. "I appreciate your confidence in my work, and I promise I won't let you down."

"I'm sure you won't. Thank you, Emma. We'll talk again when you've finished reviewing the file." He opened the door and she rushed out before he had a chance to reconsider his decision and give the assignment to someone else.

Emma nearly floated back to her office. "So what happened?" Lorraine asked. "I take it you weren't fired because no one came to pack up your office."

"No, I wasn't fired," Emma said, quickly trying to come up with a cover story that her savvy secretary would buy. "Brisbane is interested in expanding the firm's nationwide recruiting efforts, and he thought I might be able to provide a fresh viewpoint, so he asked me if I'd be interested in serving on the recruiting committee."

Emma was not sure if it was her imagination or if Lorraine really was frowning. "He had you come to his office to ask you to be on the recruiting committee? He couldn't ask you that on the phone or by e-mail?"

Emma shrugged. "We also discussed the cases I'm handling. Maybe he wanted to check out my work."

"I've heard that Louis Brisbane has an eye for the ladies," Lorraine said. "Maybe he wanted to check you out."

Emma laughed, feeling a tense situation defuse. "He was a perfect gentleman, and besides, I don't think I'm his type. I'm just a hick from Kansas City, remember?"

"Be careful," Lorraine said seriously. "He could be a wolf in lawyer's clothing."

"Don't worry. I can take care of myself."

Emma walked into her office, shut the door behind her and resisted the impulse to let out a whoop of joy. She couldn't believe her good fortune. A management committee member had singled her, Emma Davis, out for a special project. He had all but promised that good work on this matter would yield more assignments. And then, if things went well—dare she even think the word—partnership might be in her future. There was no doubt about it, Emma thought smugly, her future at Franklin & Holland was suddenly looking very bright indeed.

CHAPTER 2

"Will you hurry up!" Kathy Flood scolded Emma. "We're going to be late."

"I'm almost ready," Emma replied. "I'm looking for a pair of black flats."

"Let me help you," Kathy said, peering over Emma's shoulder as the women stood in the walk-in closet in Emma's bedroom. Addressing the black and white shih tzu running in circles around her ankles, Kathy said, "Pepper, do you see any black flats?"

The dog merely continued circling.

"Here they are," Kathy said triumphantly, retrieving a pair of shoes from the floor.

Emma shook her head. "Not those black flats. My Cole Haan black flats. Oh, here they are," she said, reaching behind a stack of boxes. "Someday, before I move out of this apartment, I swear I'm going to finish unpacking."

"Why would you ever want to move out of here?" Kathy asked. "This is the most fabulous building in the city."

"So you've said," Emma laughed, slipping into her shoes. "Now, I just need to touch up my makeup and I'll be ready to go."

"Well, don't dawdle," Kathy said. "You'll never know how many amazing men we're not meeting because you got home from work late."

"I'll be ready in two minutes," Emma promised, rushing into the bathroom.

"I'm timing you," Kathy warned.

As Emma hurriedly put on some blusher and added a bit of mascara, she reflected on how quickly she had acquired a new best friend in the big city. Two days after Emma moved into a spacious fourth-floor apartment in a newly rehabbed building in Chicago's trendy River North neighborhood, she was waiting for the elevator when a tall, slender, dark-haired woman about her age rushed out of the apartment next door carrying a pudgy dog.

"You must be 4C," the young woman had said, jerking her head toward Emma's apartment.

Emma nodded. "I'm Emma Davis. I just moved in this weekend."

"Kathy Flood, 4B," the young woman said, offering her hand. "And this is Pepper. He goes to doggy day care. How would you like to get together later for a drink?"

"I'm not sure when I'll be getting home," Emma demurred. "This is my first day on the job, and I don't know what the normal office hours are."

Kathy looked at Emma's conservative suit and large black briefcase. "Lawyer?" she asked.

Emma nodded, feeling a hint of embarrassment.

"Even lawyers don't work all night, especially on their first day. I'll come get you at eight and we'll go get a drink and maybe a bite to eat. This is a prime location. There are loads of great places close by. You're really going to like it here."

It hadn't taken Emma long to agree that she did like the neighborhood and her new friend. Kathy was bright, gregarious and eccentric. Better yet, she had introduced Emma to the world of young, upscale Chicago society and the local dating scene. The two women went out together several times a week.

"I'm ready," Emma said, walking from the bathroom into the living room.

"Bad Pepper!" Kathy scolded, pulling something out of the dog's mouth. "Don't eat Emma's *Vogue* magazine. Sorry," she said. "He didn't exactly ruin it. He just slobbered on it a little bit."

Emma shook her head. "He's the first dog I've ever heard of that eats paper."

"I think he was a billy goat in another life," Kathy said. She stood back and gave her friend the once-over. "What do I have to do to convince you to make your evening wardrobe just a bit more whimsical? After all, our goal is to meet men, not interview prospective jurors."

Emma glanced down at her black knee length skirt, white T-shirt, herringbone jacket and black flats. Then she looked at Kathy's pastel minidress, pashmina shawl and stiletto heels. She had to admit the two of them were a study in contrasts. "You look great," Emma said, "but that kind of outfit's just not me."

"You just think it's not you," Kathy said. "You'd look fabulous in this. You have great legs and your hair is too good to be true. It's almost a Pre-Raphaelite look. Hair like that deserves clothes with a little oomph. You and I are about the same size." She paused a moment, then said, "Well, I know you have bigger breasts, but I won't hold that against you. Anyway, I wish you'd let me lend you a few things. I just got a couple of great sample dresses from a new French designer."

Kathy was the artistic director for Cyn's, one of Oak Street's trendiest women's stores, and she was constantly sporting the newest styles.

"I don't think they'd suit me," Emma said.

"Why do you subscribe to magazines like *Vogue* if you aren't willing to experiment a bit?"

"So your dog has something to chew on?"

Kathy gave her friend an exasperated look.

"I love looking at the latest styles," Emma said. "But I've dressed conservatively all my life. I just wouldn't be comfortable wearing anything really flashy."

"We'll work on that," Kathy promised. "It's now the first week in May. I'm going to make it my goal to have you wearing some really great things by summer. But, for tonight, I guess your fashion metamorphosis will have to wait. The Swing Club is beckoning."

After Kathy deposited Pepper back in her apartment, she and Emma walked several blocks to a popular club that featured live, big band music. On the way, Emma filled Kathy in on her new work assignment.

"Whose estate is it?" Kathy asked.

"Somebody named Oak Greythorne. Isn't that a strange name?"

"I know who he was!" Kathy exclaimed. "The *Tribune* had a half-page obituary. I think my dad might have gone to school with him."

"Really?" Emma shook her head. "Is there anybody in Chicago who doesn't have connections to your family?"

"Probably not anyone worth knowing," Kathy replied nonchalantly. The Floods traced their roots to the 1871 fire that had nearly decimated Chicago. Kathy cheerfully admitted that the first family member to arrive on the scene was a carpetbagger who hopped a train from Detroit as soon as he heard the news that the city was in flames. Arriving before the ashes were cold, he set up a construction business and soon found himself rich. Succeeding generations of Floods built on that wealth and steadily moved up the social ladder. Although she was low-key about her lineage, Kathy had alluded to being the beneficiary of a substantial trust fund left by her grandfather, a former bank president.

"So, what's the story about Greythorne?" Emma asked. "Brisbane said something about his being 'plagued by demons.' "

"I think he had a major drug and alcohol problem

and maybe some psychological problems as well,"
Kathy replied. "If memory serves me correctly, he
built a very successful business from scratch but then
either lost it or sold it. If you'd like, I can ask my dad
about him. He probably knows more of the details."

"That'd be great," Emma said. "I've always found
it helpful to have as much background as possible
on my cases."

"No problem," Kathy said. "I'd be happy to help.
And I'm glad to hear I was right about your prospects at the firm."

"What do you mean?" Emma asked.

"Remember how I told you from the day we met
that you were going to wow the old boys at Franklin
and Holland and you kept worrying that your work
wasn't going to cut it? Well, if a senior partner thinks
enough of your work to give you an assignment after
being there only a couple of months, I was obviously
right and you've been worrying about nothing."

"Getting the assignment and doing a good job on
it are two different things."

Kathy waved a hand dismissively. "It'll be a piece
of cake. I'm sure you can finish the estate with your
briefcase tied behind your back. Well, here we are,"
she said, stopping in front of a building with a heavy
oak door. "Let's see which fabulous people are here
tonight—besides us, of course." She held the door
open and chords of "Take the A Train" wafted out.
Emma stepped inside, happy to leave the pressure-
cooker world of big city law behind, if only for a
few hours.

It was close to midnight when Emma got home. While she normally didn't like to stay up that late on a work night, she had been having too much fun at the club to leave any earlier. She and Kathy had a few drinks, enjoyed the music, and danced.

They also met several nice men. And, as often happened, Kathy disappeared with one of them while Emma caught a cab home alone. Soon after they met, Emma had asked her new friend if she routinely ended up having sex with those men. Kathy had given a typically blasé answer. "If I want to sleep with them, I do, and if not, I don't. It's that simple."

"So you're saying you have a lot of one-night stands?"

" 'One-night stands.' What a quaint expression," Kathy laughed. "It sounds so fifties. Do they still talk like that in Kansas City?"

"Yeah, they still use bundling boards, too," Emma said, bristling.

"I'm not making fun of you," Kathy said. "It's just that there's obviously a big difference in what's acceptable behavior here versus a more provincial town."

"You mean, people are more promiscuous here," Emma said.

"No, I mean that people here aren't afraid to admit that they like sex," Kathy replied.

Emma hadn't yet met anyone in Chicago with whom she cared to have an intimate relationship. In fact, she thought ruefully as she slipped into her red silk pajamas, it had been nearly five months since she'd had sex. Not since she'd finally realized that her three-year relationship with Max Englander was a dead end and she'd found the gumption to tell him to hit the road.

Breaking up with Max had been tough, but it had been the right decision. Emma had just turned thirty and had realized that she wanted more out of life than she'd been getting—or was ever likely to get—with her longtime beau. And once she'd given Max his walking papers, it dawned on her that her job-satisfaction level wasn't exactly off the charts anymore either. No sooner than she started to think about sending out a few resumes, her firm had merged with Franklin & Holland and the possibility of relocating to Chicago arose. Boy, had she ever grabbed that brass ring!

Now Max and her life in Kansas City were both ancient history. Emma curled up on her side and closed her eyes. Although she wondered a few times if she had acted too hastily in making the big move, now that she was on Louis Brisbane's team, she was certain that her judgment had been right on target.

CHAPTER 3

Brisbane's secretary sent the *Greythorne* estate file down to Emma the next day. Not wanting Lorraine to know what she was working on, Emma tucked the file into a desk drawer for safekeeping and then took it home with her that night. After grabbing a quick bite to eat, she curled up on her sofa with the file spread out around her. By the time she finished reviewing it several hours later, Emma felt profoundly sad about Oak Greythorne.

The first item of interest in the file was the lengthy *Tribune* obituary Kathy had mentioned. The obit told the tragic story of a local boy who had made good and then self-destructed. Emma leaned back against the sofa cushions and read.

Lifelong Chicago resident and businessman Oak Greythorne, 57, died yesterday at his home. The cause of death has been ruled an accidental overdose of alcohol and prescription drugs.

Greythorne was the only child of Joseph Greythorne, a longtime member of the Chicago

Board of Trade, and Gloria Adamson Greythorne.
Oak Greythorne attended the Latin School of Chicago. He earned his BA and MBA, both with distinction, from the University of Chicago.

After honing his technical and managerial skills at a number of local firms, Greythorne was one of the first Midwesterners to see the potential in the then fledgling personal computer industry. He struck out on his own, forming Greythorne Industries, which developed and produced computer hardware components. Widely hailed as one of the Midwest's best in the field, Greythorne Industries grew to over eight hundred employees.

Citing ill health, Greythorne sold his company to Ronson Components eight years ago and retired. Ronson built on Greythorne's success, taking the company public two years ago. Industry analysts have speculated that if Greythorne had retained control of the enterprise, the initial public offering could have garnered him over $200 million.

Greythorne was preceded in death by his parents. He left no next of kin. A funeral service will be held on Monday at one p.m. at Saint John Lutheran Church. In lieu of flowers, friends are asked to make a donation to the charity of their choice.

Emma gave the photo accompanying the obituary close scrutiny. It was obviously not recent. The man pictured was probably in his late forties. His hair was still dark and thick, his face unlined. His gaze was direct and he showed just a hint of a smile. He looked attractive and capable, showing no outward sign of the demons that had evidently plagued him.

"How sad," Emma murmured. She put the obituary aside and turned to a copy of Greythorne's will, which had been drafted six years earlier. The introductory paragraphs contained standard language revoking any former wills and directing the executor to pay any outstanding debts or expenses related to Greythorne's last illness. Next came the portions of the will disposing of his property:

Because I have no close relatives or anyone else with whom I have a close familial relationship, all of the property which I own at the time of my death, whether real or personal, is to be transferred to the Oak Greythorne Charitable Trust.

The primary purpose of the Trust is to assist in improving the level of health care in the greater Chicago area. The Trust shall be particularly interested in supporting primary health care, advocacy projects and research which will have a positive effect on:

- the prevention and treatment of alcohol and drug addiction, especially among young people;
- the prevention and treatment of all types of mental illness;
- increased access to appropriate levels of care

for the Chicago area's underserved populations; and

- delivery of health care services to the poor.

The Trust shall make annual grants which will address important societal issues in the Trust's field of interest and for which adequate funding from other sources cannot be obtained. The Trustee is encouraged to provide funding for projects which primarily benefit underserved populations and disadvantaged persons as well as projects which focus on prevention of the illnesses mentioned above.

Emma couldn't help but feel respect for a man who wanted to help others overcome problems that he personally had not been able to conquer. The remainder of the document set forth the procedure applicants were to follow in applying for grants from the trust. Emma merely skimmed that part since she doubted she would have any involvement in disbursing the trust's funds.

As she flipped to the end of the will, she found a provision that surprised her:

I hereby appoint my friend and attorney, Louis W. Brisbane, as both my Executor and Trustee. I request that no bond be required of him in either capacity. I empower him to sell, lease or mortgage any property without an order of the court and without notice to anyone, upon such terms and conditions as shall seem best to him, and I give him full authority to manage the Oak Greythorne Charitable Trust and disburse funds therefrom as he deems advisable. I direct that Louis W. Brisbane be equitably compensated for his service in both capacities.

"I wonder why Brisbane didn't mention that in our meeting," Emma said aloud. Not that there was anything unusual about the appointments. Many people considered their attorneys to be their most trusted advisers and asked them to serve in fiduciary capacities. Brisbane had mentioned that Greythorne was an old boyhood friend, and, since Greythorne had no close relatives, Brisbane was probably the most likely candidate to serve as both executor and trustee.

Emma frowned. But if Brisbane was not simply the attorney for the estate but also wore two other hats that made him intimately involved in the matter, why had he chosen her to help him transfer assets to the trust? She put the file down and went to the kitchen for a glass of water as she contemplated the answer to that puzzling question.

"Why me?" Emma asked. Oh, she could flatter herself into thinking that Brisbane had heard such glowing reports about her abilities that he couldn't wait to work with her. But, in fact, there were two hundred fifty other associates at Franklin & Holland, including twenty in the trusts and estates department. Why would a top-level partner, needing help on what could, in some respects, be deemed a personal matter, choose an associate who not only had little proven background at the firm but who had never even drafted a simple will?

"I don't get it." She carried her glass of water back into the living room, sat down and flipped through the rest of Greythorne's will. The final page contained Greythorne's signature. Rather large characters written with bold strokes. Emma wondered what a handwriting analyst would make of that. Delusions of grandeur? Or covering up insecurities?

The will had been witnessed by Brisbane's secretary, J. Devereaux Braxton, and someone named Julia Boswell. Emma had never heard of her. She was probably another secretary. Or possibly an associate. Emma jotted a note to herself to check the firm directory in the morning to see if anyone by that name was still listed. Not that the other witness's identity mattered one whit since no one was claiming the will was not authentic or that Greythorne was not competent when he made it. It was just Emma's nature to be thorough.

The other notable document in the file was a tentative inventory of Greythorne's assets. Even though his early sale of the business had prevented him from joining the ranks of the filthy rich, the man was certainly no pauper. His condominium was valued at $700 thousand. He had what appeared to be a rather conservatively invested portfolio of stocks, bonds, and cash equivalents that was worth about $15 mil-

lion. And he owned a hundred-unit apartment building with an estimated value of $4 million.

Emma gave a low whistle. Twenty million dollars
was a very respectable estate, and grants paid out of
the income could definitely benefit local drug and
alcohol and mental health alliances. Emma idly wondered if Louis Brisbane considered twenty million
dollars a large amount of money. Some of his clients
were probably worth many times that much.

As for her earlier quandary about why she had been
handed this assignment, it dawned on her that maybe
to Brisbane this was a relatively minor matter on which
he was willing to take a chance on an untested new
lawyer. Emma took a sip of water. That could be the
answer. Maybe to Brisbane this estate was small pota-
toes. He could have picked her because she wasn't
fresh out of law school—she did have five years legal
experience under her belt—but since she was new to
Franklin & Holland her workload wasn't as great as
most other associates at her level. She nodded and
put down the glass. That was probably it. Here she
had been looking for some sinister motives when the
reason for the assignment was probably because it
was the most efficient use of firm resources.

Brisbane had said Emma's primary duty would be
to transfer Greythorne's assets to the trust. Skimming
through the list of assets once more, Emma thought
she should be able to complete these transfers with
no difficulty. And if Brisbane was pleased with her
work, then her worth at the firm could rise markedly.

Emma breathed a sigh of relief. She was feeling much better about the *Greythorne* assignment. She replaced the documents in the file and set it aside, then glanced at the clock. It was just after nine. Since she wasn't feeling completely worn out just yet, she decided she'd spend an hour or so reviewing depositions in the *Tift v. Forage King* case before calling it a night. First thing tomorrow she would make an appointment to meet with Brisbane and get her first marching orders in the *Greythorne* case.

The next morning Tom Cane, the partner with whom she was working on *Tift v. Forage King*, called and requested her assistance in drafting a motion for an immediate injunction against a fringe political group that was picketing in front of a client's business. It was twelve o'clock before the motion and supporting affidavits were ready to be filed.

"Thanks for the help, Emma," Tom said. "And nice job."

"Anytime," Emma said. She then remembered that the morning had gone by without talking to Louis Brisbane. She hurried back to her office.

"That was a long, dragged-out project," Lorraine said upon seeing Emma. "Did you finish?"

Emma nodded. "Don't tell anyone, but emergency injunctions are not my favorite thing."

"Your secret's safe with me," Lorraine said. "I'm going to lunch now. I'll see you later."

Emma closed her office door, sat down at her desk

and dialed Brisbane's extension. The phone rang four times and then a voice mail recording came over the line.

Emma considered calling back, but then she heard the short beep and, taking a deep breath, said, "Hello. This is Emma Davis. I've finished reviewing the *Greythorne* file and I'm ready for some instructions on how to proceed. If it would be convenient for you, I could come up to your office later this afternoon, say, around five o'clock? If I don't hear from you to the contrary, I'll see you then. Thanks. Bye."

As Emma hung up the phone, she saw that her hands were shaking. "Get a grip," she told herself. Brisbane was just another lawyer and the *Greythorne* estate was just another case. She had dealt with lots of both in the past five years.

A BLT and fries from a local takeout left Emma feeling greatly rejuvenated. She spent a productive afternoon doing research for an appellate brief. At five minutes to five she picked up a legal pad and pen and casually walked out of her office. "I'm going to the library," she said to Lorraine. "I imagine you're about ready to head out for the day."

Lorraine shook her head. "Not just yet. There's a staff meeting in about ten minutes."

"Oh, all right." As Emma stood by her secretary's desk she was almost overpowered by the smell of perfume. Trying not to breathe in, she looked around her.

"It's the new Estée Lauder fragrance," Lorraine said. "Do you like it?"

Emma cleared her throat. "It's lovely, but—" She hesitated a moment. "Don't you think you maybe put on a bit too much?"

Lorraine laughed. "That's the whole point. The topic to be discussed at the staff meeting is a demand made by one of the secretaries, Barrie Holman, that the entire firm should be scent free. No perfume, no aftershave, no scented hairspray or deodorant. No air freshener or scented cleaning products."

"Why would anyone make such a ridiculous suggestion?" Emma asked.

"Because the woman is nuts," Lorraine answered. "She claims her olfactory system is supersensitive and that even the slightest hint of scent makes her sick. But that's a load of hogwash. My husband is a physician, and he says there is absolutely no medical basis for those claims. Barrie is just a psycho who wants attention. Ban deodorant?" Lorraine snorted. "Summer is coming, for God's sake. Would she rather smell rampant B.O.?"

"I can't imagine anyone would pay any attention to her," Emma said.

"Oh, but they do. She's Art Herbst's niece. He's a retired partner who is now of counsel," Lorraine explained, seeing that Emma didn't recognize the name. "Nepotism got Barrie a job here, and now she's trying to make life hell for the rest of us. The poor office manager is afraid to tell her to take a hike but the rest of the secretaries are not going to take this sitting down. We all agreed we'd douse ourselves with our favorite fragrance just before coming to the meeting. If it's true that perfumes make her sick, then this joint effort just might signal her untimely demise."

Emma laughed. "If you are going to sit in a room with dozens of other women whose scent levels roughly match yours, I'm afraid you're all going to need a few whiffs of pure oxygen to keep from passing out."

"We'll get through it even if we all have to hold our breath through the entire meeting," Lorraine promised. "Well, gotta go." She slipped the perfume bottle in her purse. "If I get there before Barrie, I'm going to give the room a few squirts for good measure."

"Good luck," Emma said. "See you tomorrow."

"Bye bye." Lorraine gave a small wave as she headed out. "Don't work too late."

As Emma rode the elevator up to Brisbane's floor she scrawled a note to herself on her legal pad, "J. Boswell?" Julia Boswell was not listed in the current Franklin & Holland directory, so she must have already left the firm. Out of curiosity, Emma would ask Brisbane who Julia was.

Emma got off the elevator on the fortieth floor and walked down the hall to Brisbane's office. Devereaux was not at her desk. Brisbane's door was closed. Emma knocked, then waited. There was no response. She knocked again. Still nothing. She hesitated, then opened the door a crack. "Hello?" she called. "Is anyone here?" She pushed the door open enough so that she could step inside.

"Hello?" she repeated. "Mr. Brisbane?" She looked around the cavernous office. The ornately carved file cabinet again caught her eye. Pausing briefly to speculate what important documents Brisbane might store in such a lavish piece of furniture, Emma completed her visual sweep of the room. The senior partner obviously was not there.

"Damn," Emma said under her breath. Perhaps Brisbane had not even been in the office that day. She supposed she should have called to confirm that he had received her earlier message. It had been stupid of her to assume that a senior partner would be sitting around waiting to talk to her. She was about to leave in defeat when she noticed a door at the far right of the room.

She walked over to the door and tapped on it. "Mr. Brisbane?" She slowly opened the door and peeked inside. It was a bathroom. Smart move, she thought. It would have been embarrassing if she'd walked in on a partner sitting on the throne.

Chastising herself for her lack of judgment, she shut the bathroom door. She was turning around when someone grabbed her arm.

Emma screamed. A big, burly man, his face mottled with anger, squeezed her arm tightly and growled, "Who the hell are you? What are you doing in here? This is a private office!"

Emma screamed again and tried to get away, but

she was no match for the man's brute strength. He grabbed her other arm and shook her roughly. Her legal pad and pen dropped to the floor. "Who are you?" the man shouted.

Emma's mouth opened, but no words came out. The man continued to shake her, and she was sure he intended to kill her. As she frantically tried to think of some way to break free, the door from the hall opened and Louis Brisbane burst in.

"Let her go," Brisbane commanded.

The burly man reluctantly released his hold on Emma. "I caught her sneaking around in here," he explained in a calmer voice.

"This is Emma Davis, one of our new associates," Brisbane said, his dark eyes honing in on the other man. "She and I are working on some cases together. She has every right to be here."

The big man merely looked at Emma and grunted.

Brisbane turned to Emma. "Are you all right? I am so terribly sorry. Please have a seat. I will be right back." He took the other man firmly by the arm and rapidly led him out into the hall. Although she was badly shaken, Emma managed to pick up her pen and legal pad and make her way over to a chair in front of Brisbane's desk. She could hear two muffled voices. They both sounded angry.

Within a couple of minutes, Brisbane stepped back inside his office. He immediately came over to Emma and put his hands on her shoulders. "I am sorry for what just happened. Are you all right?"

Emma managed a small nod. "I think so."

"Let me get you something to drink." Brisbane walked behind his desk and opened a walnut cabinet. Emma could see half a dozen liquor bottles and some barware. He took out a bottle of eighteen-year-old scotch and poured two fingers into a tumbler. "Here," he said, handing it to her. "Drink this."

Emma did not hesitate. She downed half the liquor in the first swallow, reveling in the burning sensation she felt as it went down her throat. Then she swallowed the other half.

"Would you like a little more?" Brisbane asked.

"No," Emma said, finally regaining her voice. She set the glass on the corner of Brisbane's desk. "Who was that, a bodyguard?"

Brisbane sat down in his chair and shook his head. "No, actually, he is one of my clients."

"He is?" Emma asked with disbelief. She could not believe that someone as polished as Louis Brisbane would have a client like that. The guy had looked like a Mafia goon.

"His name is Tommy Corona," Brisbane explained. "He's quite a successful contractor."

"He acts like he should be a bouncer at a bar," Emma said.

"Tommy did some semi-professional boxing in his younger days. I guess old habits die hard."

"Why was he so upset that I was in your office?" Emma asked.

"In his line of work he is used to people from other companies spying and doing all sorts of dishonest things," Brisbane said. "So, when he saw you in here, I guess he forgot he was on someone else's turf and he let his gut instincts take over." Brisbane looked at her keenly. "Are you certain you are all right? He didn't hurt you?"

Emma shook her head. "He just scared me to death. I was afraid he was going to kill me."

"Tommy wouldn't actually harm a woman," Brisbane said. "The worst that could have happened was he would have kept you here until he found out whether you belonged. Are you sure you wouldn't like more scotch?"

"No, thank you."

"I did get your message that you were ready to discuss the *Greythorne* file," Brisbane said. "But perhaps you would like to postpone that until some other time."

Emma briefly considered the offer, then shook her head. "I'd like to discuss it now, if that's all right with you."

"Fine," Brisbane said, relaxing a bit. "So, what do you think of my old friend Oak?"

"He was quite a tragic figure, wasn't he?" Emma mused. "But I admire him for wanting to help other people lead happier lives than he had."

"He always did have a big heart," Brisbane agreed. "You must have been rather close if he chose you as his executor and trustee."

Brisbane nodded. "We knew each other since grammar school. We drifted apart as adults, but we rekindled our friendship after his company became successful."

"What would you like me to do first?" Emma asked.

"Our first order of business is to transfer the securities and liquid assets into the trust's name," Brisbane explained. He handed Emma a manilla file. "Here is a sample cover letter that should be sent to each transfer agent, along with the pertinent documents from the probate file. You can send this correspondence out under your name. I would again ask that you use Devereaux for any clerical help you need in that regard."

Emma nodded. "Anything else?"

"Not for the time being. Let me know when you've completed these transfers and then we'll talk about the next step in the process."

"All right." This assignment sounded easy. Emma had been worried that she might have to learn the intricacies of fiduciary taxes or some such thing. "I'll get at this right away," Emma said. She stood up.

Brisbane came around his desk. "Again, Emma, I want you to accept my most sincere apologies for what happened earlier. I hope you will not hold that incident against me or the firm. We are so fortunate to have someone of your caliber working for us. I would never do anything to jeopardize our working relationship."

"It wasn't your fault," Emma said gamely.

Brisbane put a hand on her arm. "And would it be asking too much if we kept what happened here between us?" Seeing Emma's frown, he hurried on.

"You know how stories spread out of control. Why involve other members of the firm unnecessarily?"

Although Emma was uneasy about this request, she nodded. "All right. I guess no real harm was done."

Brisbane nodded his approval at her decision. He walked her to the door. "Keep up the good work," he said.

Emma nodded curtly and walked out. As Brisbane closed the door behind her, she nervously glanced both ways, then hurried down the hall to the elevator and pushed the down button.

What a fright she'd had. She had never been that scared in her life, not even when she was seven years old and spent a half hour stuck at the top of the Ferris wheel at the county fair.

She glanced down at her legal pad. Damn! She had forgotten to ask Brisbane about Julia Boswell. Oh, well. It probably didn't make any difference who Julia was. The *Greythorne* job was easy pickings and she'd get the credit for it. With minimal work, it would all be over.

CHAPTER 4

"Jesus Christ!" Louis Brisbane exclaimed as he paced back and forth in front of his desk. "What were you thinking? If she goes to the police or to one of the other partners, our whole operation could go down the toilet. Don't you ever stop to consider the consequences before you act?"

Tommy Corona settled back into one of Brisbane's leather chairs and shrugged. "I came in here and saw some strange dame snooping around, so I figured I'd check out her bona fides. It's no big deal. You got any scotch?"

"What do you mean 'it's no big deal'?" Brisbane repeated. "If she lodges any sort of complaint against you, it could be a very big deal indeed."

"Relax, Louie. You're being too much of a tight ass, like always," Corona said. "Now, have you got any scotch or not?"

Brisbane scowled, then walked behind his desk and retrieved the bottle and a tumbler out of the cabinet. He unceremoniously plopped the items down on the desk, then sat down in his own chair.

"I mean it, Tommy. You can't pull that Tarzan act around here. This is a silk stocking law firm, not a union hall."

"What's the difference? Fancy law firms and union organizers are both after the same thing: money. That's why you and me get along so well." Corona poured himself a generous measure of the scotch and took a long swallow. He smacked his lips. "This is good stuff." He leaned back in his chair. "I think you ought to be thanking me for looking out for your interests. What if I'd walked in here and found that little lady pawing through your personal files?"

Brisbane immediately swung around and looked at the ornately carved file cabinet. "She wasn't anywhere near the file cabinet, was she?"

"Oh, so now you're starting to show a little concern, eh?" Corona chuckled. He drained the rest of the scotch and poured himself another two fingers. "No, she wasn't near the files. She was over by the bathroom when I came in. But she could have been tossing the whole place and hiding important documents in her undies. You really ought to pay more attention to security, my friend. It's not very smart to leave the place unattended."

"Devereaux had a doctor's appointment and had to leave early, and I was down the hall talking to a colleague," Brisbane said. "You're certain Emma wasn't near the file cabinet or my desk?"

"Not that I saw," Corona answered. He put his feet up on Brisbane's desk. "Would you like me to have a little follow-up chat with her to find out exactly what she was doing in here before I arrived? That broad's quite a looker. I might enjoy renewing her acquaintance, if you know what I mean. Just say the word."

"That won't be necessary," Brisbane said. He ran his hands through his hair. "Christ, I need a drink." He took a fresh tumbler out of the cabinet and poured the scotch.

"Your hands are looking a little shaky there, buddy," Corona said. "You need to chill out."

"How can I chill out when you keep doing things that could give me a heart attack?" Brisbane snapped. He took a swallow of liquor, then visibly relaxed.

"So what kind of cases have you got that broad working on?" Corona asked.

Brisbane took another sip. "Coincidentally, she's working on one of our pet projects."

Corona raised an eyebrow. "Which one?"

"Oak Greythorne."

Corona swung his feet off the desk and slapped his knee. "You're shitting me! So she's the patsy who's going to transfer dear departed Brother Greythorne's property to the trust. That's brilliant. Nobody would suspect her of doing anything shady."

Brisbane smiled. "I chose her very carefully. This is a delicate operation. It's much more public than most of our joint enterprises. We have to be very careful that everything looks like it's on the up-and-up."

"While all the while the money is going down and down into our pockets," Corona said. He leaned over and clinked his tumbler against Brisbane's. "A toast to our new little helper. What's her name again?"

"Emma Davis."

"To Emma Davis," Corona said, hoisting his glass in the air. "May she do us proud and make us lots of dough." He drained the rest of the scotch, slammed the tumbler down on Brisbane's desk and leaned forward, chuckling. "And if she fucks anything up, may she be fish food by morning."

Brisbane raised his own glass. "I'll drink to that."

CHAPTER 5

The next afternoon Emma had just returned from grabbing a late lunch when her phone rang.

"So, are you enjoying that beautiful skyline?" Coleen Kennedy asked.

"As long as I don't have to look down from it," Emma said, smiling.

Coleen had been Emma's best friend in Kansas City. A petite and feisty redhead, Coleen was an assistant attorney general. For the past two years she had been assigned to a specialty task force devoted to catching people who preyed on and formed illicit relationships with teenagers over the Internet. A typical work day for Coleen involved several hours of cruising Internet chat rooms posing as a promiscuous fifteen-year-old girl named Carla.

Coleen loved her work. "The research required for the job is the perfect antidote against aging," she said. "After all, how many thirty-year-olds get to read *Seventeen* and watch Britney Spears videos? I'm Kansas City's answer to Peter Pan. I'll never have to grow up."

Emma and Coleen kept in almost daily contact via e-mail, and chatted on the phone about every other day.

They talked for a bit before Coleen casually said, "I saw Max last week."

"Oh? How is he?" Emma asked, secretly hoping that her ex-boyfriend was pining away from loneliness.

"He's fine."

"That's good. What's he up to these days?"

"Actually, he's seeing someone new. I saw them together at a fund-raiser for Big Brothers–Big Sisters."

Emma took a moment to process the information that Max was dating again. "Oh. Well, good for him. What's she like?"

"She's a nurse. In her late twenties. Dark hair. Seemed nice."

"I hope she's not looking to get married because Max made it very clear that marriage was not on his agenda."

Coleen made no reply.

Emma waited, then pressed for more info. "What is it? Come on, tell me. I won't be upset. I'm the one who gave him the boot, remember?"

"Okay," Coleen said. "Max told Debbie Friedman that this girl 'could be the one.'"

"'Could be the one'?" Emma repeated. "What the hell does that mean?"

"I assume it means she could be the one he settles down with, the love of his life, his inamorata—"

"All right, all right," Emma interrupted. "I get the picture. Geez." She pushed her hair behind her ears.

48

"I had three years of virtual stagnation with the man. Then the minute I dump him and leave town, he finds someone else and falls head over heels. I didn't think he was capable of head over heels." Emma paused and a horrible thought washed over her. "Oh, my God! Maybe it was just me that he couldn't fall head over heels for."

"It wasn't you," Coleen said. "He wasn't the right one for you. Even at the beginning, there never seemed to be any sizzle."

"And now he's frying up new bacon, and I don't have so much as a pilot light."

"You'll meet someone," Coleen promised. "Give it time."

"I just hope I meet someone before Max and Nurse Naughty send out their first birth announcements," Emma grumbled.

"Come on," Coleen said. "Chicago's full of eligible bachelors."

"Oh, all right," Emma replied. "But on the off chance that you've just found out that any of my other ex-boyfriends are also head over heels for someone besides me, keep it to yourself, okay?"

They hung up soon after, and Emma brooded for a few minutes about Max. Coleen was right. There hadn't been any sizzle. That's why Emma had broken it off and moved to Chicago. Now all she had to do was meet Mr. Right.

After her chat with Coleen, Emma drafted letters requesting that the bulk of Oak Greythorne's assets be transferred to the charitable trust. Putting the documents in a large red file, she told Lorraine she was going to the library, then took the elevator to the fortieth floor.

The bruises on her upper arms were still painful, and Emma had not yet completely shaken off the trauma of Corona's assault. She tried to remain calm during the brief elevator ride, but as soon as the doors opened, she could feel the blood rushing to her head and her knees growing weak. She furtively looked to the left and right before stepping off the elevator. Then she walked crisply down the hall to J. Devereaux Braxton's workstation.

Brisbane's secretary looked up from her computer screen as she saw Emma approach. "May I help you?" she asked in her perfect diction.

Emma removed the documents from her file and handed them to Devereaux. "I've drafted correspondence asking the various transfer agents to switch title of Oak Greythorne's assets to the trust," she explained. "I've clipped the necessary probate forms to each request. I'd appreciate it if you would mail them out for me."

Devereaux took the documents and quickly flipped through them. "Does this cover all the securities and cash accounts?" she asked.

"Not quite," Emma responded.

Devereaux frowned. "What do you mean by 'not quite'?"

"Before I mail the transfer requests, I thought it might be a good idea for me to verify the exact value of each asset as of the date of death," Emma explained. "Mr. Brisbane didn't explicitly tell me to do that, but I always like to be thorough. I am still waiting to hear from three or four financial institutions as to the value of the securities they are holding. I should be able to verify those values within a day or two and then I can finish the rest of the transfers."

"Fine," Devereaux said curtly, setting the stack of documents to one side. "I'm sure Mr. Brisbane would like to get the transfers executed soon, so bring the additional letters to me as soon as you complete them."

"I will," Emma said at once. "I'll finish them as soon as I can." What was it about this woman that made her feel so uncomfortable? She supposed it was that Devereaux had a haughty air about her, as if she were signaling to Emma that she worked for a Very Important Personage at Franklin & Holland and Emma had better not forget it.

Devereaux turned her attention back to her computer screen. She obviously did not think this new associate was anyone whose favor she needed to curry.

"Thanks for your help," Emma said. She turned to go, then turned back.

Devereaux looked up again. Her expression was not cheerful. "Is there something else?" she asked.

"Yes. There's something I've been wanting to ask either Mr. Brisbane or you. In looking through the file I noticed that you were one of the witnesses to Oak Greythorne's will. The other witness was someone named Julia Boswell. I wondered if you could tell me who she was."

Devereaux's already unfriendly face turned positively stony. "Why do you ask?"

"I'm just curious," Emma replied. "As I said, when I work on a project I like to be thorough. Was Julia Boswell an employee here?"

"She was an associate here for a very short time," Devereaux replied.

"Did she help draft the will?"

"I really wouldn't know the answer to that."

"How long ago did she leave?"

"She's been gone a number of years. I really couldn't say how many."

"Do you know where she went?"

Devereaux's scowl deepened. "I have absolutely no idea. Now if you'll excuse me, I am working on a rush project for Mr. Brisbane. I will see to it that these letters get mailed out today. Bring me the remaining letters as soon as you've completed them and I'll see that they are sent out as well."

"Thanks a lot for your help." Such as it was, Emma added silently.

Devereaux again turned her attention to her computer screen. Emma took her now empty folder and walked briskly down the hall to the elevator. She would be glad to get back to the thirty-fourth floor. Even without the presence of Tommy Corona, the fortieth floor seemed to give off a lot of negative vibes.

After work that day, Emma went to an informal

gathering at a nearby pub for litigation team attorneys. In the past she had often found firm social events to be stilted affairs and had not been sure she wanted to attend this one. But several other associates had assured her that, even though they worked like dogs, Franklin & Holland litigators were a pretty congenial bunch who knew how to have a good time. "Besides," one associate confided, "Tom Cane always buys at least one round of drinks for the entire crowd and sometimes springs for some appetizers." After hearing this hearty endorsement, Emma decided it might be a good opportunity for her to get to know some of her colleagues better.

Nearly forty F & H attorneys were already milling around in a private room off of the establishment's main bar when Emma arrived at five thirty. As Emma ordered a Goose Island ale at the bar, she heard someone call, "Emma! Over here!"

Emma looked around to see where the voice was coming from and spied Jill Bedner, a cheerful brunette about Emma's age, motioning from a corner table. Another woman Emma hadn't met was sitting with her. Emma waved back. The bartender handed her the beer. Emma held out a ten-dollar bill. "Are you one of the lawyers?" the bartender asked.

Emma nodded.

"You've got an open bar until six thirty," the bartender said. "Compliments of that gentleman over there." He pointed toward the other side of the bar.

"Thanks, Tom," Emma called, catching the partner's eye. She carried her drink over to Jill's table.

"This is Annah Bull," Jill said, indicating the slender brown-haired woman sitting next to her. "She's up for partnership next year. Annah, this is Emma Davis, a fifth-year lateral transfer from Kansas City."

The women shook hands. "Nice to meet you," Emma said. "So, you're up for partnership. That's great."

Annah took a sip of her martini and shrugged. "You'll get there, too, in a few years. There's really no magic to it. You just have to put in your time."

"Annah is much too modest," Jill said. "She's a real barracuda in the courtroom. I second-chaired a case with her a couple of years ago, and the judge ruled in her favor on so many objections that opposing counsel almost punched her out during a break. He weighed about three hundred pounds, but Annah stood her ground and made him back off. It was wild! I wish I had a video."

"I'm sorry I missed it," Emma said.

"Jill's on her second drink, and I think they're going straight to her head," Annah said. "In truth, the incident was not nearly as exciting as she makes it out to be. How long have you been at F and H, Emma?"

"Almost three months."

"How are you enjoying it?"

"Very much," Emma said. "The work has been extremely interesting and challenging. The thing I'm still having a little trouble adjusting to is the sheer size of the firm." She looked around her. "I don't think I've met more than half the people here, let alone the three hundred or more lawyers who work in departments other than litigation. I have to admit that I feel like a very little fish in a very big pond."

"I don't mean to sound snobbish," Annah said, "but the lawyers outside of litigation don't matter all that much. It's unlikely you'll ever work with most of them so there's not much point in getting to know them. We litigators are sort of an incestuous lot. We pretty much stick together and the rest of the firm be damned."

"The litigation partners are all quite nice," Jill said. "Especially Tom Cane and Mike Hoover. But there really isn't a bad one in the lot. And believe me, you can't say that about some of the other teams."

Emma leaned forward. "One of the disadvantages of transferring into a huge firm is that you don't know anything about the office dynamic. Do either of you have any advice on which partners to try to avoid?"

Jill thought a moment, then said, "Well, I've heard Louis Brisbane is bad news."

Emma felt her cheeks flush. "Really? Why is that?"

"I don't know anything firsthand," Jill replied, "but I've heard he's a real SOB to work for and that he's especially nasty to women associates. Around the time I started at the firm five years ago there was a story going around that he drove one female associate almost to the brink of insanity."

"How did he do that?" Emma asked.

Jill shrugged. "I don't know. She was on another team. Trusts and estates, maybe. Did you hear about this, Annah?"

"It sounds vaguely familiar," Annah said. "But then again, it could just be one of those urban myths. My second year at the firm one of the night secretaries started a story that the ghost of one of the firm's long-deceased partners haunted the kitchen. The story about Brisbane driving an associate to the madhouse might be equally bogus."

"You said you thought she might have been on the trusts and estates team," Emma said, trying to quiet the voice that was shouting the words "Julia Boswell" in her ear. "You didn't hear what her name was, did you?"

Jill racked her brain. "If I did, I can't remember it. Sorry. I just remember hearing that she wasn't at the firm very long and she left under somewhat mysterious circumstances. Like one day she was there and the next her office had been cleaned out and all traces of her had vanished."

"Sounds like a plot for a good mystery novel," Emma said. As she picked up her glass, her hand was shaking. She drained the rest of the beer in one long swallow.

"You must've been thirsty," Annah said. "Would you like another?"

Emma nodded. "I'd love another one." As Annah hailed a waiter, Emma sat quietly, her hands clenched into fists. Rumor had it that Louis Brisbane had nearly driven a female trusts and estates associate mad. The young woman had left the firm suddenly between five and six years ago. Oak Greythorne's will had been witnessed by a woman named Julia Boswell, a former associate who had left the firm in that approximate time frame.

Was the story an urban myth? Emma felt a chill come over her. Or was it all true? And if so, was she going to be the next Julia Boswell?

CHAPTER 6

Late the following afternoon, as Emma was working on a brief, she got a frantic call from Kathy. "Could you do me a huge favor and pick Pepper up from doggy day care?" she asked breathlessly. "I'm stuck in a meeting with our new ad agency reps, and there's no way it's going to be over before the center closes at seven."

Emma looked at the small clock on her desk. "I was planning to work late today myself, but I guess I could take some work home and finish it there. Sure, I'll pick Pepper up for you."

"You're a lifesaver," Kathy exclaimed. "I'll call the center and give them authorization to release him to you."

"Authorization?" Emma repeated. "The center's owners really take their responsibilities to the dogs seriously, don't they?"

"Of course. You don't think they'd just hand the dogs over to anyone who walked in off the street, do you? Do you realize how many dognappers are out there?"

"Apparently not," Emma replied. "Well, Pepper will be in good hands with me. He'll be waiting safely at my place whenever you finish your meeting."

"Thanks. You're a doll. See you later."

Emma worked until about five thirty, then dropped her car off at home and walked to Yuppie Puppy Day Care, three blocks north of her apartment building. After verifying that Kathy had given permission for her friend to fetch her dog and requiring Emma to show photo ID, a perky young woman with a ponytail went into another room and came back leading Pepper on a leash.

"Bye bye, Pepper," the young woman said, handing Emma the leash. "See you in the morning."

As Emma and Pepper made their way out the front door, Emma shook her head in amazement at the way well-heeled young professionals spoiled their pets. She paused on the front steps of the building to secure her briefcase strap more firmly on her shoulder, then started down the sidewalk for the short walk home.

Emma and Pepper walked down the first block without incident, the dog prancing happily at the end of his leash. In the second block, Emma's briefcase strap started to slip. As she instinctively tried to catch it, Pepper suddenly lunged forward. Before Emma could stop him, he pulled free and was racing down the sidewalk at top speed, his leash bouncing behind him.

"Shit!" Emma exclaimed. Kathy would never forgive her if something happened to her cherished pet. "Pepper!" she screamed, racing after the wayward animal as fast as she could. "Pepper, come back!"

Emma drew in her breath. "Oh, no!" The dog was nearing the corner. Please don't go in the street, she implored silently.

As if the dog had heard her, instead of entering the intersection, he turned right and stayed on the sidewalk. "Thank God," Emma murmured. As she rounded the corner, her lungs burning from the exertion of running, she saw Pepper slow his pace. Maybe he was running out of steam, too. At least she hoped so. If she was lucky, she might be able to catch him before he got his second wind.

Emma picked up the pace, and as she closed the distance between herself and the dog, Pepper abruptly veered off of the sidewalk and ran toward a somewhat dilapidated beaux-arts office building where a tall, dark-haired man was sitting on the lawn holding a set of blueprints. As Emma opened her mouth to ask the stranger if he could grab Pepper's leash, the animal ran up to the man and stuck his nose right in the fellow's crotch.

Emma was mortified. "Pepper, stop it!" she yelled. As she jogged into the yard, the dog removed his nose from the man's private parts and took a bite out of his blueprints.

"Pepper! Bad dog!" Emma scolded, reaching down and grabbing the animal's leash. "I am so sorry," she said to the man. "I don't know what came over him. He's usually much better behaved than this."

The man laughed, standing up. "It's all right. No harm done. He's a friendly little guy, isn't he?"

Emma looked up at the man. He was about six three, slender but well built. Wearing dark jeans and a black T-shirt, he was very nice looking. As the man stared down at her with a captivating smile, Emma realized that she was gawking and that he was waiting for her to say something.

"Yes, Pepper is very friendly," she agreed.

"I'll bet you taught him to do that. You probably meet a lot of interesting people that way."

Emma blushed. "He's not even my dog. He belongs to a friend. She had to work late today, so I picked him up for her. He goes to Yuppie Puppy Day Care. You've probably seen it." God, that sounded lame. Emma wished she could crawl in a hole and take the dog with her.

"Well, he's a cute little guy," the man said, leaning down and patting Pepper on the head. "I have two cats. He was probably drawn to their scent."

Emma looked at the gaping hole in the man's blueprints. "Unfortunately, he loves to eat paper. My friend swears he was a billy goat in another life. It looks like he damaged your prints." Firmly holding onto Pepper's leash, she reached into her briefcase and pulled out a business card. "Here's my card. Please send me a bill for the damage."

The man took the card and looked at it. "Emma Davis, attorney-at-law. Franklin and Holland. I'm impressed. That's one of the city's best firms. Have you been there long?"

Emma shook her head. "Only a few months. I'm new in town."

"Do you live near here, or is this just the dog's neighborhood?"

Emma felt herself relax. "The dog and I both live a couple of blocks from here."

The man smiled and stuck Emma's business card in his jeans pocket.

"I'm serious about paying for the damage," she said.

"Don't worry about it," the man said. "These are just preliminary plans. I worked them up last week and wasn't happy with them, so I came over here to take a closer look at the building. Now that I've seen it, I can see I need to make some fairly significant changes. Your buddy didn't do any real harm by tasting them."

Emma looked at the building, then back at the man. "Are you an architect?"

The man nodded. "Forgive my manners." He reached into a back pocket, pulled out his own card, and handed it to Emma.

"Flynn Fielding," she read aloud. "So, what are the plans for this building?"

"It was built in 1915 and was a showpiece in its day, but over the years it changed hands a lot and got remuddled."

"Remuddled?" Emma repeated.

"That's what happens when remodeling of historic buildings goes astray. Original woodwork and floors ripped out or covered over with crap, that kind of thing. A lot of these buildings end up being torn down. Fortunately this one survived and the new owners want to restore it to its original glory."

Emma looked at the building again. "There must be a real sense of satisfaction in your work."

Flynn Fielding nodded. "There is. I can't imagine doing anything else."

Pepper was straining at his leash and began to bark.

"Looks like your friend is anxious to get home," Flynn said.

"I guess he is," Emma said. Funny, she was not at all anxious to break off this conversation. "Well, it was very nice meeting you, even though it was under less than ideal circumstances."

"It was nice meeting you, Emma Davis," Flynn said. "Maybe I'll see you around sometime."

"Maybe," Emma said. I hope so, she added silently.

Ninety minutes later, Emma filled Kathy in on her event-filled walk home from Yuppie Puppy. "I was so embarrassed."

"What's to be embarrassed about?" Kathy asked. "You met a nice man. I don't suppose you got his name?"

"Of course I got his name," Emma replied indignantly. She retrieved the card from her briefcase and handed it to Kathy. The reaction was instantaneous.

"Oh, my God!" Kathy screamed. "You actually met Flynn Fielding. I don't believe it! Don't you know who he is?"

"Yeah, he's an architect. It says so on the card."

Kathy jumped up from her chair. "He's not just an architect. He's the hottest architect in the whole city. He's been voted one of Chicago's most eligible bachelors by several magazines. I can't believe you met him. Wait here. I'll be right back." She rushed out the door toward her own apartment and returned a few minutes later carrying a manilla folder full of clippings. She sat down next to Emma and began riffling through the papers. "Here," she said, pulling out a magazine article and handing it to Emma. "Look at this."

Emma scanned the article. "Historic Buildings Come Alive Again in Flynn Fielding's Talented Hands."

"And this one." Kathy handed her another article.

"Flynn Fielding Shares His Favorite Projects."

"And how about this?"

"Flynn Fielding's Latest Challenge."

Emma looked at her friend. "Why do you have all these? Is that whole folder full of stories about Flynn Fielding?"

"Of course not," Kathy said, patting the folder. "This is my wish list."

"Wish list?" Emma repeated.

"You know," Kathy said. "Men I wish to go out with."

Emma laughed. "Isn't that kind of high schoolish?"

"Hell, no. It's good to have lofty goals. It's like taping pictures of supermodels to the fridge to keep yourself from overeating. You're never going to look like them, but it's something to strive for. This file contains photos of the sort of men I aspire to date. Even though I might have to settle for less, it's still good to aim high. And believe me, Flynn Fielding is about as high as you can get."

"Let me see that file," Emma said, taking it out of Kathy's hands. "Who else is in here?" She leafed through the clippings. "New CEO of Harris Bank. Hospital chief of staff. University of Chicago vice chancellor." One of the photos stopped Emma in her tracks. "Who is this?" she asked, holding it up so her friend could see it.

"It's Prince Albert of Monaco, of course," Kathy replied.

"Why is Prince Albert on your wish list?"

Kathy shrugged. "Because I think Princess Kathy has a nice ring to it." She saw the strange look on Emma's face and said, "Why? What's wrong with having him on my list?"

"Well, first of all, I've never heard that he spends much time in Chicago. And more important, don't they say he swings in the other direction?"

"Who cares about that? If I could be a princess, I'd be willing to make a few concessions." Kathy grabbed the photo out of Emma's hand. "You're missing the whole point here. You just met one of the premier bachelors in the Midwest and we have to figure out how to get you a date with him. I know. Why don't you call him tomorrow and insist that you pay for the damage to his blueprints? Then you could arrange to meet him for dinner to settle up."

"I can't call him," Emma protested. "I'm too embarrassed."

"That's silly. You said he was a good sport about it."

"Yes, he was an extremely good sport. But your dog bit a hole the size of Comiskey Park in his blueprints. I'm sure Flynn Fielding never wants to see me, or Pepper, again."

"You can't pass up this opportunity," Kathy insisted. "Remember I told you how Pepper has a sixth sense with people? Well, he's obviously given Flynn his stamp of approval. You simply have to go out with him."

"I can't call him."

"Well then, I'll call him for you."

"No!" Emma said vehemently.

"Honestly," Kathy sputtered. "And you wonder why you don't have many dates. You have to seize the moment."

"I think your dog already seized more than enough from this particular guy."

"All right, fine," Kathy said, shoving all of the clippings back into her folder. "Sit home alone and let life pass you by. See if I care. Come on, Pepper. Let's go home. Emma obviously needs some quiet time alone to think about her pathetic, lonely life. And then maybe she'll realize that help is only a short phone call away."

Emma spent a couple of hours working on her

brief, watched a bit of TV, and went to bed. Before she drifted off to sleep, she thought about her chance meeting with Flynn Fielding, architect, eligible bachelor, animal lover, and all-around nice guy. She hated to admit that Kathy was right but she very much wanted to see Flynn again. Emma dozed off wondering how to go about asking him for a date. As it turned out, she didn't have to.

Emma was at her desk late the following morning when her phone rang. "Emma Davis," she answered.

"Hello, Emma Davis," a smooth voice said. "This is Flynn Fielding. We ran into each other last night."

Emma's heart started racing. Flynn didn't sound angry. That was a good sign. "I remember. How are your blueprints?"

"I'm in the process of redoing them. But I didn't call to talk about my blueprints."

"You didn't?"

"No, I called to ask if you'd like to have dinner with me tomorrow night."

Emma's face lit up and she raised a fist in the air. "I'd like that."

"Great. I'll pick you up around eight. Where do you live?"

Emma gave him the address.

"See you then."

"See you then," Emma repeated.

"Bye."

She hung up the phone feeling happier than she'd felt since moving to Chicago. Flynn Fielding, a man from Kathy's wish list, had asked her out.

She snatched up the phone. She couldn't wait to tell Kathy the good news and, after that, would send Coleen a quick e-mail.

Max Englander, eat your heart out.

CHAPTER 7

By early that afternoon Emma had completed the letters needed to transfer the remainder of Oak Greythorne's tangible assets to the trust. She slipped them into a folder and walked by Lorraine's desk. "I have to run an errand. I shouldn't be gone long."

"Take your time," Emma's secretary said. "I have plenty of things to keep me occupied."

Emma was about to head down the hall when she noticed something new on her secretary's desk. "I didn't know they made scented candles in the shape of grand pianos," she said.

"I thought it was cute," Lorraine said. "I don't know if I've ever mentioned this, but I'm a huge music buff. In fact, I started taking piano lessons myself a couple of years ago. I took lessons as a kid but then sort of gave it up. I'll never be talented enough to perform anywhere, but I really enjoy it. I collect piano trinkets and I couldn't resist this candle. It also has a quite powerful vanilla scent."

"I can smell it," Emma said. "So, what's happening

with Barrie Holman's proposition to make this a scent-free office?"

"No action has been taken yet," Lorraine replied, "but I'm happy to report that since our last staff meeting, at least eighty percent of the secretaries on this floor are displaying at least one scented item at their desks. And I'm hoping that with a little persuasion, we can increase that to ninety percent."

"Good luck," Emma said, chuckling.

Emma took the elevator to the fortieth floor and made her way down the hall to Louis Brisbane's office, feeling only a bit jittery about the memory of Tommy Corona.

She intended to simply drop the letters off with Devereaux Braxton and return to her office, but when she approached the woman's work area she saw that Brisbane himself was standing there. Emma felt a chill go through her, remembering the talk at the bar. She would have preferred not having to speak to him.

"Emma, how nice to see you," Brisbane said genially. "What do you have for me?"

"These are the rest of the *Greythorne* transfer letters."

"Excellent. That was quick work." Brisbane took the folder out of Emma's hands and briefly scanned the contents. Then he set the folder on Devereaux's desk. "Please mail these out today," he instructed his assistant.

"Certainly," Devereaux replied.

Breathing easier now that her errand was completed, Emma turned to go. "Do you have a few minutes?" Brisbane asked.

"Ah . . . sure," Emma said, fighting back her nervousness. She tried not to think about Jill's story. *It's an urban myth and I won't think about it. This man is a senior partner and a well-respected lawyer, not Count Dracula.*

"Then please come in." Brisbane opened the door to his office and ushered her inside.

Entering the office, Emma avoided looking toward the rest room where Corona had confronted her.

"Have a seat," she heard Brisbane say. He settled into his own plush leather chair.

Emma chose a chair where she could both have her back to the rest room door and avoid directly staring out of the enormous windows behind Brisbane's desk. Facing the ornate file cabinet, she folded her hands primly in her lap and crossed her ankles.

"I'm very impressed with the work you've done so far on the *Greythorne* estate," Brisbane said. "It is obvious that you are both efficient and thorough. Those are admirable qualities in an attorney."

"Thank you," Emma said, relaxing.

Brisbane leaned back in his chair. "I don't know if you're aware of this, but for the past twenty years I have not been formally associated with any particular team here at the firm. I dabble in most types of work, and in the ten years I've been on the management committee I've found that more and more of my time is occupied with administrative matters. As a result I have less time for the actual practice of law."

Emma nodded.

"I have always enjoyed doing estate work," Brisbane went on. "It's not contentious like litigation, nor is it strictly transactional like real estate. In every estate I've handled, I have always felt good about helping carry out the decedent's last wishes. That is the primary function of trusts and estates work, you know, determining and carrying out the intentions of the deceased."

Emma nodded again.

"And even though the decedent's family members are going through a trying and difficult time, they are almost always grateful for their attorney's help in wrapping up their loved one's affairs. It really is a very satisfying business. If I had been practicing fifty or seventy-five years ago, before law firms turned into multinational corporations, I could see myself being a small-town probate attorney."

"I'm sure you would have made an excellent small-town lawyer," Emma said politely, wondering where this was going.

"Oak Greythorne would have liked you," Brisbane said. "He appreciated intelligent women, particularly those who were well-mannered and not always speaking out of turn. And if they were attractive, well, so much the better."

Emma flinched at his last remark. Hadn't Lorraine warned her that Brisbane had a reputation as a ladies' man? In case the conversation was moving in that direction, she'd better try to derail it. "Greythorne never married," she said.

"No, he did not."

"Was there a reason for that?" Emma asked.

Brisbane considered the question for a minute before answering. "It's not something I ever discussed with him. My guess would be that his illness prevented it. I think he realized that he was a troubled man and he was not the type of person who wanted to inflict his problems on others."

"With all the help available today for mental health problems and drug and alcohol abuse, it seems such a shame that he either didn't seek treatment or wasn't able to find help," Emma said.

"That is a pity," Brisbane said.

"Did you see him very often?"

Brisbane shook his head. "No. He would call or come to see me a couple of times a year, usually to ask my advice about some investment, but other than that I had no contact with him. The last time I saw him was last year, around Thanksgiving."

Brisbane suddenly fell silent and seemed lost in thought. Emma wondered if he was mourning for his old friend or thinking about something else. Whatever was on his mind, the silence dragged on long enough that Emma began to feel uncomfortable.

"Is there something else you'd like me to do to wrap up the estate?" she finally asked.

The question seemed to startle Brisbane. "What was that? Oh, yes, there is. The next task I have for you has to do with the apartment building." Brisbane referred to a manilla folder in front of him. "We have a buyer willing to pay more than the assessed value of the property. Quite frankly, the building is not in the most desirable neighborhood. Values in that area have been stagnant for quite some time, and, in fact, some have fallen in the past five years. We'll do well to liquidate that asset and put the money into the trust, where it can directly benefit the charitable endeavors that Oak Greythorne designated."

Brisbane leaned back in his chair. "The buyer wants to gut the building and remodel it; therefore, it is desirable that the building be empty before possession is transferred." He handed Emma several sheets of paper. "Here is a list of all existing tenants, their monthly rent and a notation of when their leases expire. I would like you to write each of these people a letter offering to buy out the remainder of their leases. Offer them three thousand to start. Most of them should take that and run. Offer those who don't up to six. If anyone is still balking at that figure, let me know and we'll deal with them on an individual basis. Our goal is to have the building vacant by September first. Any questions?"

Emma looked over the list of names. "What if someone just flat out refuses to move?"

The sides of Brisbane's mouth curled. "As I said, we'll deal with each person individually. I really don't anticipate any problems. Everyone has their price."

As with the account transfers, this project seemed straightforward enough. Emma nodded. "I'll get the letters out first thing next week."

"Splendid." Brisbane stood up and Emma followed suit. "I am very pleased with your work, Emma," he said. "I hope this will be just the first of many projects we work on together."

"I hope so, too." Emma didn't quite know why, but she really wanted to get out of Brisbane's office. "Then if you'll excuse me, I need to be getting back downstairs. I have a meeting with Tom Cane in a few minutes." This was a lie, and Emma hoped that Brisbane wouldn't call his partner to verify it.

"Don't let me keep you." Brisbane stood up and looked out the window. "There must be a fire at the building next door," he said excitedly. "There are half a dozen fire trucks and a lot of people standing outside. They must have evacuated it. Come look."

Emma hesitated.

"Come here," Brisbane said, motioning for her to join him at the window.

Swallowing hard, Emma walked around the large desk and stood in back of Brisbane.

"You can't see from there," Brisbane said. He put his hand on her back and gave her a firm nudge forward. "Come right up here and take a good look."

Emma clenched her fists together and forced herself to take deep breaths. She took the briefest peek down at the street, then stepped back. "Must be a fire, all right," she said.

Brisbane turned and looked at her, a strange expression on his face. "You're trembling," he said. "Are you all right?"

"I'm fine," Emma said in a squeaky voice. "It's just that I'm afraid of heights."

"So that's why you didn't want to look through my telescope the first time you were up here," Brisbane said in a kindly tone. "I couldn't for the life of me figure that out. Most people are absolutely fascinated by my telescope." He gave Emma a paternal pat on the arm. "I'm sure once you've worked here for a while you'll get over your phobia," he said. "At least I hope you do. It can't be much fun working in a terrific building like this if you can't enjoy the view."

Emma nodded. She really needed to leave. "I'd better get going or I'll be late for my meeting."

"Yes, you run along now. Again, thank you for your assistance with the *Greythorne* file. I'll be in touch again soon."

Emma had to restrain herself from racing out of the office. But once she was safely on the elevator, she was able to relax. By the time she got off the elevator she was starting to feel ashamed that she had questioned the man's character.

Louis Brisbane had been a perfect gentleman. He had seemed sincerely grateful for the work Emma was doing on the *Greythorne* estate, and he also seemed truly sad that his friend's life had been cut short by his personal demons. In short, it appeared that Brisbane was a good manager who had not lost his common touch. As Emma walked down the hall toward her office, she was convinced that Annah Bull was right. The story about the woman associate was clearly just an urban myth.

CHAPTER 8

On Saturday afternoon, Kathy employed the precision of a drill sergeant in helping Emma prepare for her first date with Flynn. Sitting in a comfortable chair in Emma's bedroom, with Pepper in her lap, Kathy insisted that her friend model virtually her entire wardrobe, then rejected one outfit after another.

A black sheath. "Too boring."

A tan suit. "Too schoolmarmish."

A peach-colored Laura Ashley. "Too Kansas City."

"Watch it," Emma said. "You're getting a little personal."

Kathy shrugged. "You said you wanted my honest opinion."

"I know, but you don't have to be mean."

"Quit wasting time," Kathy said. "Let's see some more clothes."

Half a dozen additional rejects later Kathy was starting to get impatient. "Don't take this wrong, but every single thing you've shown me so far makes you look like a Sunday schoolteacher. Are women who graduate from law school issued some kind of edict prohibiting them from ever wearing fashionable clothes?"

"I'm getting tired and cranky," Emma complained. "I don't know what you have in mind, but it's obviously not part of my wardrobe."

"I'd be glad to lend you something, but I figured you'd be more comfortable wearing your own clothes." Kathy set Pepper on the floor, then stood up. "Let me take a look. You must have something in there with some pizzazz." A few minutes later she emerged triumphantly from the walk-in closet. "You were holding out on me!" she exclaimed. "This is perfect."

Emma's mouth dropped open when she saw the pastel floral dress Kathy was holding up. "That's a summer dress," she protested. "I bought that last year for a Fourth of July party in Kansas City. This is Chicago and it's early May. It still gets cool at night here. I'd freeze to death in that."

"Honestly," Kathy said, handing the garment to Emma. "That's what fashionable wraps are for. I'll bet I've got one that's just the right color. You slip into the dress and I'll be right back."

When Kathy returned moments later, Emma was standing in front of the mirror, critically eyeing her reflection. "I'm not so sure about this—" she began.

"It's exquisite!" Kathy gushed. "Absolutely stunning. Turn around."

As Emma dutifully spun around, the silky fabric

of the dress clung to her curves like a second skin and the hem of the garment flared out slightly just above the knees. "Very sexy," Kathy said approvingly. "Here, let's try this." Kathy draped a pale peach shawl around her friend's shoulders. "What do you think?"

Emma looked in the mirror. "Wow, it looks terrific." She ran her fingers over the soft fabric. "This is the softest pashmina I've ever felt."

"It's not pashmina," Kathy said. "It's shahtoosh. Much softer and more elegant."

"And completely illegal to import into this country!" Emma exclaimed. "Where did you get this?"

"My aunt Bitsy bought a whole suitcase full of them in Paris last year. It's no big deal."

"It'll be a big deal if customs officials haul me out of the restaurant in handcuffs in the middle of dinner," Emma countered. "That would make quite an impression for a first date."

"You're overreacting again," Kathy said. "Don't you ever stop thinking like a lawyer? Look, it's not like you personally went to Tibet and slaughtered the animals this came from. They'd already gone to the big pasture in the sky and had no more use for their fur so why shouldn't we enjoy it? It's just the right accent for that dress and it's very warm, too."

"The shawl *is* a nice complement to the dress," Emma admitted, rubbing her face in the soft folds of fabric.

"It's fabulous," Kathy agreed. "Sister, you are

going to have Flynn Fielding eating out of your hand before you even order cocktails. Now, let me see your shoes and bag."

A short time later Kathy nodded approvingly at the full ensemble. "Perfection," she said.

After treating herself to a long soak in a hot bubble bath and taking extra care with her hair and makeup, Emma was ready for her big night. Flynn Fielding picked her up precisely at eight o'clock. "That's a great outfit," he said admiringly as he watched her wrap the shahtoosh shawl around her shoulders.

"Thanks," Emma said, happy that she had let Kathy help with her ensemble. "You're looking quite dashing yourself," she said, thinking how handsome he looked in his dark suit.

Flynn smiled. "Now that we've established we're a damn fine-looking couple, I'm starving. Shall we go?"

"Let's."

As they waited for the elevator, Flynn looked over his shoulder. "Why do I have the feeling someone is watching us?"

"Probably because someone is," Emma whispered. "My friend Kathy—you know, Pepper's owner—was dying to get a glimpse of you, so it wouldn't surprise me if she were looking through her peep hole. It's the apartment right there." Emma motioned behind her.

"I see," Flynn whispered back. He turned and waved with both hands. "Hi, Kathy," he called. "How are you? Love your dog." As the elevator door opened, he blew a kiss toward Kathy's door, then pulled Emma inside the elevator. "Do you think she got a good look?"

Emma burst out laughing. "I think she got an eyeful. That was great!"

During the short drive to the restaurant Emma leaned back against the plush leather upholstery of Flynn's silver Lexus and marveled at how seemingly minor incidents could yield big results. If Kathy hadn't worked late, or if Pepper hadn't run away, Emma would not be heading out for a night on the town with a man on Kathy's wish list. It was those unexpected twists and turns that made life so interesting.

Flynn had made a reservation at NoMi, a restaurant in the Park Hyatt on North Michigan Avenue, across from the city's old water tower, that featured upscale Continental cuisine. In Emma's opinion, it was a perfect venue for a first date. Quiet enough to facilitate conversation yet lively enough not to make two strangers feel they were being rushed into intimacy.

Flynn ordered a bottle of white Bordeaux. After the sommelier poured a glass for each of them, Flynn raised his glass. "I propose a toast. To your friend's dog and chance encounters. May they both prosper."

Emma laughed and clinked her glass against Flynn's. "Cheers."

By the time the waiter brought their salads, Emma and Flynn were chatting about their childhoods like old friends.

"My dad is an insurance adjuster in Kansas City," Emma explained. "He's always worked closely with a lot of lawyers in the course of defending claims and had a good rapport with many of them. That's how I first became interested in the profession."

"I don't imagine Franklin and Holland does much insurance defense work," Flynn said with a smile.

"That's true," she said. "Although there are times when I think that doing insurance defense work at a small firm would be a lot less nerve-wracking than trying to make it at a place like Franklin and Holland."

"What's so important about making it at a big firm?" Flynn asked. "All the associates I've ever known do nothing but bitch about the long hours, the sadistic partners, the bureaucracy. Why do so many of you put yourselves through that torture? It's always sort of reminded me of lemmings marching toward the sea. Deep down they have to know there's nothing good up ahead, but they keep marching anyway."

"Oh, but there might be something good up ahead," Emma said, taking a sip of wine.

"What's that?"

"In a word, partnership. It's the holy grail. It means independence, financial security, respect in the legal community. Assuming that you haven't fallen into drug or alcohol dependency or picked up any serious mental health problems along the way."

Flynn laughed. "Sounds like a delightful way of life."

"It has its moments," Emma said. "What about

you? How did you come to make your living saving incredible old buildings?"

The waiter brought their entrees, roasted halibut for Flynn and Carnaroli risotto for Emma.

"My story is similar to yours," Flynn said, taking a bite of his fish. "My dad pointed the way. He was a bricklayer and a mason. I grew up doing all sorts of odd jobs at building sites and learned the business from the ground up. My dad did a lot of restoration work on older buildings, too, so I gained an appreciation for both old and new architecture. By the time I was about sixteen, I discovered I had some facility for drawing plans, and things just sort of progressed from there. I put myself through college by working construction jobs. Everything from pouring cement to operating a crane. It was a great training ground. It made me appreciate all the different talents that go into making a building that's attractive, utilitarian and that will last." Flynn paused a moment, then said, "God, that was a long-winded answer. I'm sorry."

"No, it's interesting," Emma said. "Are you from Chicago?"

Flynn shook his head. "Iowa. Home of corn fields and covered bridges. It was a great place to grow up, but I honestly think Chicago is the best place to be right now. There are so many opportunities here." He poured more wine for both of them. "You must think so, too, since you moved here. Or were you running away from something?"

Emma flushed. "Why would you think that?"

Flynn smiled. "It just popped into my head. So, why did you come here?"

Emma took a sip of wine. "I guess I was ready for new challenges. I liked my firm in Kansas City, the people and the work. If they hadn't merged with Franklin and Holland, I don't know that I would have ever left there. But as soon as I heard about the merger, I couldn't get the idea of moving to Chicago out of my head. Everything about it appealed to me. Bigger city, bigger firm, bigger cases—"

"Bigger salary," Flynn cut in.

"Well, yes," Emma said. "Also much bigger cost of living. But it was something I wanted to try."

"And you're happy you did?"

"So far, yes. I'm very happy I made the move."

"Me, too," Flynn said, looking at her over his wineglass. "And I'm especially happy your friend has a spoiled dog that goes to doggy day care and that he ran away from you. Because that led to the happy coincidence of my meeting you."

Emma smiled at him. "That *was* a happy coincidence," she agreed.

Flynn held up his wineglass again. "To Pepper."

Emma touched her glass against his. "To Pepper," she repeated.

"And to us," Flynn said in a softer tone.

"To us," Emma murmured. And to many more nights like this one, she added silently.

Emma and Flynn lingered over coffee and dessert at the restaurant, then stopped at a nearby bar for a nightcap. It was midnight when Flynn walked Emma back up to her apartment. "I had a great time," he said as they stood outside of Emma's door.

"So did I," Emma said.

"I hope we can do it again soon," he said.

"Me, too."

Flynn leaned down and kissed her on the lips. "Good night, Emma."

"Good night."

Emma was barely inside her apartment when the telephone rang.

"Why didn't you invite him in?" an indignant voice demanded without even giving Emma a chance to say hello.

"Do you mean to tell me you've been peering out your door all night?"

"Well, I wouldn't say *all* night," Kathy replied.

"You're crazy," Emma said, kicking off her shoes and sinking down onto the sofa. "Has anyone ever told you that?"

"Constantly. I just pay no attention. So answer my question, why didn't you invite him in?"

Emma sighed. "Because we'd had a perfect evening and I didn't want to spoil it with the awkwardness that sometimes comes at the end of the evening on first dates. This was a nice way to end it."

"End it?" Kathy fairly screamed. "You mean end the evening, right? Not end the relationship."

"Yes, I mean end the evening. And I wouldn't say that there is a relationship yet." Emma smiled. "But there might be one in the offing."

"So he was nice?"

"Very nice. And very smart. And very good looking, although I don't know how he'd compare to, say, Prince Albert of Monaco."

"Damn," Kathy said. "Of all the days for me to ask you to fetch Pepper from doggy day care. If it hadn't been for that stupid meeting at work, I might have run into him myself. Now I'm relegated to living out my fantasies about him vicariously through you."

"Life's a bitch, isn't it? Listen, I'm beat and I'd like to go to bed now. What do you say we have brunch tomorrow at the Drake and I'll give you all the glorious details of what you missed."

"You sure know how to rub it in, don't you?" Kathy grumbled. "I'll come get you around eleven. And you'd better not leave anything out. I want to hear about his every word."

"You'll get the full story. 'Night, Kathy."

"Good night. And Emma? I'm happy you met a nice guy. You deserve it."

"I'm happy, too." Emma agreed. She hung up the phone and leaned back against the sofa cushions and smiled. Very happy.

CHAPTER 9

On Monday, Emma typed a letter to the tenants of Oak Greythorne's apartment building offering to buy out their tenancy. After getting Brisbane's approval, she asked Devereaux to mail the copies. Then she spent several long days researching a products liability case she was working on with Tom Cane. On Thursday she came back to her office at lunchtime to eat a sandwich that she had picked up from a downstairs deli and check for messages.

"Your messages and mail are on your desk," Lorraine said as Emma passed. "And another floral arrangement arrived. I didn't know where to go with it, so I put it on your credenza. If this keeps up, you should think about opening a greenhouse."

Emma laughed and walked into her office. Flynn Fielding was in San Francisco attending a symposium on architectural conservation. Although he couldn't be with Emma in body, he was very much with her in spirit. Not only had he called her every day since their first date, he had also sent a daily dose of flowers. Emma's desk held a vase filled with long-stemmed red roses. A small table near the window displayed a hibiscus plant with enormous salmon-colored flowers.

The most recent arrival featured an exotic mix of orchids and ginger. Emma opened the attached envelope and removed the card. "Counting the minutes till tomorrow night. Flynn." Emma smiled and put the card on her desk.

"The guy is obviously a true romantic," Lorraine said from the doorway. "You'd better hang on to him. They're very rare in this town."

"They're very rare in any town," Emma said.

After eating her lunch, Emma returned to the conference room where she'd been working with Jill Bedner. They kept plugging away, reviewing file after file, until six thirty.

"I swear if I have to look at one more document, my eyes are going to permanently glaze over," Emma complained, slipping the stack of papers in front of her into a manilla folder. The table was covered with documents and the floor contained dozens of boxes.

"I hear you," Jill Bedner agreed. "Let's finish this box and then call it a day."

"It's a deal," Emma said.

In the case Tom Cane had assigned to Emma and Jill, the client was one of several paint manufacturers that had been named as defendants in a class action filed by school districts seeking damages for the costs of removing lead paint from their buildings. Since the paint in question had been in the schools for at least forty years, the schools' success in the lawsuit turned on being able to prove that each of the defendants was one of the companies that manufactured the paint. Six months into the discovery phase of the lawsuit, Tom's new client had become disenchanted with the way its attorneys were handling the defense and had hired Franklin & Holland as successor counsel.

In order to get up to speed on the case, which was scheduled for trial in just six months, Tom Cane told Emma and Jill to drop whatever they were doing and review an entire truckload of documents to determine if there was evidence their client had manufactured any of the paint. Although Jill was a pleasure to work with and Emma was looking forward to second-chairing the case with Tom, after two solid days of staring at chemical formulas, paint chips and sales orders, she felt like her head was going to explode.

"I never knew there were so many different paint formulas or manufacturers," Emma said, paging through a 1950s paint catalog.

"I know," Jill said. "The next time I walk through the paint department at Home Depot, I'll have a lot more respect for what goes into making the stuff."

Emma finished perusing the documents in the folder in front of her, jotted a few notes on a legal pad, then put the folder back in a box on the floor. "I'm quitting," she said. "The rest can wait till tomorrow."

Jill closed her folder and returned it to the box. "If

we put in a good day tomorrow, we should be able to finish and we won't have this project hanging over our heads this weekend."

"Amen to that," Emma said. "I most definitely do not want to spend the weekend here getting up close and personal with paint chips."

"Me neither. I'm spending a three-day weekend in Wisconsin," Jill said. "I have a friend whose family has a place in Minocqua and we're going up there. It's supposed to be seventy and sunny and they have a boat so I'm gonna make like a tourist."

"Sounds like fun," Emma said.

"It's something different," Jill agreed. "Like you said, we all work hard here and we need to get away once in a while."

"Maybe one night next week we can get a beer and celebrate being done with these damn documents," Emma suggested.

"I'd like that."

Ten minutes later Emma grabbed her briefcase, shut off the light in her office and headed for the elevator. It had been a long day. She was looking forward to some mindless chatter with Kathy. After they'd eaten she might even let her friend offer some advice on appropriate apparel for Emma's second date with Flynn.

When Emma got off the elevator a few minutes later, the building's underground parking ramp was fairly deserted. As she walked briskly toward her car, Emma mentally reviewed her wardrobe. Flynn had seemed to like the summer dress she'd worn on Saturday. Unfortunately, she had nothing else like it. Maybe she should try something plain but chic. Emma smiled. It had been years since she had spent this much time agonizing over what to wear on a date. She felt like a teenager. And it was a wonderful feeling.

As she approached the row where her car was parked, Emma's mental fashion show was interrupted by loud voices. She slowed her pace and looked in the direction where two men were arguing. She took a few more steps, then froze. One of the voices belonged to Louis Brisbane. The other to Tommy Corona.

Acting purely on instinct, Emma rushed between the nearest two vehicles, crouched down on the pavement and nervously peered out. She saw a black Cadillac SUV two rows away. Corona was behind the wheel. Brisbane was standing next to the open passenger's door. The discussion grew more heated.

"Stupid bastard!" Emma heard Brisbane exclaim. "What were you thinking?"

"You told me to handle it, so I handled it," Corona replied. "Next time you can do your own fuckin' dirty work and leave me out of it."

"Maybe I'll do just that," Brisbane replied. "You take too many chances."

"The problem with you is that you're gettin' to be a regular pussy in your old age," Corona said. "My aunt Edna's got more balls than you."

Emma had to strain to hear Brisbane's response. "You'd better watch it, Tommy. Nobody's indispensable, including you."

"The same goes for you, my friend," Corona shot back.

Brisbane slammed the door and began walking toward Emma's hiding place. The Cadillac's engine roared to life and the big vehicle also headed her way. Her heart pounding wildly, Emma moved to the back of a nearby vehicle and wedged herself in between its trunk and a cement post.

As Brisbane walked past the car that was shielding her, Emma held her breath, praying he wouldn't look her way. Corona gunned the engine of the Cadillac and zoomed around the corner. As he passed Brisbane, he rolled down the window, gave him the finger, then squealed toward the exit. Brisbane walked to the elevator without responding to Corona's gesture or glancing in Emma's direction.

Emma remained in her hiding place for several minutes to assure herself that neither man was coming back. Then she crawled out from behind the vehicle and unsteadily rose to her feet. She had been crouched down so long that it felt as if she had lost all circulation in her legs. She hefted her briefcase strap onto her shoulder and jogged to her car as quickly as she could. Within minutes she emerged from the parking garage onto the street and finally allowed herself to breathe a sigh of relief. She hoped that running into Tommy Corona was not going to be a regular occurrence. The violence pent up inside of him seemed ready to explode for any reason at all.

Thirty minutes later, Emma and Kathy were having a glass of wine at a bistro near their apartment building. "What do you think they were arguing about?" Kathy asked after hearing what had happened in the parking garage.

"I have no idea," Emma said, taking a large swallow. "But they were seriously pissed at each other." She set down her wineglass and sighed. "I'm so embarrassed at how I reacted. If anyone had seen me hiding behind that car they would have called the cops."

"I don't blame you at all for reacting that way," Kathy said. "After what Corona did the last time you saw him, what were you supposed to do, rush over and give him a hug?"

"I could have kept walking to my car," Emma replied. "They were having such a heated discussion that they probably would never have seen me. But the second I heard that voice I just panicked and crouched down like a scared rabbit. Maybe I'm not cut out to live in a big city."

"It's not the city, it's the company the senior partners at your firm keep," Kathy said.

"I guess so," Emma agreed. She kept replaying the incident in her mind. Brisbane and Corona had sounded like they were ready to kill each other. She wondered what they had been arguing about. More important, she wondered why a well-respected attorney like Brisbane would want to have a common thug like Corona as a client.

CHAPTER 10

The following morning, Emma took time out from working on a brief to see if Franklin & Holland's client database could yield any information on the type of legal matters Louis Brisbane was handling for Tommy Corona. She typed "Corona, T." into the client name field, then hit "search." A message immediately flashed on the screen: "Forty records were found matching your search."

Emma randomly clicked on a number of the listed cases. The majority involved contracts between Corona Construction and the owners or developers of real estate. A handful appeared to be civil lawsuits in which Corona Construction was either the plaintiff or defendant. In all cases, Louis Brisbane was shown as the supervising attorney.

Emma stared at the screen, feeling vaguely disappointed that Tommy Corona was a legitimate Franklin & Holland client. The man scared the daylights out of her, and it would have made him and his connection to Brisbane all the more sinister if there had been no official record of him in the client database.

Her curiosity now piqued, Emma did a quick Internet search to find out more about Corona and his company. Her search turned up a wealth of articles. In fifteen minutes she was able to glean the highlights of Tommy's career.

Tommy Corona was born on the south side of Chicago, the son of a bricklayer. As Brisbane had mentioned, young Tommy had done some amateur boxing. At age twenty he took a job with a well-respected construction firm. After ten years he struck out on his own. Corona Construction was now one of the largest such companies in the greater Chicago area, having been the general contractors on many notable projects. Publicly, at least, Corona seemed legit.

Emma did find one article that gave her pause. Five years earlier, following a lengthy undercover operation, the United States Attorney's office had indicted a dozen prominent Chicago businessmen with ties to organized crime. At least two dozen others had also been under investigation but there was insufficient evidence to bring charges against them. One was Tommy Corona.

Emma shuddered. The fact that Tommy Corona probably had ties to the Mob definitely did not make her feel better about Corona's business relationship with Louis Brisbane.

Emma switched back to her word processing program. Her time was too precious to waste more of it thinking about a crass bully—and possible crook—like Tommy Corona. If Louis Brisbane wanted to represent Corona, that was his business. It had no bearing on Emma's work at the firm or her working relationship with Brisbane—even if she preferred not to have a working relationship with him.

Soon after Emma returned from lunch, the phone rang.

"Emma Davis."

"Hello, Emma Davis," Flynn's voice came over the phone. "How are things on the thirty-fourth floor today?"

"Things are fine," Emma said, smiling. "When did you get back?"

"I'm at the airport waiting for my baggage," Flynn replied. "I just wanted to make sure we were still on for dinner."

"We sure are. Thanks so much for the flowers. That was very sweet."

"I'm glad you liked them."

"I loved them. And my secretary is just dying to meet you. She says either you're one of a very elusive breed or I actually sent myself all those flowers to make all the other women in the office feel bad."

Flynn laughed. "What's your secretary's name?"

"Lorraine."

"Well, you tell Lorraine that I may be elusive but I'm still a gentleman."

"I'll do that," Emma said.

"See you at seven?"

"Seven it is."

*   *   *

After leaving the airport, Flynn drove directly to the construction site of a high-rise office building called Converse Towers. It was his largest project to date and it had been plagued with delays, the most recent a problem with the quality of the black marble in the entryway. The developer was threatening everyone with legal action if the building wasn't ready for occupancy by November first. Flynn had been monitoring the situation while he was out of town and was anxious to see firsthand what progress was being made to replace the marble.

At the site, Flynn parked his car and made his way to the trailer that served as the general contractor's office. Once inside he headed to the table where the owner of the construction company was going over some papers and demanded, "I want to know when that marble is going to be in and this time I want a straight answer, not more of your double-talk!"

Tommy Corona looked up at him. "Sounds like somebody got up on the wrong side of the bed. Or are you this ornery because you can't find anybody to share the bed with you?"

Flynn put his hands on the table and leaned closer to Corona. "I mean it, Tommy. I'm sick of your jiving. We're all going to have our asses hauled into court if we don't meet the November first completion date, and we can't meet it if your people don't finish that marble work."

"What's the matter?" Corona sneered. "Is Mr. Fancy Architect afraid of a lawsuit? Shit, I get sued all the time. It's part of doing business. No, it's more than that. It's part of the American way of life."

"I have never been sued, and I don't intend to start now," Flynn said. "I want you to give me a firm date when that marble will be in and then I want you to do whatever is necessary to have it in by then."

"I'll have it in by the end of the month," Corona said.

"You'd better," Flynn said.

"And what if I don't?" Corona chuckled. "Are you gonna come and kick sand in my face?"

Flynn reached over and grabbed Corona by the collar. "No, I might just sue your lousy ass for everything you've got."

The veins bulged in Corona's neck. "Get your fuckin' hands off me," he spat.

Flynn let go of the burly man and took a step back. "And what if I don't? Are you gonna tell the teacher I was bad?"

"Don't mess with me, Fielding," Corona growled. "Or I'll hang you from a crane and leave you there until the crows devour your lousy carcass."

Flynn walked over to the door. "You've got until the end of the month and not one day longer." He left without giving Corona a chance to retort.

It seemed to Emma that the afternoon dragged on interminably. She left work at five thirty, early by Franklin & Holland's associates' standards, so she wouldn't be rushed getting ready for her date. She had allowed Kathy to lend her a clingy dress with short sleeves and a neckline that was fairly low without being too revealing. Kathy had also graciously furnished another shawl.

"You don't have to say a requiem mass over this one," Kathy said as she draped the wrap around Emma's shoulders. "It's silk and cashmere."

Emma was dressed and ready to go by six thirty. She spent the next thirty minutes rushing back and forth to the bathroom to check her hair, touch up her makeup, reapply lipstick and perfume and generally look at herself critically in the mirror.

"Get a grip," Emma told herself as she sat back down on the sofa after her seventh inspection. "You're acting like an idiot." She was contemplating an eighth inspection when the doorbell rang.

"You look wonderful," Flynn said, leaning down to kiss her lightly. "It's good to see you."

"It's good to see you, too," Emma said happily.

"Are you ready to go?"

Emma nodded.

Flynn offered his arm. Emma took it and they stepped into the hallway and rang for the elevator. Flynn motioned toward Kathy's door. "Is she watching us again?" he whispered.

"I don't know," Emma hedged. "I guess it's possible." She hoped Flynn wouldn't think that peering out of a peephole at Emma's new beau was too sophomoric. "She's rather protective of me since I'm new in town and all."

"Why don't we stop in and say hi so she can see that I'm a nice guy and that you're in good hands?"

The elevator door opened.

"Are you serious?" Emma asked. "You don't have to do that."

"It won't take long and besides, we're not in that big a hurry. Come on." Flynn took Emma's hand and pulled her down the hall to Kathy's door. "Go ahead."

Emma took a deep breath, hoped her friend hadn't chosen this evening to give herself a mud mask facial, and knocked on the door. "Kathy, are you home? It's me."

Kathy opened the door within seconds, looking as if she were ready to be photographed for *Town & Country*. "Why, Emma, what a nice surprise. Aren't you looking lovely tonight. And who is this handsome creature?"

"This is Flynn Fielding. Flynn, my friend Kathy Flood. Pepper's mother."

Flynn and Kathy shook hands.

"Would you like to come in?" Kathy asked.

"We're just on our way to dinner," Flynn said, "but Emma's told me so much about you that I insisted on meeting you. I hope we didn't disturb you."

"Of course not." Kathy's dog trotted up behind her. "I understand you've already met Pepper," Kathy said.

"I have indeed," Flynn said. He leaned down and took a closer look at the dog. "What does he have in his mouth?"

Kathy turned and looked. "Oh, that's his pacifier.

He found it on the sidewalk when we were out walking a couple of days ago and now he carries it everywhere, even to doggy day care."

"We really should be going," Emma said, taking Flynn's arm. She was afraid that if they stuck around much longer, Kathy might pull out the file containing her wish list. Explaining a dog sucking on a pacifier was one thing; explaining why Flynn's photo was keeping company with Prince Albert of Monaco's was quite another.

"It was nice to meet you, Kathy," Flynn said.

"The pleasure was all mine," Kathy said, batting her eyes seductively. "Have a good time, you two."

"We will," Emma said.

"She seems nice," Flynn said as he and Emma rode down in the elevator.

"She's very nice," Emma agreed. "I'm lucky that I met her. She grew up in Chicago and she's been a big help in making me feel at home here."

Over a quiet dinner at Vinci, a restaurant with floor-to-ceiling wine racks and soft lighting, Flynn told Emma about the symposium he attended in San Francisco. "It's just amazing how much the conservation and preservation of old buildings has caught on," he said. "There were three hundred architects at this conference. Twenty years ago you might have had thirty. This is really an exciting time to be in my business."

"I love old buildings," Emma said, taking a bite of her lamb chop. "I grew up in a Victorian house. I'd love to own one myself someday."

"It's my dream to restore a house for myself," Flynn said.

"Why haven't you done it?" Emma asked.

Flynn smiled. "Good question. I suppose for the same reason the shoemaker's children go barefoot. The press of business. I feel more of an obligation to take care of paying clients' needs than my own. But I am going to do a place of my own someday."

"So for the time being you live in a high-rise like lots of other young people."

Flynn nodded. "It's a very nice high-rise. I designed it five years ago. I have a great lake view, it's bright and airy and I enjoy being right in the city rather than stuck out in some suburb. But I definitely view it as a temporary residence. Before too much longer I'm going to make rehabbing my own house a priority."

"I've always thought it would be fun to decorate and furnish a house from the ground up," Emma said. "I've still got a lot of stuff from my first apartment. Family castoffs, thrift store junk. It would be great to be able to start from scratch and pick out just what you wanted from furniture stores, antique shops, flea markets. Of course, all that takes time, and excess time is a commodity I don't exactly have right now."

"Maybe you will someday," Flynn said.

"Maybe," Emma agreed. "You're looking a little tired. Do you have jet lag?"

Flynn shook his head. "No, after I got back this

afternoon I had a rather unpleasant discussion with someone working on one of my projects."

"I'm sorry to hear that. Did you get everything worked out?"

"I hope so," Flynn said. "I was thinking we could take a drive up to the construction site tomorrow. That is, if you're interested in seeing a work in progress."

"I'd love to see it."

"Then it's a date."

Kathy called Emma bright and early to get the details about the date and was appalled that Emma had again not invited Flynn in for some après-dinner activities. "What's the matter with you?" Kathy shrieked. "I grudgingly went along with your reasoning about taking things slow on a first date but this is carrying it way too far. He's going to think you're a nun or something."

"We stopped for coffee and dessert, so it was kind of late when we got home," Emma explained. "He was fine with it. In fact, he didn't even ask to come in."

"You don't think he's gay, do you?" Kathy asked.

"No, I don't think he's gay," Emma said, trying not to laugh. "I just think he's a nice guy who's not in a big hurry to jump in the sack."

"I'll kill myself if he's gay," Kathy said.

"Don't break out the strychnine just yet," Emma said. "I'm seeing him again this afternoon. He's going to show me around a couple of his building sites."

"Thank God! Don't blow it this time. After all, three strikes and you're out."

"I'll remember that," Emma said.

She spent the morning puttering about. Keeping in mind what Kathy said, she vacuumed the apartment—just in case. She wasn't anywhere near as inexperienced as Kathy seemed to think. She just happened to be going out with the right sort of guy.

Flynn picked Emma up early in the afternoon. He had suggested that she dress casually so she wore a pair of jeans and an oversized sweater. First Flynn took her to the construction site of a prairie style home he had designed. The property was perched on a bluff overlooking Lake Michigan, about ten miles from the Loop. The house had just been framed in. Flynn showed Emma the blueprints and pointed out various features.

"There will be two staircases," he explained. "An open staircase in the front and a closed staircase leading down to the kitchen. The front one will be right there," he said, pointing. "It will be five inches wider than standard to make it easier to move furniture to the second story. Also the stair risers will be a bit shorter than normal. The owners are middle-aged now, but they wanted a home that will accommodate their changing needs as they age, and shorter steps put less stress on old legs."

"It's wonderful that someone would have the foresight to think about having a house that will still be suitable when they're old," Emma marveled.

"Buyers are getting more savvy and more demanding all the time," Flynn replied. "The master suite will be there, overlooking the lake, and there will be sliding glass doors leading out to a deck." He looked down at Emma's white sneakers. "It might be a little muddy to walk around there."

"Dirt washes off," Emma said. "Let's go."

Flynn took her hand and led her around the perimeter of the property. They stood at the top of a bluff looking down at Lake Michigan. It was a sunny, warm May day and the breeze wafted through Emma's hair. "This is a wonderful location," Emma said. "I'd love to live in a place like this."

"I thought you wanted an old house," Flynn said.

"A new house with some traditional features would be okay, too," she said. "I'm really not that hard to please."

"That's good to know," he said. "Come on. Now that you've seen the kind of thing I do in single-family housing, I'd like to show you a larger-scale project."

They drove about six miles west to a partially completed, ultramodern high-rise called Converse Towers. "Wow!" Emma said as they got out of Flynn's Lexus. "You designed this?"

"Yeah, and I'll have to admit I'm rather proud of it. It's my largest project to date."

"How many stories are there?" Emma asked as they walked into the site.

"Thirty-five," Flynn replied.

"When is it scheduled to be finished?"

"Good question. The developer has insisted it be ready for occupancy by November first, but I'm afraid the angels are going to have to be on our side in order for that to happen. We've been plagued with numerous delays, including a teamsters' strike. The latest problem is the quality of the black marble in the entryway. A good portion of it has to be removed and replaced. Remember I told you I had an unpleasant discussion yesterday afternoon?"

Emma nodded.

"Well, it was with the general contractor who keeps promising me he'll take care of the marble but never delivers."

Emma looked up at the building and gave a low whistle. "This is amazing," she said. "I can't imagine what it takes to design something like this."

"Come on," Flynn said, taking her by the hand. "Let's take a closer look."

As they approached the building, Emma noticed a huge crane that was used to lift steel girders into place. "That's got to be the biggest crane I've ever seen. How many people does it take to run that?"

"Just one," Flynn replied.

"You're kidding! One person can run that monster?"

"Sure," Flynn said. "Come on, we can go up in it."

Emma froze in her tracks.

"What's the matter?" Flynn asked. "They're really amazing machines. Wouldn't you like to see how it works?"

Emma shook her head.

"Oh, come on," Flynn cajoled. "When are you going to get another offer like this?" He tried to pull her forward but she planted her feet firmly and would not budge. Flynn looked at her closely. "What's wrong?" he asked.

Emma turned away from the crane. "You're going to think this is silly," she said quietly, "but I'm afraid of heights."

"Really?"

Emma nodded. "I always have been. Ever since I was a little girl. I almost get sick looking out of my office window." She turned back and looked up at Flynn. "That's childish, isn't it?"

Flynn immediately put his arm around her. "Of course it's not childish. It's not something you're doing on purpose. Don't ever be embarrassed by it and don't let anyone make fun of you. A lot of people are afraid of heights. It can be overcome, you know. There are programs that help desensitize you by taking you to progressively higher levels. Have you ever tried something like that?"

Emma shook her head. "I've thought about it a few times, but I've never done it."

"Maybe that's something I could help you with," Flynn offered. "Heights don't bother me in the slightest. I'd be happy to work with you if you want."

Emma took a deep breath. "I'd like that," she said. "It is a bothersome phobia. The only way I can ride in glass elevators is if I keep my eyes shut."

"Come on over here. We don't have to go up in

the crane but I can at least point out some of its features."

Emma followed him around the building. As they got closer, the name on the crane came into view and she stopped short.

"Now what's the matter?" Flynn asked. "Don't you trust me? I promise I won't make you go up in it."

Emma swallowed hard. "Corona Construction is the general contractor for this building?"

"Yes."

"Tommy Corona's company?"

"That's right. Do you know him?"

"I'm afraid so." Emma told him about her encounter with Corona.

Flynn's reaction was instantaneous and violent. "Jesus Christ! What was that slimeball doing at your law firm?"

"He's a client of Louis Brisbane, the partner I'm working with on that big estate."

Flynn put his hands on her shoulders. "Listen to me carefully, Emma. Tommy Corona is a very bad man. I don't want you anywhere near him. He's a successful contractor and those of us in the business have no choice but to put up with him, but he's rumored to have Mob connections. I can't believe anyone in your firm would represent him."

The unease that Emma had felt about Corona escalated, but she tried to remain calm. "I'm not working on any of his cases, and if I'm lucky I'll never run into him again," she said.

"If you do, run the other way and then call me immediately," Flynn said. Sensing that he had upset her, he put his arm around her and said, "I think we've seen enough here. How would you like to start on the Flynn Fielding fear of heights desensitization program?"

Emma nodded. "I'd like that. As long as we start slowly."

"No problem," Flynn said as they headed back toward the car. "Our next stop will be Navy Pier."

"Why are we going there?"

"Because they have a one-hundred-fifty-foot-tall Ferris wheel."

Emma's mouth dropped open. "There is no way I am going on a one-hundred-fifty-foot-tall Ferris wheel."

"It's very romantic, especially at night," Flynn said.

"How about if we skip the Ferris wheel for now and find some other place to be romantic?" Emma countered.

Flynn leaned down and kissed her. "You've got a deal."

CHAPTER 11

"I just can't believe you!" Kathy exclaimed. "Would it help if I lent you my copy of the *Kama Sutra*? Or maybe you just need a course in remedial dating."

It was the following afternoon, and Kathy, Emma and Pepper were on their way to have tea with Kathy's grandmother. As Kathy drove, she continued the stream of sarcastic comments that had begun several hours earlier after she learned that Emma had still not had sex with Flynn Fielding.

"Honestly, instead of dragging that gorgeous man home and into your bedroom, you spent two hours riding up and down the glass elevators at Water Tower Place. What was that good for?" Kathy tossed her head indignantly.

"I told you, Flynn is trying to help me overcome my fear of heights," Emma explained. "I've never been able to tolerate glass elevators, and by the end of the night riding on them didn't bother me at all. I think that's great progress."

"You don't look like the sort of person who would be afraid of intimacy," Kathy prattled on as her green

BMW Z3 squealed around a corner, "but I guess that's a possibility. Have you ever considered therapy? Because I think it might help—"

Emma's patience finally snapped. "Enough!" she shouted.

The sudden harsh noise made Pepper yelp and squirm frantically in Emma's lap while his owner gave her friend a hurt look. "You don't have to yell at me." Kathy pouted.

"Apparently I do," Emma replied. "I've been trying to carry on a normal conversation with you for the past four hours, but all you've done is call me all sorts of terrible names and imply that I should be taken to the nearest psychiatric ward just because I haven't yet had sex with someone I've known for all of ten days."

"Well, you have to admit it is a little odd—" Kathy began.

"No, it's not," Emma interrupted. "It's not odd at all. This is what's normal for Flynn and me, so will you please stop trying to make me feel like I'm a freak of nature and just let our relationship take its normal course?"

Kathy set her jaw.

"Please," Emma said. "I want a friend who can be happy that I'm dating a very nice guy who seems to be genuinely interested in me, not a self-appointed therapist who insists on analyzing every last thing I do."

Kathy slowly nodded. "You're right. I'm sorry. I guess I was so excited that you were actually going out with a great man that I've been trying to experience the relationship vicariously. That's selfish of me. I'll try to chill out. And by the way, I am sublimely happy for you."

"Thank you," Emma said. "I really appreciate it."

"Don't mention it. Just promise me that if anything hot and heavy ever does develop with Mr. Fielding before the next millennium, you'll let me know ASAP."

"I promise," Emma said. She settled back in her seat and scratched Pepper's head. "So tell me again why your grandmother insisted that I come along with you to have Sunday tea."

"Well, for the last three months I've been telling my whole family how wonderful you are, so naturally Grandma wants to meet you. She's very social."

"How old is she?"

"Eighty-two but you'd never know it. She's sharp as a tack—that goes for both her mind and her tongue."

Kathy turned onto Goethe. "Well, here we are," she said, pulling into a driveway and cutting the engine.

Emma stared out of the window at the enormous three-story brownstone in the heart of Chicago's Gold Coast. "Your grandmother lives here? Oh, my God! It looks more like a foreign embassy than a private residence. How many rooms are in there?"

"I've really never counted. Fourteen or fifteen, I think. Plus five bathrooms. It's about nine thousand square feet."

"Your eighty-two-year-old grandmother lives alone in a nine-thousand-square-foot house with five bathrooms?"

"No, she has a live-in housekeeper." Kathy opened the door and reached for Pepper. "Come on, let's go."

Emma put her hand on Kathy's arm. "I don't mean to be gauche, but about how much would this house sell for?"

Kathy shrugged. "In the neighborhood of four to five million."

Emma let out a low whistle. "That's some neighborhood. I thought you said your grandfather owned banks. He must have had to rob a few of them to afford a place like this."

"The house has been in my family since it was built in 1890, so I guess we kind of take it for granted. William Flood, my carpetbagger ancestor who made a killing after the fire, was a friend of Potter Palmer, the man who developed this neighborhood. There's a saying here in Chicago that Palmer was the guy who put the gold in the Gold Coast," Kathy explained. "Anyway, Palmer used to own the house next door, and he talked William into building this place. Succeeding generations of Floods have lived in it ever since."

"So your father grew up here?" Emma asked.

"Yes."

"I can't imagine living in a place like this," Emma said as she continued to stare in awe at the building.

Kathy patted her friend's hand. "I know. You're

not in Kansas anymore. Now come on. Grandma doesn't like to be kept waiting."

A stylishly dressed woman in her sixties ushered them into the house. "This is Barbara Nelson," Kathy said. "She's been Grandma's right hand for over twenty years. Barbara, this is my friend Emma Davis."

"It's a pleasure to meet you, Emma," Barbara said. "We've heard so many good things about you from Kathy. Rose is in the parlor. Go on in. I'll be along with the refreshments shortly."

As Barbara tended to the food, Emma stared at the foyer's dark paneling, the open staircase and the stained glass windows. "How high are the ceilings in here?" she whispered.

"Fourteen feet," Kathy replied in a normal tone. "Why are you whispering?"

"Because I feel like I'm in a historic monument."

"The house is on the National Register of Historic Places," Kathy said. "But speaking out loud is permitted. Come on, let's go see Grandma. You can have a full tour later if you'd like."

"You'd better believe I'd like a tour," Emma said. "I'd even be willing to pay admission."

"For you I think we can waive the admission fee," Kathy said, giving her friend a gentle nudge down the hall.

Rose Stewart Flood was a tall, slender woman with thick honey-colored hair and a regal bearing. She had alert green eyes, flawless skin, and was attired in a mint tweed Chanel suit. "It's delightful to meet you,

Emma," she said as she sat back in one of the over-stuffed chintz chairs in the airy, feminine parlor. Rose reached into a Staffordshire jar, pulled out a dog biscuit and tossed it to Pepper, who was sitting on an antique Persian rug at the old woman's feet. "Kathy hasn't stopped raving about you since you moved into her building. Would you like a glass of wine, dear?"

"Only if someone else is having one," Emma said politely as she and Kathy settled themselves on a sofa that matched Rose's chair.

"Of course we're all having wine," Kathy piped up. "Would you like me to go get it, Grandma?" she asked.

"No, I'll get it." The old woman nimbly got up from her chair and walked briskly to the door. "Make yourselves at home. I'll be right back."

As soon as Rose was out of earshot, Emma leaned over to Kathy and whispered, "I can't believe how great your grandmother looks. You'd never think she was a day over sixty."

"She's always taken great pride in her appearance," Kathy explained. "Besides, she has a plastic surgeon virtually on call."

"That's not very nice," Emma said, laughing in spite of herself.

"No, but it's true," Kathy said. "Her medical center should rename its cosmetic surgery clinic after her."

Rose returned shortly with a bottle of Riesling. She was flanked by Barbara, who was wheeling a cart loaded with tea, sandwiches and sweets, along with fine china, flatware, heavy linen napkins and a chew bone for Pepper. The four women fell into an easy conversational patter as they helped themselves to the refreshments.

"Grandma, Emma is working on Oak Greythorne's estate," Kathy said. "Do you remember him?"

The old woman reached down and gave Pepper a small piece of a cookie. "I certainly do," she said. "I always felt sorry for him. He seemed like such a troubled soul, even as a child."

"In what way was he troubled?" Kathy asked.

"He was extremely moody," Rose replied. "One day he would be the nicest, most polite boy you'd ever want to meet, and the next he'd be crying uncontrollably over little or nothing. Or then again, he'd be belligerent and uncooperative. I remember thinking what a trial it must have been for his poor mother. It certainly made me appreciate my three boys. Your father and uncles might have raised a little hell now and then, but they were very well grounded."

"Were Dad and Oak friends?" Kathy asked.

"Yes—in grade school anyway. By the time they became teenagers they didn't seem to see too much of each other anymore."

"Even though I never met Oak, I feel sorry for him, too," Emma said. "It sounds like he was very bright and managed to build a prosperous business, but then his mental condition deteriorated and he was forced to sell it."

"It's a damn shame," Rose agreed. "I'm sure I have some old albums that contain pictures of Oak when he was a boy. Would you be interested in seeing them?"

"Very much," Emma said.

Rose turned to her companion. "Barbara, would you mind hunting the albums down? They'd be in the rear bedroom on the third floor. Bring the ones labeled 'James—grammar school.'"

Barbara stood up. "I'll see what I can find."

"You don't have to go to the trouble of trying to find them right now," Emma said.

"It's no trouble," Barbara assured her. "Rose is impeccably organized. I'm sure I'll be able to find them in a flash."

"And she won't even have to expend any energy getting to them," Rose said with a smile. "You see, we have an elevator. I'm told it was quite an extravagance in 1890. Apparently, it was the talk of the neighborhood."

"I don't doubt that for a minute," Emma said.

Fifteen minutes later, Emma, Kathy and Rose were enjoying another glass of wine when Barbara returned with three photo albums. "I believe these are the correct ones," Barbara said, placing them on the coffee table in front of her employer.

Rose picked up the first one and began paging through it. "Oh, yes. Look at this. I can't believe it's been almost fifty years since these were taken. Here," she said, "I'll come over and sit between you girls so we can all look at once." Kathy and Emma moved to the ends of the sofa and Rose stationed herself between them.

"This was a class trip to the Lincoln Park Zoo," Rose explained, pointing to a black and white photo. "The boys must have been about ten years old. This is my son James—Kathy's father—and this is Oak Greythorne."

Emma peered intently at the photo. James Flood was an attractive dark-haired boy with a big smile on his face. Oak Greythorne had lighter hair and a very serious expression.

Rose turned the page. "These pictures were taken at the Yacht Club. I believe this was James's eleventh birthday. Here is Oak again. He looks as if he was in a better mood that day. Look, here he and James are hamming it up for the camera."

"They were both nice-looking boys," Emma commented.

"They were cute little rascals, weren't they?" Rose agreed. She turned another page. "And here they are at another party. It must have been later that summer. Oak looks rather upset here, don't you think?"

Emma leaned closer for a better look at the picture. "Yes, he looks downright distraught," she said. "It looks like James has his arm around him, as if he were trying to console him or cheer him up. Who is this?" she asked, pointing to another boy behind James and Oak. "He looks like the class bully."

"Which one?" Rose asked. "Oh, him. Yes, he was always something of a bully. That is Louis Brisbane."

Emma's mouth dropped open. "Louis Brisbane was a friend of Oak and James?"

"Yes, they were all in the same class at the Latin School," Rose replied.

"Brisbane is the senior partner at my law firm. He's the one who gave me the assignment of working on Oak's estate," Emma explained. "Come to think of it, Brisbane did mention that Oak had been an old friend. But I certainly never expected that Kathy's father was in the same class. What a small world."

"So Brisbane was a bully, eh?" Kathy asked. "What kind of things did he do?"

"Oh, that was so long ago that I'm not sure I can think of anything in particular," Rose said. "But I do remember that Louis was always extremely competitive. Wanted to win at all games at all costs and got very angry if he didn't. I don't think James ever liked him much. You'll have to ask your father for details, Kathy. I'm sure he could give you more specifics."

"Do you recall if Oak and Louis were close friends?" Emma asked.

Rose thought for a minute. "I always got the impression that Louis and Oak had sort of a love-hate relationship. I never thought Louis was very nice to Oak, and sometimes he seemed to do things that he knew would provoke Oak's outbursts—much the way nasty people might tease a mad dog, to use a rather crude analogy. That's what I meant when I said Louis was a bully. He seemed to prey on those who were weaker than he."

"Sounds like being a senior partner at a large law firm was the perfect career path," Kathy joked. "Now he preys on lowly associates like Emma."

Rose turned to Emma and said seriously, "Be cautious in your dealings with Brisbane. I haven't thought of him in many years, but a leopard rarely changes its spots. Unless I miss my guess, he would not be above using people to achieve his own ends."

Emma felt a chill go through her as thoughts of Tommy Corona danced through her head. If Brisbane was a bully, what did that make someone with Mob connections? And what about Julia Boswell? Could it be possible that Brisbane had caused the young associate to have a nervous breakdown?

"Thanks for the warning," Emma said. "I'll keep it in mind."

CHAPTER 12

Emma spent the following day taking depositions in the lead paint case, and it was five thirty when she got back to her office. Lorraine had left, and the floor was largely deserted. Emma sat down at her desk to check her mail.

Nine of the tenants in Oak Greythorne's building had already returned the forms indicating that they were willing to terminate their lease early in exchange for a three thousand dollar payment. The fine response to the mailing was good news since it meant Emma was that much closer to being finished with the project and Brisbane.

Emma returned a couple of phone calls and when she looked at the clock on her desk it was six fifteen, time to go home. She shut off her computer, took her purse out of her desk drawer and walked to the door.

Flipping off the overhead light, Emma opened the door and found herself nose-to-nose with an angry-looking young man wearing jeans and a green sweatshirt. Emma let out a small yelp of surprise and took a step backward. The man followed her into the office.

"Are you Emma Davis?" the man demanded as the office door clicked shut.

Emma stared at him, paralyzed with fear. Was this one of Tommy Corona's henchmen?

"Answer me!" the man said. "Are you Emma Davis?"

She took a deep breath. "Yes," she said in a squeak. She edged her way over to her desk and managed to get behind it, putting some space between herself and her uninvited visitor.

The young man paced back and forth in front of the desk. Emma looked at him closely. He looked to be about her age, close to six feet tall, had a reasonably good build, and his brown hair was long.

"How dare you make a mockery out of a great man," he said, pointing his finger at Emma. "You're not fit to shine his shoes."

Emma tried to think of an appropriate response. It was not going to be easy to try to reason with someone who considered Tommy Corona a great man. "I'm not sure I understand what you mean," she said, struggling to keep her voice even.

The man scowled at her and continued his pacing. "I guess you thought you were going to pull a fast one, but you're not. I'm going to keep you honest, lady. Just like I did with all the others."

Emma swallowed hard. There had been others. What had he done to them? And what did he intend to do to her?

"Not one of you is willing to admit the truth," the man went on. "It's one big conspiracy. And you're just another part of it."

Emma frowned. Now he had lost her completely. Maybe he was on some sort of drugs. She glanced around her. Her phone was about four feet away. She wondered what the odds were that she could get to it and call 911 before the man stopped her.

"I tried to tell people what happened and nobody would listen to me," the man went on. "They treated me like I was nuts. Well, I'm not nuts," he said in a louder tone as he took a step toward Emma. "And you are going to listen to me whether you want to or not."

"I'm listening," Emma said as calmly as she could. She backed up so that she was standing next to the wall behind her desk. "What is it you want to tell me?"

The man reached into his jeans pocket. Emma drew in her breath. Was he going for a weapon? What if he had a gun?

Emma held her breath as the man slowly pulled his hand out of his pocket. As the hand emerged, Emma saw that instead of a weapon he was holding a folded piece of paper. She exhaled. The man unfolded the paper. Emma craned her neck to see what it was, then her eyes widened in amazement. It was one of the letters she had sent to Oak Greythorne's tenants.

An feeling of enormous relief washed over her as she realized that she was facing not one of Tommy

Corona's soldiers but a disgruntled tenant. The tension faded from her body.

Emma moved back toward her desk. "Are you one of the tenants in Mr. Greythorne's building?" she asked.

The man's eyebrows knitted together. "Of course I am. Why did you think I was here?"

"Until now I really wasn't sure," Emma admitted. "Would you mind telling me your name?"

"Lee Hennick."

Emma nodded. She remembered seeing that name on the tenant list. "All right, Lee. It's obvious that something about my letter upset you. Is it the amount of money that we offered in exchange for the early termination of your lease? Because I am authorized to say the amount is negotiable."

Lee's face turned mottled. "I don't care about the money!"

"Then what is it?" Emma asked. "Tell me and maybe I can help you."

"I don't need any help. I didn't come here to talk about me. I came to talk about him."

"Who?"

"Oak Greythorne," Lee replied.

"What about him?"

"Nobody cares about him," Lee said. "I went to the police and told them what happened and they just blew me off."

Emma rubbed her hands over her cheeks. Just when she thought she was getting somewhere, the guy was back to talking in riddles. She guessed she would have to try to take it one step at a time and see if she could eventually get a coherent story out of him.

"Let me get this straight," she said slowly, as if she were speaking to a small child. "You went to the police and told them about Oak Greythorne."

"You're damn right I did."

"And they blew you off."

Lee nodded. "I'm wondering if maybe somebody paid them off."

"Why would someone pay off the police?"

"To keep the truth from coming out, of course," Lee said.

"The truth?" Emma repeated, feeling as if she were Alice down the rabbit hole. "The truth about what?"

Lee slammed his fist down on Emma's desk. She jumped back toward the wall. Maybe her visitor wasn't so harmless after all.

"The truth about how Oak Greythorne was murdered. But nobody believes me, so the rotten bastards who did it are still out there someplace."

Emma's mouth gaped open.

Lee leaned over the desk and looked her in the eye. "Now, what I want to know is what you and your fancy law firm are going to do to help me prove Oak was murdered."

Emma stared at Lee for what seemed to her like an eternity. She was so stunned at his claim that Oak Greythorne had been murdered that she didn't know how to respond. All she could think was that this young man was deeply troubled.

"Lee," she said gently, "Oak Greythorne wasn't murdered. He battled substance abuse all his life. The authorities ruled that his death was the result of an accidental overdose of prescription drugs and alcohol."

"That's bullshit," Lee exclaimed. "I knew Oak Greythorne. He'd gotten his life together. There's no way he would have accidentally OD'd. The man was murdered, and I'm not going to let you leave this office until I've convinced you of that."

From the vehemence of Lee's expression, it was clear to Emma that he truly believed the man was murdered. Emma sat down in her chair. "All right," she said. "You go ahead and try to convince me that Mr. Greythorne was murdered." She motioned to the chairs in front of her desk. "Would you like to sit down? I think you'd be more comfortable if you did."

Lee hesitated a moment, then took her up on her invitation.

"How did you happen to know Oak Greythorne?" Emma asked.

"I met him at AA."

"Alcoholics Anonymous?"

Lee nodded. "About six months before he died, Oak started coming to AA meetings near where I live."

"Maybe I'm missing something," Emma said, "but I thought the whole point of AA was that people could remain anonymous. How did you find out Oak's identity?"

"Anonymity is an option, not a requirement," Lee explained. "A lot of people talk after the meetings and get to know each other."

"Is that what happened with you and Oak?"

Lee nodded. "Yeah. When he came to his first meeting, he looked sort of lost and out of place. I'd been going to meetings there for a few years and was very comfortable with the group, so afterward I went over and asked if he'd like to get a cup of coffee or something. He said he would. We went to a coffee shop and talked for about an hour. When we were ready to leave, I told him where I lived and he laughed and said that was a real coincidence because he owned the building. We hit it off so well that he ended up asking me to be his AA sponsor."

"Really?" Now Emma was truly intrigued. Lee Hennick wasn't just a crackpot. It sounded like he had actually known Oak Greythorne fairly well in the last months of his life.

"Was this the first time Oak had gone to AA?" Emma asked.

"No, I think he'd been in and out of twelve-step programs for a long time, but in the past he'd always relapsed. This time he was determined not to let that happen."

"What made him choose to attend meetings near your apartment building? I believe he lived much closer to downtown."

Lee shrugged. "He never said. Maybe he just needed to start fresh with a new group. Or maybe he felt ties there because of his apartment building.

He really seemed to like the area. For a guy with money he was pretty down-to-earth."

"How often would you see him?"

"Usually at least twice a week."

"Always at AA meetings?"

"Yeah. And sometimes we'd talk on the phone."

"He'd call you when he felt like he needed a drink?"

"That happened a couple times the first month after I met him," Lee said, "but after that he'd just call and talk about sports or other things. I think he was kind of lonely and sometimes just wanted to talk to somebody."

"It sounds like the two of you got along very well."

"We did. We had a lot in common." Lee paused a moment, then added, "We both had other problems besides drinking."

A warning flag rose in Emma's head. "I don't mean to pry, but do you mind expanding a little bit on that last comment?" she asked.

Lee looked down at the floor, then back at Emma. "Besides abusing alcohol, Oak Greythorne and I were both lifelong manic-depressives. We both had regular panic attacks."

"I'm sorry," Emma said. "You've been like that all your life?"

"Pretty much. I had my first panic attack in third grade. Oak told me he had his when he was seven."

"That must be rough," Emma said.

"You learn to live with it," Lee said, "and you learn that you have to take your meds. I'm on Prozac and lithium."

"Do you take the meds every day?"

Lee nodded. "You're supposed to, and usually I do, although I admit I haven't taken any the last couple days because I was so pissed off about your eviction letter."

Emma grimaced. "Did Oak Greythorne ever tell you what prescriptions he was taking?"

"He mentioned Prozac and Xanax, but I think he'd tried a bunch of different drugs over the years."

"Do you know if he took them regularly?"

"I don't know for sure, but I assume so because right before he died he told me that the past six months had been the longest period of sobriety he'd had in a long time. From my own experience, I don't think someone with his medical history could have maintained sobriety without being properly medicated."

Lee stared off into space as if he were deep in thought. After a pause, Emma asked, in order to get the conversation moving again, "What do you do for a living, Lee?"

He shook off his contemplative state. "I'm an assistant manager at an Office Depot store. Been there four years. I've been the employee of the month three separate times."

"Good for you. That's great. So what kinds of things would you and Oak talk about?"

"Lots of stuff. Ourselves. Like I said, sports. He liked the Cubs. He was a big Sammy Sosa fan. Was really looking forward to this season."

Emma nodded. While it was interesting for her to learn more details about Oak Greythorne, so far she'd heard nothing to support Lee's theory that the man had been murdered. "Anything else?"

"Sometimes we talked about the future. I said I'd like to be a store manager someday and he told me he'd been thinking about starting up a new business."

"Really?" Emma could not conceal her surprise. "What kind of business?"

"Some kind of Internet company. He was fascinated with all the new technology and how fast things were changing and developing. He said he'd had a knack for building businesses and he thought he was ready to try his hand at another one. He even said there might be a job for me," Lee said proudly.

"Did he give you any details about this proposed business?" Emma asked.

Lee shook his head. "It was still in the planning stages, but in the month before he died, he was really upbeat about it. That's why I know he didn't OD. He had too much to look forward to."

"In that last month of his life, did Oak mention that anything was bothering him?"

"About a week before he died he was real upset. I'd never seen him like that before."

"What was he upset about?" Emma asked.

"He said he was going ahead with the plans for his new business and nobody was going to stop him."

Emma frowned. "What did he mean by that?"

"I don't know."

"Was someone trying to stop him from going back into business?"

Lee shook his head. "I asked him that, but he wouldn't give me a straight answer. He just said, 'I'm not going to let some asshole run my life. I'm going to do as I please.' "

"And you have no idea who he might have been referring to?"

"No."

"Before that time, had he ever mentioned being upset with someone?"

"No."

"When was the last time you saw him?"

"Four nights before he died."

"How was his mood at that time?"

"Terrific. A lot more upbeat than it had been a few days earlier."

"Did he explain the reason why his mood had improved?"

"No. When he came to the meeting, I told him he seemed to be in good spirits. He said he'd been doing a lot of thinking, and the plans for his business were really starting to fall into place. That was the last time I talked to him," Lee said, his voice cracking with emotion.

Emma swallowed hard. "Thinking back to the last

few times that you saw him, was there any indication that he'd gone back to drinking?"

"Absolutely none," Lee said firmly. "He was so damn proud of his sobriety. There's no way in hell he willingly drank alcohol."

"But there was a great deal of alcohol in his system when he died," Emma said. "Surely you're not suggesting that someone forced him to drink it?"

Lee sat up straight in his chair and leaned closer. "I don't know how the alcohol got in his system," he said. "But I'd bet my life on the fact that Oak didn't just suddenly decide to go on a bender. Maybe he was tricked or forced into drinking but, in my heart, I just know that somebody put him up to it. And whoever that son of a bitch is, he should be charged with murder. And that's what I told the cops."

Emma took a deep breath, then exhaled. She was at a loss. Oak Greythorne's death seemed like a classic case of an addictive personality succumbing to his weaknesses. But Lee Hennick clearly believed Oak had been the victim of foul play. And in spite of herself, Emma found the story plausible, at least to some degree.

"Do you remember the name of the detective you spoke to?" Emma asked.

Lee nodded. "Richard Porter. He was a first-class jerk. He smirked the whole time I was talking to him. Like he thought I was cuckoo and he couldn't wait to get me out of there."

"Did you tell Detective Porter exactly what you just told me?"

"Yeah. He thanked me for being a concerned citizen and said he'd check out my story. I called him back at least half a dozen times, but the receptionist never put me through to him and I never heard a word from him."

"Did you tell anyone else you believed Oak had been murdered?"

"No. From the way the detective blew me off, it was clear nobody was going to give me the time of day. I decided I'd try to put it out of my mind and I almost did—until I got your letter about wanting to buy out my lease. Then I just got madder and madder until finally I decided I was going to come and see you." Lee looked Emma in the eye. "There is no way Oak Greythorne would have sold that building to a developer. He would have never done that to his tenants. He told me he liked owning a building that provided affordable housing. He wouldn't have wanted it gentrified."

Emma sat quietly, thinking about everything Lee had said.

"So, did I convince you?" Lee asked.

"I'm afraid you haven't," Emma said, "but I must admit I am intrigued by your story."

"You'll check into it?" Lee asked eagerly.

In spite of her better judgment, Emma found herself nodding. "Yes, I'll do some checking," she said.

"That's great," Lee said, pumping his fist in the air.

"Don't get your hopes up," Emma cautioned. "There's better than a ninety-nine percent chance that Oak Greythorne did die of an accidental overdose."

"But you are willing to consider the possibility that it wasn't accidental?"

"The extremely remote possibility," Emma corrected.

"That's good enough for me," Lee said. He got to his feet and stuck out his hand. Emma gave it a vigorous shake.

"It was nice meeting you," Lee said, as pleasantly as if he and Emma had met at a gallery opening.

"I'll look into this for you," Emma said, getting up from her chair, "but don't expect miracles."

"I don't need a miracle; just somebody who'll take me seriously—and you've already done that." He walked toward the door, then turned back. "Oh, by the way, you can tell whoever is calling the shots for Oak Greythorne's estate that it'll be a cold day in hell before I terminate my lease early. I don't care how much money they offer me. The new owner will have to carry me out kicking and screaming."

"I'll make a note of that for the file," Emma said.

"Have a good night," Lee said as he headed out the door. "Talk to you soon." He closed the door quietly behind him.

Emma walked behind her desk, slumped down into her chair and looked at the clock. It was six forty. She felt as though she'd been trapped for an eternity when, in fact, less than a half hour had passed.

Emma knew it was a mistake to have agreed to check out Lee's story. As she'd warned him, the overwhelming odds were that Oak's death was accidental. She could only hope that Lee would ultimately be able to gracefully accept this finding rather than morphing back from Dr. Jekyll into Mr. Hyde.

Yet Emma couldn't shake the feeling that there could be something to Lee's story. Disturbing facts jumped out at her: sober for six months, starting a new business, having a new friend. That didn't fit the profile of a man who died of a massive overdose.

After mulling over the problem of Oak Greythorne's death for some time, she had a brainstorm. Snatching up the phone, she dialed a familiar number.

"Coleen Kennedy."

"You're still at work?" Emma exclaimed.

"Not all of us have an active social life and a lucrative private sector job," Coleen groused. "Some of us who toil as public servants are actually still working."

"Is Carla trolling for prospects?" Emma asked.

"Yup. I've got a live one in Minneapolis. I told him I'd meet him if he could get tickets to the Alicia Keys concert. He's supposed to get back to me tonight. So, why aren't you out with Mr. F? There's nothing wrong, I hope?"

"Things are going great. So great it's almost scary. No, the reason I called was that I need some advice about a possible criminal investigation, and I thought maybe my friend the expert would be willing to help me out."

"Sure. What kind of case?"

"Well—" Emma hesitated. "It's a little complicated. And you have to promise not to lecture me when you hear what I have to say." Taking a deep breath, she told her friend the highlights of her conversation with Lee Hennick.

"Good God, Emma!" Coleen exclaimed. "He sounds like a lunatic. Why in the world would you tell him you'd check into his story?"

"I told you I don't want a lecture," Emma said. "I called to pick your brain on how to discreetly get information about Greythorne's death."

There was a long pause on the other end of the line, then Coleen said. "All right. I'd start by talking to the detective that the guy allegedly spoke to. You'll get further if you talk to him in person rather than over the phone. Do you have a copy of the death certificate?"

"Yes."

"Good. The name of the deceased's physician should be listed. Talk to him or her. See if you can verify that Greythorne was making progress treating his problems. I assume there was an autopsy."

"There was."

"Then you should talk to the medical examiner who performed it. Find out if there was anything that looked the least bit suspicious even though they ruled it accidental. You might also want to talk to a few of Greythorne's neighbors and get their take on his mental condition around the time he died. That's all I can think of off the top of my head, but if anything else comes to me I'll let you know."

"Thanks, Coleen. This is really helpful."

"Emma, you be careful. You could be dealing with a sick puppy."

"It's okay. This guy is just upset. I don't think he'd hurt anybody."

"What about that other thug who grabbed you in the partner's office?"

"I haven't seen any more of him," Emma said.

"Well, that's good. Oh, one more thing. Since you're looking into the death of a gentleman of some means, don't forget the most important rule in any criminal investigation."

"Which is?"

"Follow the money."

"Follow the money," Emma repeated. "Gotcha. Thanks a lot, Coleen. I'll keep you posted on what I turn up."

"Be very careful," Coleen said again. "You don't know who you might be dealing with."

Emma hung up the phone, Coleen's words running through her head. Follow the money. Follow the money. As the mantra repeated itself over and over, a sick feeling grew in the pit of Emma's stomach.

In the Oak Greythorne estate, a healthy portion of the money led back to Louis Brisbane.

CHAPTER 13

Lee Hennick walked out of the skyscraper that housed Franklin & Holland's offices and headed west. He couldn't afford the exorbitant rates charged by the building's parking garage, so he had left his car at a surface lot a few blocks away.

Lee walked briskly along, his spirits lighter than they had been since receiving Emma's letter offering to buy out the remainder of his lease. He thought about Oak Greythorne, a wonderful man whose hopes for a fresh start had been snuffed out by some unknown monster.

Then he thought about Emma. She seemed caring and down-to-earth. Lee liked her. Oak would have liked her, too. Although she obviously had not wanted to get his hopes up, Lee was confident that Emma would be able to reveal Oak's death for what it was: a cold-blooded murder.

Lee was so caught up in his thoughts that he did not notice the black Cadillac SUV crawling along the curb about a block behind him. As Lee entered the parking lot to retrieve his car, the Cadillac double-parked in front of a dry cleaners and turned on its four-way flashers. When Lee pulled his car out onto the street and headed north, the Cadillac turned off its flashers and followed several car lengths behind.

As the SUV and its quarry continued their trek northward, the driver of the Cadillac took out his cell phone and punched in a speed-dial code.

The call was picked up after three rings. "Brisbane here."

"It's me," Tommy Corona said. "I thought you'd want an update on that wacko who went to the police crying that Greythorne was murdered."

"Don't tell me he went back to the police," Brisbane said. "I thought your contact assured you that the detective he spoke to didn't believe a word of his story."

"He didn't go back to the police. He went to see somebody in your building."

"What?" Brisbane exclaimed. "Who did he see?"

"I don't know," Corona said. "I've had one of my guys tailing him off and on since his visit to the PD. About an hour ago, I got a report that he was spotted going into your building. My guy fucked up and lost him in the lobby, so I don't know for sure what floor he went to, but I thought it might be worth checking out so I took over the tail myself."

"Where is he now?"

"Headin' north on Wells."

"Shit," Brisbane muttered. "The last thing we need

is that guy nosing around, stirring up trouble." He paused a moment, then said, "Wait a minute. This character lives in Oak's building, doesn't he?"

"Yeah."

"So he would have gotten a letter from my office offering to buy out his lease. Maybe he stopped in to drop off his acceptance form."

"It woulda been a lot cheaper to mail the form back than to drive downtown and pay for parking," Corona pointed out. "This guy don't look like he's got a lot of extra dough."

"Maybe he didn't understand something in the letter and wanted to talk to someone about it. It's possible he spoke to Emma Davis. The letter went out under her name."

"You don't suppose Mr. Wacko spilled his guts to your cutie patootie associate, now do you?" Corona said. "It wouldn't be good for the little lady to start hearing stories about Oak's death bein' something besides an accidental overdose."

"I hope to Christ that didn't happen," Brisbane said. "I'd better have a word with Emma to see if she talked to him and, if so, what all he said. Are you still tailing him?"

"Affirmative," Corona said.

"Where are you now?"

"He's just signaling to turn into Office Depot. I guess he's going back to work."

"All right," Brisbane said. "I don't think he can do us any harm there. Why don't you call it a day."

"Do you want me to talk to him?" Corona asked.

"With a little persuasion I'm sure I could find out what he was up to downtown."

"Leave him alone for now," Brisbane said. "I'll see what I can find out on my end. In the meantime, it might be a good idea to keep one of your guys on him—preferably one that can't be given the slip so easily. Losing somebody in the lobby. Jesus. What kind of people are you hiring these days, Tommy, former Wal-Mart greeters?"

"Believe me, the guy who fucked up will have his mistake brought home to him in a very memorable way," Corona snickered. "It won't happen again."

"I hope not."

"You're sure you don't want me to lean on this twerp a little?" Corona pressed. "I'm feelin' in the mood for some action."

"Save your energy for later," Brisbane said. "The guy is probably harmless. But if it starts to look like he's a real threat, you can take him out."

"Just say the word," Corona said.

"Thanks for calling. Keep up the good work."

"The pleasure's all mine," Corona said.

CHAPTER 14

When she walked into her office Tuesday morning, Emma had a surreal feeling as she replayed the previous afternoon's encounter with Lee Hennick. She found that she was actually looking forward to checking into Lee's story. It beat billing hours looking at paint chips.

After briefly rehearsing what she intended to say, she dialed the number that Lee had provided. Not surprisingly, Detective Richard Porter was not in.

"Would you like to leave a message?" the dispatcher asked curtly.

"Yes, would you please ask him to call Attorney Emma Davis?" She gave the phone number.

"Will he know what this is in regard to?"

"Tell him I'd like to speak to him about a man named Oak Greythorne, who died a few weeks ago."

"I'll give him the message." Before Emma could say anything else, the dispatcher hung up.

Emma spent the next half hour pulling together her notes on the lead paint case. Feeling stiff and cranky from being cooped up inside on such a nice day, she got up and walked over to her window. Taking a deep breath, she looked out at the horizon, then down at the street. To her delight, she felt only the slightest pang of fear or vertigo.

"Flynn's desensitization therapy is working," she said aloud. She could notice a marked improvement in her reaction to heights after just a few days. She wasn't quite ready for the Navy Pier Ferris wheel, but maybe there was hope for her yet.

She was just about to go down the hall for some coffee to celebrate her newfound courage when her phone rang. She walked back to her desk and answered, "Emma Davis."

"Ms. Davis, this is Detective Richard Porter. I had a message that you called me."

"Yes, sir. Thank you for calling back. I wanted to talk to you about the circumstances surrounding the death of a man named Oak Greythorne."

"I've already checked, and I don't have an open file on anybody named Greythorne."

"I know you don't, but I'd like to talk to you about it anyway. Could you spare me about fifteen minutes?"

"You mean you want to talk in person?" The incredulity in the detective's tone was apparent. "I'm pretty busy. Can you tell me what it's about?"

"I'd really rather explain it in person," Emma said. "Just give me fifteen minutes. Whenever you can fit me in. I'll be happy to accommodate your schedule."

There was a pause on the other end of the line. "Oh, all right," the detective said. "One o'clock. And if you're a minute late, you missed me."

"I'll be there. Thank you so much."

As Emma hung up the phone, she felt a tingle of excitement. For better or worse, she was on her way to finding out the truth about Oak Greythorne's death.

The rest of the morning passed in a blur. Tom Cane had signed a new client, a manufacturer of infant car seats, that was being investigated by the Consumer Product Safety Commission. Tom tapped Emma and Jill Bedner to go through an entire file cabinet of documents prior to releasing to the CPSC to make sure the company was not disclosing any privileged material.

"Didn't we just spend at least thirty hours in this very conference room looking at paint chips?" Jill grumbled. "Instead of paint, now we're looking at pictures and descriptions of baby seats."

"I know," Emma said, paging methodically through a file. "And for this we went to law school? How was your long weekend in Minocqua?"

"Great," Jill replied. "I tried windsurfing."

"You're brave. That looks much too dangerous for me. Did you like it?"

"Yeah, I liked it a lot. The lakes are still awfully cold up there, so I had to wear a wet suit, but it was very exhilarating. I'd like to take lessons. How about you, did you have a good weekend?"

"Yes. I stayed in town," Emma said, thinking of Flynn. "It was amazing how fast the time sped by."

"Unlike this morning, which seems to be dragging on forever," Jill said. "Hand me some more files. We're going to have to pick up the pace if Tom really expects us to finish this by noon."

By working hard, Emma and Jill completed their document review by twelve thirty. "It's been fun," Jill said as she stood up and rubbed her neck. "Let's do this again sometime—preferably in about ten years."

"I'm with you," Emma said.

"I'm going to lunch," she announced to Lorraine as she headed out a few minutes later. "I have a couple of errands to run so I might be gone a little longer than usual."

"I have plenty to do," Lorraine replied. "Don't hurry back on my account."

As Emma took the elevator down to the parking garage, she felt a twinge of conscience at having to tell her secretary yet another fib. Lorraine was a wonderful assistant and Emma had absolutely no reason to question her loyalty, but the *Greythorne* case was just too sensitive to risk the possibility that someone might inadvertently leak even the slightest bit of information.

On the drive to the police station, Emma tried to rehearse what she was going to say to the detective. She soon realized that no matter what approach she took, she had to avoid sounding as if she were as disturbed as Lee Hennick.

Regardless of his reaction to Emma's visit, Detective Richard Porter won high marks for punctuality. It was precisely one o'clock when a tall black man around fifty dressed in dark slacks, a white shirt and conservative blue floral tie walked out to the bench where Emma was sitting. "Ms. Davis?" he asked.

Emma nodded.

"Richard Porter." Emma shook the detective's offered hand. His grip was firm and deliberate. "There's a conference room right back here where we can talk," the detective said.

Emma followed him into a small room furnished with a table and four chairs. Detective Porter waited until Emma had taken a seat before he sat down across from her.

"As I mentioned on the phone, I wanted to talk to you about Oak Greythorne," Emma said.

"Drug and alcohol overdose," the detective said. "I did a little checking to refresh my memory after your phone call."

"The cause of death was officially ruled to be an accidental overdose," Emma agreed. "But at least one friend of the deceased is convinced it was murder."

"That would be Lee Hennick," Detective Porter said.

Emma nodded.

"Do you represent him?"

"No, actually I represent the *Greythorne* estate."

"I'm glad to hear he's not your client," the detective said, leaning back in his chair. "That guy is a real fruit loop."

"You remember speaking to him, then."

"I see a lot of kooks in this job, but he made quite an impression," Porter said. "I decided to cut him some slack since he was clearly very upset about Mr. Greythorne's death."

"Did you check into the circumstances surrounding Greythorne's death?" Emma asked.

"I spoke to the medical examiner and confirmed that he'd concluded the death was the result of an accidental overdose and that there was absolutely no indication it was anything else. That was good enough for me."

"Do you know who found the body?" Emma asked, realizing that her file did not mention this detail.

"The cleaning lady found him the next morning," Porter replied. "He was on the sofa in the living room. There were two pill bottles in front of him and two bottles of booze, one empty and one half full."

"Did police officers go to Greythorne's home?"

The detective nodded. "The cleaning lady called 911 and two officers responded. They confirmed the guy was dead and had the body removed."

"Did the officers search the home or look for signs of foul play?" Emma asked.

"There were no signs of foul play," Porter said firmly. "Every detail about the scene supported a finding that the deceased accidentally OD'd."

"So you're saying there is absolutely no possibility that Oak Greythorne was the victim of foul play."

"I've been in this business twenty-five years, Ms.

Davis," Detective Porter said. "And I learned early on that there are very few absolutes. It's true that sometimes when the cause of death looks too obvious, that can be a cause for suspicion. But based on my experience, in Oak Greythorne's case things were exactly as they seemed. After a lifetime full of problems, the guy self-destructed. End of story."

"But what about Lee Hennick's claim that Greythorne had just completed the longest period of sobriety of his life and that he was even talking about starting a new business?"

"I'm afraid your time is up," the detective said. "As much as I've enjoyed our little chat, I've got a dozen active files that need my attention." He got to his feet. Emma reluctantly followed suit.

"As I said," the detective went on, "I have genuine sympathy for Mr. Hennick. Greythorne's death was clearly a blow for him. But his stories about conspiracy and murder are just plain bunkum. That young man is obviously ill and in need of treatment. I sincerely hope he gets it."

Emma nodded.

"But until then," the detective went on, "I'd strongly suggest that you be very cautious in your dealings with him. He is unstable, and unstable people sometimes do unexpected and violent things."

"Thank you for your time and your concern," Emma said, shaking the detective's hand.

"Go back and close your estate with a clear conscience," Detective Porter instructed as he walked Emma back out to the waiting room. "It appears your client was his own worst enemy and his problems finally caught up with him. It's a story that repeats itself in this city several times a day. Young Mr. Hennick is tilting at windmills if he thinks otherwise."

Emma couldn't help but feel down as she drove back to the office. While she had not expected the detective to launch a full-scale investigation into Greythorne's death, she had held out the slim possibility that perhaps Greythorne was the victim of foul play. Her talk with Detective Porter brought her back to reality.

"Did you finish all your errands?" Lorraine asked cheerfully as Emma walked past her secretary's desk.

"Yes, I did," Emma replied. "Now I'd better get to work on a draft of the summary-judgment motion in the *Forage King* case. I promised Tom Cane I'd get it to him by the end of the week."

Emma spent the next few hours immersed in her work. Around four thirty she was ready for a break and went to the kitchen for a bottle of sparkling water. She returned to her office planning to turn her attention back to her writing project when, on impulse, she decided to try to reach the medical examiner who had performed the autopsy on Oak Greythorne. She dug through her briefcase and found the name and phone number.

The M.E. who had actually conducted the autopsy was not available, but an amiable receptionist put Emma through to one of his assistants, Daniel Harvey. Emma explained that she was the attorney for the *Greythorne* estate and that Greythorne's heirs wanted to know the details about how he died.

"His death was such a shock that they had a hard time coping with it, but now that a little time has passed, they'd really like to know as much as possible about his final hours," Emma fibbed. "Any light you can shed on it will be much appreciated."

"I understand," Harvey said. "We get a lot of requests like that. Just give me a minute to pull the file."

A few moments later Harvey returned to the phone. "Thanks for holding. I've got the full report here. Should I just skim through it for you and give you the highlights?"

"That would be great," Emma said.

"Okay. Let's see what we've got. Mr. Greythorne's blood alcohol content was .31."

"That's awfully high, isn't it?" Emma asked.

"Yes. A man his size would have had to consume a large quantity of alcohol in a relatively short time to register that BAC."

"How much alcohol are we talking about?" Emma prodded.

"Oh, I'd say at least ten ounces in an hour."

"That is a lot." Emma shuddered at the thought of consuming so much booze. "Anything else?"

"He also had approximately six Xanax tablets in his system. Combined with the alcohol, his chances of survival were virtually nil unless someone had happened to come along very soon after he ingested the pills and called 911."

"Would the Xanax tablets alone have killed him?" Emma asked.

"It's unlikely," Harvey replied. "But the combination of pills and that much alcohol was bound to be lethal."

"I see. Is there anything else of interest in the report?"

"It doesn't appear so."

"Thank you for the information," Emma said.

"You're welcome," Harvey said. "If it's any consolation, he didn't suffer. He simply went to sleep."

"Thank you again. I'll pass that information on to Mr. Greythorne's loved ones."

Emma hung up the phone feeling even more dejected than after returning from her visit with Detective Porter. She might as well admit defeat. It was obvious that trying to track down information suggesting that Oak Greythorne's death had been anything but accidental was nothing but a wild goose chase.

Oak Greythorne hadn't suffered. He had simply fallen into a coma and passed into oblivion. Somehow that information did not make Emma feel any better. Given all the factors she knew about, something wasn't adding up. She just wished she could put her finger on what it was.

CHAPTER 15

Emma left work promptly at five to go home and prepare for another date with Flynn. A leisurely soak in a bathtub filled with aromatic herbal salts helped erase the stress of the day. After toweling off, she walked over to her closet and contemplated the always unfathomable question of what she should wear. Her first impulse was to go with a simple black short-sleeved dress, but as she reached for it she could hear Kathy's voice scolding her. "Borrrring. Why don't you just hang a sign on your back that says 'Lawyer'? Or, better yet, just wear a long black robe."

"Okay, okay," Emma mumbled under her breath. Forget the black dress. What else looked promising? As she stared at her far-from-meager wardrobe she wished she had taken Kathy up on her standing offer to lend her an outfit.

Kathy was always saying that a woman's wardrobe made an important statement about her. Most of Emma's garments seemed to say, "Hi, I'm from Kansas City and I don't like to take chances with my clothes or my life." Emma had to admit that was probably not the type of statement that would keep the interest of one of Chicago's hottest architects. And she most definitely wanted to hold Flynn Fielding's interest.

Just as she was ready to call Kathy and ask if she could come home from work early to handle a clothing emergency, Emma spied a sleek royal blue sheath jammed between two black suits. She pulled the dress out of its hiding place, stood in front of the mirror and held it up. It had cap sleeves, a neckline that was low without being scandalous and was fashionably short without making its wearer look like a tart. Emma had worn it just once before, two summers ago, to a college friend's wedding. It had a sophisticated air, perfect for a late spring dinner in Chicago. All it needed was a good pressing, and it would be ready for whatever Flynn Fielding had in mind.

Half an hour later, Emma again stood in front of the mirror, admiring her reflection. She had redone her makeup and her hair was loose and flowing. She looked good. Damn good, in fact. "How do you like them apples, Max Englander?" she asked, tossing her head. She truly bore her former boyfriend no ill will—although she had to admit that she much preferred to think of him spending a cold and lonely night alone rather than out on the town (or worse yet, in bed) with a new girlfriend. Maybe by this time the nurse Coleen had mentioned had traded him in for an eligible doctor.

Ten minutes later, all thoughts of Max were forgotten as Emma slid into Flynn's car. "Where are we going?" she asked.

"To Morton's," Flynn replied as he pulled away from the curb. "Did I tell you how great you look in that dress?"

"Only three times so far, but that's okay. I don't mind some repetition of that kind of remark. I've never been to Morton's."

"It's one of the best steak places in town. Oh, God, you do like steak, don't you?" Flynn asked with concern. "Because I've had a real craving for it all day. But if you don't like it, I can cancel the reservation and we can go somewhere else."

"I'm from Kansas, remember?" Emma teased. "Of course I like steak."

"That's a relief," Flynn said. "If you'd insisted on something else I'd have obliged, but I have to admit that my heart wouldn't be in it and I'd spend the rest of the night dreaming about nice pink meat."

"Then by all means you should live out your dream," Emma said, a bit seductively.

"You're unbelievable," Flynn said, reaching over and taking her hand. "A woman who appreciates both old buildings and red meat. How did I get so lucky?"

"Fate," Emma said, running her fingers up and down his palm. "And a little help from Kathy's dog."

The restaurant was lively and boisterous, the wine full-bodied, the steaks huge and tender, the conversation relaxed. "So, you've now become an expert on

paint," Flynn said as he finished the last of his por-
terhouse. "Maybe I could use you as a consultant on
some of my projects."

"I'm afraid my expertise is limited to identifying
the leading manufacturers of lead-based paint,"
Emma corrected, taking another bite of prime rib.
"Not a particularly useful tool in today's society."

"The schools seem to have a really weak case,"
Flynn said.

"I'll have to see if there's some way to get you on
the jury," Emma said teasingly.

"I'd love to come watch part of the trial," Flynn
said. "Would you mind if I did that?"

Emma put down her fork and stared at him. "You
want to watch the trial? Why? Most trials are
boring."

"I'd like to see you work," Flynn said. "Would it
be okay if I came?"

"Sure." Emma smiled at him, ecstatic at the
thought that Flynn might still be part of her life in
six months. "I'd like that."

"Good. Let me know when it starts and I'll be
there. Are you up for some dessert or coffee?"

Emma shook her head. "I am absolutely stuffed."

"Me, too," Flynn said. He signaled for the check.
After paying it, he took Emma's arm and they
walked out to the car. "Are you ready for another
exercise in desensitizing you to heights?" he asked.

"That depends," Emma demurred. "I'm not ready
for the Navy Pier Ferris wheel yet."

Flynn laughed. "Don't worry. We're going to work

up to the Ferris wheel very slowly. How about something a little less scary?"

"All right."

"Good." He opened the car door and Emma slid in. A few minutes later, Flynn turned onto Lake Shore Drive, then pulled into the underground parking ramp of a high-rise building. He swung into a parking space and cut the engine. "Here we are," he said. "Are you ready to be desensitized?"

"Where are we?" Emma asked.

"At my place," Flynn said.

"And what are we going to do here to cure me of my fear of heights?" Emma asked.

"I live on the thirtieth floor," Flynn replied, getting out of the car. "Let's go up and see." He came around to Emma's side of the car and opened her door.

"I'm not going out on a balcony," she warned.

"I don't have a balcony," Flynn said, taking her hand and helping her out of the car. "But I've got a view most people would kill for. Come on up and I'll show you. I promise if you get scared we'll think of something else to do." He brushed his lips against her hair.

"Let's go," Emma said breathlessly.

Flynn's apartment was on the top floor of a building he had renovated. As he opened the door Emma saw a scurry of movement off to her right. "What was that?" she asked, taking a step backward.

"My cats, Groucho and Harpo," Flynn replied.

"Hey, fellas, come and meet Emma." Two large felines, one black and one yellow, poked their heads out from behind a chair.

"Let me guess," Emma said. "The black one must be Groucho."

"Very perceptive. Come on into the kitchen and I'll get us some wine."

Emma took a seat at the granite-topped island. Flynn poured two glasses of merlot and sat down next to her. The two cats peered at them from the doorway.

"How long have you lived here?" Emma asked, sipping her wine.

"Five years."

"It's great. Are all the units this nice?"

Flynn laughed. "Not quite. I'm afraid I claimed the best one for myself. Are you ready to see the rest of it?"

"Sure."

"Come on. I'll give you the full tour." Flynn took her hand and led her into the enormous living room, which had floor-to-ceiling windows overlooking the lake. "Isn't it beautiful?" he said.

Emma nodded.

"Why don't we move a little closer and take a better look." Flynn gently pulled Emma forward. She allowed herself to be led to within three feet of the windows.

"What do you think?"

"It's very nice."

"I don't think you're really looking, Emma," Flynn said. "Let's move a little closer. It's okay. I'll be right there with you."

Emma closed her eyes, took a small step forward, then another. Flynn stood behind her, their thighs touching. "One more little step," Flynn urged. Emma took a deep breath, then complied. "That's great, Emma. Now just look at that spectacular view."

Emma was trembling but forced herself to open her eyes. She looked out at the lake first, then directed her gaze downward to the street below. Looking down had always given her the most severe attacks of vertigo. As she looked at the cars wending their way along Lake Shore Drive, she felt herself growing dizzy.

Flynn pressed himself even closer against her and put his arms around her. Emma began to relax. They stood there for a full two minutes. At the end of that time Emma was feeling considerably bolder and her breathing relaxed.

"That's terrific, Emma!" Flynn hugged her. "I knew you could do it. I am so proud of you!"

Emma was ecstatic that she had passed this test with flying colors. She turned and put her arms around Flynn's neck. "Thank you," she said. Then their lips met. Flynn's arms were around her, and they pressed themselves against each other.

"How would you like to see the rest of the apartment now?" Flynn whispered in her ear. "Perhaps starting with my bedroom."

"I'd love to," Emma murmured.

Flynn took her hand and led her down the hall.

His bedroom was decorated with sturdy Mission oak furniture. The focal point was a king-sized bed. Flynn unzipped Emma's dress. She stepped out of it and he tossed the garment onto a nearby chair, then shed his jacket. Emma began to unbutton Flynn's shirt but when she had trouble with a couple of the buttons Flynn finished the job. The rest of their clothes came off in a matter of seconds and they fell back onto the bed.

Flynn kissed Emma's neck, then worked his way downward. "You are so beautiful," he said. "You have an absolutely incredible body."

"So do you," Emma said, running her hand down his taut stomach.

"Oh, God, I can't wait," Flynn said, moving between Emma's thighs. "I want you so much."

"I want you, too," Emma said, pulling him down to her.

Their lovemaking was both urgent and tender and left them both breathless. "You are amazing," Flynn said later as he sensuously rubbed Emma's back. "Not only do you like historic buildings and red meat, you're terrific in bed, too. Is there anything negative about you?"

Emma laughed and burrowed her head into his neck. "I think I'm still afraid to ride the Navy Pier Ferris wheel, but the way you just sent me into orbit I might be able to fly right over the top of it."

Flynn pulled her close. "Come here. Something tells me it's time for another blastoff."

CHAPTER 16

Flynn took Emma home around seven the next morning. "Be good at work today and play nice with the other lawyers," he said as he kissed her good-bye.

"I will," Emma promised, giving Flynn's thigh a friendly squeeze.

As she rode up the elevator, Emma couldn't help but feel a little like Holly Golightly returning home from a night of sin. It had been a very long time since she'd crept home at dawn after a night of glorious lovemaking. Much too long. In fact, the more she thought about it, the more Emma realized it was very possible that she had never had such a night. But now that she was the main squeeze of Chicago's hottest architect, the future held endless promise.

Emma had barely emerged from the shower when her phone rang. "Did you spend the night with him?" Kathy demanded.

"Good morning, Kathy," Emma said, toweling herself off. "Lovely day, isn't it?"

"Answer me. I have to know. I've been up all night."

"Really?" Emma laughed. "That's funny. I was

awake a lot of the night myself. And the short answer to your question is yes."

Kathy's shriek of exultation left no doubt in Emma's mind that she was very pleased with her friend's news. "Way to go, Emma! Good for you. I knew you'd get it right eventually. How was it?"

"On a scale of one to ten?" Emma paused. "I'd give him a twelve and a half."

"Excellent! Are you seeing him again tonight?"

"Not until tomorrow night. He wanted to get together tonight but he has a dinner meeting with clients and frankly I need a good night's sleep."

"Good girl. It's always good to play a little hard to get, even after you've slept with a man. It helps keep them interested. If you need to borrow an outfit, just let me know."

"I don't view the clothes issue as quite so important anymore," Emma said.

"You're right, of course. I can't wait to hear all the lurid details."

"I'm afraid I haven't time for lunch today. I'm really swamped. What about getting a bite after work?"

"As a matter of fact, that fits right into my plans," Kathy said. "I talked to my dad last night. He'd love to meet you and reminisce about Oak Greythorne. I told him we'd come to the house tonight for supper."

Emma was stunned into silence. She had been so busy, she had completely forgotten to tell her friend that she had decided to call a halt to her investigation into Oak Greythorne's past.

"Did you hear what I said?" Kathy prompted. "I thought you'd be thrilled. You were so keen about the idea of finding out as much as you could about Greythorne's past the other night and I thought who better to talk to than someone who knew Oak way back when."

"It was really sweet of you to set this up," Emma said, "but I'm afraid it's a lost cause." She briefly explained her discussions with Detective Porter and the assistant medical examiner. "So since it looks like Lee Hennick's claims have no basis in reality, I hate to waste your father's time."

"Just because you now have a boyfriend doesn't mean you can't still keep in touch," Kathy grumbled. Then she softened again. "But hey, even if you don't give a hoot about Greythorne, we can still go to my parents' house. They would love to meet you. Grandma told them how delightful you are."

"That was sweet of her," Emma said.

"She said you were by far the most normal friend I'd brought to visit her in a very long time."

"I'm flattered—I think."

"So what do you say? We'll leave about six thirty."

"Great. I'll see you then."

After Emma hung up, she flipped her desk calendar to the following week and scribbled a note to herself for Wednesday. "Talk to L. Hennick." She put down her pen and grimaced. She was not looking forward to giving Lee the bad news that his friend had, in fact, died of an accidental overdose. She'd have to spend some time over the next week thinking of a gentle way to deliver that unpleasant message.

Emma put in a strenuous day working on her cases. By five thirty she had accomplished a great deal, but there was still a lot of paperwork left on her desk. She knew she should probably put in a few more hours of work, but she didn't want to renege on her promise to have supper with Kathy's parents.

As she shut down her computer and took her purse from her desk drawer, the door to her office swung open and Louis Brisbane stepped inside. An overwhelming feeling of nervousness swept over Emma and she took a deep breath to steady her nerves.

"Hi, there," Emma said, hoping her voice sounded normal. "I was just leaving. What can I do for you?"

"I was on my way out myself," Brisbane said. He walked over and stood in front of Emma's desk. "I just thought I'd stop in and let you know that ten more tenants in Oak Greythorne's building have accepted our offer to buy out their leases."

"That's great," Emma said. "Sounds like things are moving right along."

"Indeed they are, thanks to all your efforts."

Emma nodded her thanks, then came around her desk and headed toward the door. Brisbane stepped in front of her, blocking her path.

Emma swallowed hard. "Is there anything else?" she asked. "I'm late for an appointment."

"I have a friend who is a captain at the police

department," Brisbane said, "and he mentioned that you paid a visit to one of the detectives there. I just wanted to make sure that there was nothing wrong and to offer my services in the event you were experiencing any sort of difficulty."

How the hell did he find out about her meeting with Detective Porter? Emma wondered. She did some fast thinking to come up with an explanation that Brisbane would find plausible.

"Thank you for your concern, but there's nothing wrong," she said. "A couple of days ago, one of the tenants in Mr. Greythorne's building stopped in to see me. He was quite upset about the tone of the letter. He had some wild story about how Mr. Greythorne had been murdered and he said he would not even consider ending his lease early unless I agreed to talk to the police to try to find out what really happened to Mr. Greythorne. That's why I went to the police station, to speak to the detective that this tenant had talked to a few weeks ago."

"And did the detective confirm that Oak Greythorne's death was in fact an accident?" Brisbane asked.

"Of course," Emma said. "I knew he would. As I said, the only reason I spoke to the detective was so that I could report back to the tenant that he had been misinformed. I hoped that by taking the time to follow up on his concerns I would be able to convince him to sign the lease termination."

"Why didn't you come to me after this tenant approached you?"

"I didn't want to bother you," Emma said. "It was nothing I couldn't handle myself."

"What is the tenant's name?"

Emma hesitated. She hated to divulge Lee's name, but if Brisbane had contacts at the police department he probably already knew Lee's identity and was just checking to see if she would give him an honest answer. "Lee Hennick," she replied.

Brisbane nodded. "And is Mr. Hennick now willing to terminate his lease?"

"I haven't gotten back to him yet. I've been rather busy with other work. I plan to speak to him in the next few days."

"Keep me posted," Brisbane said. "And, if necessary, offer Mr. Hennick an additional three thousand dollars to help him make up his mind."

"I'll do that," Emma said. "Now if you'll excuse me, I've really got to run."

Brisbane stepped aside. "Keep up the good work, Emma," he said as he held the door open for her. "If Mr. Hennick gives you any trouble or if you hear from any other tenants who are balking about ending their leases, I'd appreciate it if you'd refer them to me immediately. I have much more experience than you in dealing with difficult people. I'm sure I could make them see things our way." He smiled but his eyes were cold.

"I'll remember that," Emma said. "Good night." She raced out the door and headed for the elevator, her heart pounding. The fact that Brisbane had almost immediately found out about her talk with the detective was very unnerving. Did the man have spies everywhere? Was he having her followed? She shuddered. She couldn't wait for her work on the *Greythorne* estate to end.

Kathy was in high spirits during the drive to her parents' home. "Say, would you and Flynn be interested in attending a fund-raiser for the Lincoln Park Zoo? I'm trying to put together a table of charming singles."

"When is it?"

"The first Saturday in June. It should be a lot of fun. Great food and wine and top-notch music. It's black tie so you can wear a really elegant dress. Maybe I can lend you something."

"I'll mention it to Flynn," Emma replied as Pepper stood up on her lap so he could look out the car window.

"I just love summer parties," Kathy said. "The store is getting in some beautiful sample gowns next week from a new French designer. They'd be perfect for the zoo gala. They all look like Impressionist paintings. Lovely floral designs and rich colors. You'd look just great in one. I'll bring a couple home so you can try them on."

"I suppose they're all extremely revealing," Emma said.

"Of course a summer evening dress is going to be revealing. That's the whole point. Who wants to wear a dress with long sleeves and a high neck when it's ninety degrees out? This is a high-class charity benefit, not a reenactment of the Pilgrims' landing. Just wait till you see these dresses. You'll be dying to wear one of them."

"I can't wait," Emma said.

Kathy's parents, James and Elizabeth Flood, lived in a Tudor mansion in Wilmette, a wealthy enclave about fifteen miles to the north of the Loop. The couple greeted their young guests warmly.

"It's wonderful to meet you, Emma," said Elizabeth, a statuesque brunette casually dressed in white slacks and a blue knit top, shaking Emma's hand. "Kathy hasn't stopped talking about you since you met. And Rose was quite taken with you—and let me tell you, she is not easily impressed."

"I don't think Mother has spoken so highly of anyone since she met Jackie Kennedy back in the eighties," James Flood said. Kathy's father was tall and handsome, with thick dark hair just starting to gray around the temples. "Very few people measure up to her standards—God knows I rarely did."

"Remind me to come here more often," Emma said, laughing. "I seldom get this kind of praise lavished on me."

"When do we eat?" Kathy asked. "I'm starving. And do you have something for Pepper?" She set the animal down on the marble floor of the foyer.

"We can eat as soon as you get seated in the dining room," Elizabeth replied. "And I have a box of Pepper's favorite treats in the kitchen."

"In that case," Kathy said, heading down the spacious entrance hall, Pepper hot on her heels, "what are we waiting for?"

Over supper, the conversation remained light and centered mainly on Emma's background and her move to the city. Not until Elizabeth served dessert was the ostensible reason for Emma's visit even mentioned.

"So, Emma," James said, pouring another glass of wine for everyone, "Kathy tells me that you're handling Oak Greythorne's estate."

"I've been helping Louis Brisbane with portions of it," Emma said. "I understand that you went to school with both Oak and Louis."

James nodded. "They were an interesting duo. They were very much alike in some ways and polar opposites in others. Both were very bright and very ambitious, but while Oak's psychological problems caused him to sometimes lose control, Louis was always very methodical about forming a plan and then executing it."

"Were they close friends?" Emma asked.

"Oh, yes. They were very close all through school."

"Grandma seemed to recall that in grade school Louis was a bully who purposely taunted Oak and upset him," Kathy said. "Is that the way you remember it?"

James took a sip of his wine. "That's an interesting observation. I never thought of it in those terms. Of course a child wouldn't see it that way. Yes, I guess

I'd have to say that Mother's observation is probably correct. There's no doubt that Louis knew how to push Oak's buttons, and sometimes the result was rather volatile."

"Was Oak diagnosed with psychological problems back then?" Emma asked.

"The precise nature of his ailment was always kept under wraps," James answered. "I believe he was seeing a psychiatrist, but I never heard any details about his illness or any treatment he received. In those days there was still a stigma about mental health problems, and people suffering from them kept it very hush-hush."

"How would Oak's problems manifest themselves?" Emma asked.

"He had terrible mood swings. I'm sure that now they'd call it bipolar disorder. At the time we just thought he was the moodiest kid in town. One minute he could be on top of the world, singing and whistling and talking about what he was going to do after school, and the next minute he'd be either crying or screaming at somebody."

"How sad," Emma said. "But he managed to do well in school in spite of his problems?"

"Yes, he was an excellent student," James replied. "It seemed that classes were very easy for him. That was always a point of rivalry between Oak and Louis. While Oak seemed to be able to coast through tough courses, Louis had to study much harder to get top grades."

"That's interesting," Emma said.

Everyone had finished their dessert. "Why don't we move onto the patio and have some more wine?" Elizabeth suggested.

"Sounds good to me," Kathy said.

A few minutes later, they were seated in comfortable chairs on the Floods' patio overlooking their spacious back yard which, befitting the rest of the house's décor, looked like an English country garden.

"Where were we?" James asked as he settled back in his chair. "Oh, yes. The dynamic between Louis and Oak. When Oak's psychological problems were dormant, he was by far the more personable of the two. It was always a struggle for Louis to make new friends."

"Really?" Emma asked with surprise. "Brisbane seems like such a smooth character, like he could schmooze with anybody in the world."

"He acquired that ability," James explained. "He wasn't born with it. Oak, on the other hand, was. I'm sure that's why Oak was so successful in building his own company."

"Mom, did you ever meet Oak?" Kathy asked.

"Yes, a few times at this function or that," Elizabeth replied. "He seemed like a nice man."

"When was the last time you saw him?" Emma asked James.

Kathy's father rubbed his palm over his chin. "Probably ten years ago. Before he sold his company. After that he turned into something of a recluse."

"You didn't happen to hear any rumors shortly

before he died that he was thinking of going back into business?" Emma inquired.

"Was he? No, I didn't hear anything about a new business. It's a shame he wasn't able to follow through on that. If he could have kept his mental problems under control, I'll bet he could have successfully built another company. He was a true entrepreneur."

Emma's wine glass was empty. She looked over at Kathy. "I think we've taken up enough of your parents' time. We should probably be getting back downtown."

Kathy nodded. "I'm ready whenever you are."

Everyone got up, walked back into the house to the kitchen, and deposited their glasses on the granite counter. Pepper lay contentedly on a throw rug gnawing on a rawhide bone.

"Thank you so much for supper and for taking the time to share your memories of Oak Greythorne," Emma said to James. "I really appreciate it."

"It was my pleasure," James replied. "I felt damn sad when I read that Oak had died. Even though I hadn't seen him in years, I always liked him and it just seemed as if he'd been dealt an unfair hand."

Emma nodded. "That's the impression I have, too. It's a shame he died alone and that he had no close relatives."

"Oak almost married when he was in college," James said.

"He did?" Emma found this information intriguing. Hadn't Brisbane at least intimated that Greythorne had never formed any strong romantic attachments? "Who was the girl?"

"Her name was Janice Hall," James said. "She was an art history major. She was pretty, blond, vivacious. I think she was very good for Oak."

"What happened?"

"I'm not exactly sure," James said, "but apparently their breakup was quite unpleasant. I heard that Janice really wanted to get married, but Oak refused, thinking his mental condition was likely to doom the marriage."

"What happened to Janice after that?" Emma asked.

"I don't know. I believe she left town. I have never heard anything about her since then. It's funny how old memories come flooding back. I'll bet I hadn't thought about her in thirty years, but now I can picture her in my mind as clearly as if I just saw her last week."

"Was her family from Chicago?" Emma asked, eager to find out all she could about this mystery woman. "Did she have siblings? Do you remember her parents' names?"

James shook his head. "I'm afraid I can't help you out there. I know Oak met her at the University of Chicago. My sense is that she was not from here, but I can't say for sure."

"That's all right. You've been very helpful," Emma said.

"Oh, I remember one more tidbit that you might find interesting," James said as Kathy picked Pepper up and they all meandered toward the front door. "Louis Brisbane was besotted with Janice, too."

Emma's mouth dropped open. "You're kidding."

"No, it was probably the fiercest rivalry he and Oak ever had. Louis's nose was quite out of joint when Janice chose Oak over him."

"Thank you so much," Emma said, pumping James's hand warmly. "It was lovely meeting you both and you've been extremely helpful."

"My pleasure," James said. "Feel free to give me a call if there's anything else I might be able to tell you."

"I might just take you up on that," Emma said.

On the drive back downtown, Emma pondered what James had just said. Here was yet another connection between Brisbane and Oak Greythorne. It seemed that the lives of the two men kept intersecting. She would love to know more about the mysterious Janice Hall. Emma started thinking about ways she might locate Janice, then she stopped short.

Louis Brisbane seemed to know what Emma was doing almost before she did it. If she launched a search for the woman who both Brisbane and Oak Greythorne had once loved, there was a good chance the senior partner would get wind of it.

Emma shook her head. Not a smart idea. There was no reason to arouse Brisbane's suspicions or his anger. After all, he was the head of Emma's law firm. And even though he and his buddy, Tommy Corona, gave her the creeps, she still had absolutely no reason to think that Oak Greythorne's death had been anything but an accidental overdose. There was no sense in sticking her nose into things that didn't concern her—except to satisfy her ever-growing hunch that there was more to the *Greythorne* case than met the eye.

CHAPTER 17

By the next morning, Emma's curiosity had gotten the better of her and she decided to make just a few more inquiries into Oak Greythorne's past. The firm's library contained a copy of a Chicago city directory. Emma photocopied the page listing the names of other residents in the building where Oak Greythorne had lived. She was somewhat daunted to see that over a hundred people were listed, but she was determined to try to flesh out some details of the elusive Oak's life. As soon as she got home, before getting ready for her date, she began phoning his former neighbors.

Emma had given careful thought about the type of ruse people were not only likely to believe but would also make them want to furnish Emma with information. She thought she had come up with a winner. She tried it out on the first neighbor, a Mrs. Allan Chapman.

"Hello, Mrs. Chapman?" Emma said brightly when an elderly-sounding woman answered the phone. "My name is Emma Davis. I am an attorney representing the Oak Greythorne estate. Mr. Greythorne passed away in early March. Do you remember him? He lived on the seventh floor of your building."

Yes, Mrs. Chapman remembered Oak.

"Great. I don't know if you are aware that Mr. Greythorne left all of his property in a charitable trust for the purpose of furnishing medical care for the less advantaged members of our community. . . . Yes, that is a very worthwhile endeavor, isn't it? Mrs. Chapman, the reason I'm calling you is that I am in the process of developing a brochure explaining the mission statement of the trust and I would very much like to personalize it by including a few comments from the people who knew Mr. Greythorne.

"You could comment about what type of neighbor he was or give your observations of him as a businessman. Any type of reminiscence would be much appreciated. Would you be able to help me with that?"

While Mrs. Chapman did not question the premise for Emma's call, she unfortunately had little to offer. She had lived in the building three years. She knew who Oak was, but not much else. She was sorry she couldn't offer more.

"That's quite all right, Mrs. Chapman. I appreciate your taking the time to talk with me. You wouldn't, by any chance, know someone else in your building who might have had a closer relationship with Mr. Greythorne?"

"Why, yes. I've heard Frank Marsden speak highly of Mr. Greythorne. You might want to call him."

"Thank you very much."

Frank Marsden, Emma found out, was a retired Cook County bailiff. He had lived in Oak's building for nearly thirty years. "He was a nice man," Marsden said. "I was sorry to hear he passed on."

"How well did you know him?" Emma asked.

"The way people in the same building usually know each other. We weren't buddies, but we'd see each other a few times a week, in the elevator or getting the mail or in the garage. We'd always greet each other and sometimes we'd have a little chat."

This was better than nothing. Emma pressed on with her questions. "Was there anything in particular about him, a quality or a trait, that you'd like to share?"

"He was generous," Marsden replied. "For the last ten years or so at Christmastime I've taken up a collection to buy presents for needy kids and he always gave me a very substantial check. He liked kids a lot. You could tell by the way he treated the kids who lived in our building and any kids who visited. He'd always take the time to talk to them and sometimes give them a little something. It doesn't surprise me that he left his money to charity. He was that kind of guy."

"When was the last time you saw him?" Emma asked.

"About six weeks before he passed away. My wife and I spent two months in Florida visiting her sister so we were out of town when it happened. One of our neighbors sent us the obituary."

"Did he seem in good spirits the last time you spoke to him?" Emma asked, disappointed that this gregarious man had not been around during Oak's final days.

"Very much so," Marsden answered. "In fact it seemed to me that he'd been more outgoing, happier even, the last year or so."

"Really?" Emma said. "What makes you say that?"

"I don't know. He just seemed more at ease with himself. He was never one to talk about his troubles but you could tell a lot of times he wasn't exactly feeling on top of the world. It seemed to me that he was peppier and more cheerful toward the end."

"Did he ever mention anything to you about going back into business?" Emma asked.

"We never talked about business," Marsden said. "We'd mostly talk about my grandkids—I have five—and sometimes politics. And the Cubs. He loved that team."

"Thank you for your time," Emma said. "Do you know if there was anyone in your building whom Mr. Greythorne was particularly close to? I'd really like to get a few more comments for our brochure."

"Talk to Lucille Adina," Marsden answered at once. "She raised eight kids and has a heart as big as Lake Michigan. She always kind of mothered Oak. She'd worry that he wasn't eating right and bring him home-cooked meals. She was probably closer to him than anyone in the building."

"Thanks so much," Emma said. "It's been nice talking to you."

"Good luck with your brochure," Marsden said. "I'd be interested in getting a copy when it's done. I might even donate a few bucks to the trust. Those of us who can live comfortably should never forget that there's lots of people who can't."

"I'll make sure you get a copy as soon as it's done," Emma fibbed. "Thanks again."

One tip was leading to another. She quickly located Lucille Adina's name on her list and dialed the woman's number. After four rings, however, an answering machine picked up the call. "Damn," Emma sputtered. She left a brief message with both her work and home numbers, then hung up. That was enough for one night. After all, she had a hot date ahead of her. She was just starting to change her clothes when there was a knock at her door.

"I know you're pressed for time," Kathy's voice boomed through the door. "But this is important. I've got evening gowns for your approval."

That ended Emma's dilemma about whether to make any more calls. She opened the door. "I was so excited when you called this afternoon to tell me that Flynn agreed to come to the zoo gala that I couldn't wait to help you pick out an outfit," Kathy said. She thrust three gowns into her friend's arms. "Here. They're hot off the plane from Paris. Try them on."

Emma looked askance at the offerings. "These all look like slips," she said. "Where's the rest of them?"

"All right, Sister Emma," Kathy said. "Knock it off with the prudish act. Get your clothes off and get into these dresses pronto. I have to return any rejects to the store tomorrow. You may think these are too avant-garde for your taste, but trust me, scores of Chicago women are dying to get their hands on these things."

"All right," Emma said. "Let's see what we've got here."

The first dress was a luscious peach floral with a plunging V neck in front and rhinestone straps in the back. Emma gamely put it on, then stood self-consciously holding the front together to prevent her breasts from being exposed. "This is obscene," Emma said.

"You could use tape," Kathy suggested.

"Tape what?" Emma asked, perplexed.

"Tape your boobs down so they don't pop out," Kathy said.

Emma shook her head. "This thing was designed for someone who has a chest like an ironing board."

"I hate people with big boobs," Kathy grumbled. "Next dress."

Dress number two was a white see-through creation that had a modest enough front neckline but the back plunged below Emma's tailbone. "How could you sit down in this?" Emma asked. "Your whole ass would show if you sat down."

"You've made your point, Sister Emma," Kathy said with exasperation. "Next."

Emma picked up the third dress. It was a muted turquoise floral that had spaghetti straps and a built-in underwire bra. Emma held it up to her body and melted. "This is gorgeous," she said.

"So get that other thing off and put it on," Kathy ordered.

The gown was even more stunning on. Emma looked in the mirror, pirouetted around several times, then looked at Kathy. "I love it!" she exclaimed. "It's sexy but not vulgar. This is something I could actually wear in public."

"See! I told you you'd love these dresses."

"I love it!" Emma said, spinning around. "I've never had a dress like this. How much is it?"

Kathy waved her hand dismissively. "It's on me."

"No. I want to pay for it. How much?"

"Your money is no good," Kathy insisted. "This is my treat."

"Thank you." Emma gave her a big hug. "You're the best friend ever."

"I know," Kathy said modestly.

"What are you wearing to the ball?" Emma asked.

"I've picked out a stunning little number," Kathy said coyly. "I predict it will make quite a splash."

"So, have you invited a date?"

"You would have to ruin a happy occasion by bringing that up. I don't know yet."

"What do you mean, you don't know? It's only a couple of weeks off. Don't you think you'd better invite someone?"

Kathy shrugged. "What's the hurry? I can always invite some mediocre person at the last minute.

They're never booked very far in advance. At the moment, I'm optimistically still holding out for Mr. Right. Are you sure Flynn doesn't have a friend?"

"I don't know. I could ask him," Emma said.

"I can't wait to see Flynn all gussied up in a tux."

"By the way, Flynn says since he's coming to your pet benefit, maybe you'd be willing to do something for him in return."

"What's that?" Kathy asked suspiciously.

"He's one of the people in charge of putting up a Habitat for Humanity house this weekend," Emma explained. "I'm going to be working there on Sunday. We thought maybe you'd like to come along."

"What would I have to do?"

"I don't know. Whatever is needed. Moving supplies, nailing, you name it."

"Do I look like I know anything about nailing?" Kathy asked.

Emma laughed. "They need all kinds of grunt workers. I'm not exactly a master carpenter myself. Why don't you come and keep me company? We'll have fun, and it's for a good cause."

"Oh, all right. Why not? What time do we start?"

"Eight o'clock."

"Eight o'clock on a Sunday morning? I think I'd like to reconsider."

"You can't reconsider. I'll call you at seven and make sure you're up."

Kathy sighed. "Okay."

"And be sure to wear old clothes."

Kathy looked at her friend dumbly.

"You do have old clothes, don't you?"

"Of course I have old clothes. If you can believe it, I have some things that are actually three years old."

Emma laughed. "Old work clothes. Loose-fitting jeans and an old T-shirt. And comfortable shoes. None of your usual designer stuff. You won't be able to move in it and it's likely to get ruined."

"Old clothes," Kathy repeated. "Right. I'll see what I have. I guess I can always stop at a thrift store."

"I have more than enough old clothes for both of us," Emma said, laughing. "I'll pick out something suitable. You can consider it my payback for this lovely dress. Now if you'll excuse me," she said, heading for her bedroom, "I have to hurry and get ready for my date. Flynn is picking me up in fifteen minutes and I wouldn't want to keep him waiting."

"God, no, don't do that." Kathy swept up the two rejected gowns and headed for the door. "If you make him mad he might cancel out on the zoo gala and I am so looking forward to having one of Chicago's most eligible bachelors at my table. So get a move on, sister. My social reputation is at stake."

CHAPTER 18

The following morning, Emma was on her way to a meeting with Tom Cane and Jill Bedner when Lee Hennick called. The young man sounded perturbed.

"I tried being patient. I told myself I was going to wait for you to call me. But obviously you're not going to call me, so this morning I decided I just had to know what you'd found out."

"I'm sorry I haven't gotten back to you," Emma said, "but I haven't found out anything concrete yet. I'm still working on it."

"You're not just stringing me along, are you?" Lee asked. "Like that detective did?"

"I promise I'm not stringing you along. I really am working on it. And I think I might be making some progress."

"Really?" Lee's tone brightened immediately. "What kind of progress?"

"I've talked to some of Oak's neighbors, and at least one of them confirms what you said, that in the last year of his life Oak seemed happier and more stable than they'd ever seen him."

"See, that proves he wouldn't have OD'd," Lee said.

"We don't know that yet for sure," Emma said, "but like I told you, I'm working on it."

"When do you think you'll know something for sure?"

"I'm afraid I can't give you an answer to that, but I promise I'll do the best I can. I'll get back to you just as soon as I have something definite to report."

"All right," Lee said. "But if I haven't heard from you by the beginning of next week I'm calling you again. Oak didn't give up on himself, and I'm not going to give up on him either."

"That's fair enough," Emma said.

"All right. I'll talk to you then. And thanks."

"You're welcome."

Emma hung up the phone and hurried off to her meeting. When she returned later that morning, she had several phone messages. One was from Lucille Adina. Tossing the other message slips on her desk, Emma eagerly dialed Oak's former neighbor.

Lucille sounded like everyone's favorite grandmother. "How wonderful that you are soliciting testimonials about Oak for your brochure," she said after hearing Emma's bogus pitch. "Of course I'd be delighted to talk to you. Oak Greythorne was a wonderful man. I miss him every day."

"That's great," Emma said. "How would you describe Oak as a neighbor?"

"I'll be home all afternoon," Lucille said. "What time would be convenient for you to stop by?"

Emma frowned. Although she was anxious to hear what Lucille had to say, she was not particularly keen on giving up a good chunk of her afternoon to do it. "I really hate to put you to the trouble of having me come over," Emma hedged. "I'm sure it would be more convenient for you to do this over the phone."

"Nonsense. It would be no trouble at all. I raised eight children and I love having people visit. You just name your time and I'll be ready for you."

Emma quietly sighed. Obviously the only way she was going to get Lucille's story was to have a tête-à-tête. "Would three o'clock be convenient for you?"

"Three it is. See you then."

"Great. Bye." Emma hung up the phone feeling as if she'd just been outfoxed by a sly telemarketer. She looked at the clock. She'd promised Tom Cane she'd have time to do some rudimentary research on a legal issue that had just arisen in the lead paint case and get back to him by the end of the day. Emma had no idea how long her meeting with Lucille Adina would last but she had a feeling the woman was quite loquacious, so it was possible she wouldn't be getting back to the office too early. She guessed she'd better work through lunch to make sure she finished Tom's project before she left.

By quarter to three Emma had finished the research project and e-mailed Tom the results. She was taking her purse out of her desk drawer when the telephone rang. Emma picked it up.

"Louis Brisbane here."

Emma's gut tightened.

"I was calling to say that I thought it was time to send a follow-up letter to those tenants who have not yet responded to our offer to buy out their leases."

"It hasn't even been two weeks since the first letter went out," Emma said, grateful that Brisbane couldn't see the look of disdain on her face. "I'd prefer to wait a little longer to do a follow-up."

"That sounds reasonable. Why don't you plan on sending a second mailing the middle of next week."

"Will do."

"Have you heard back from Mr. Hennick?"

Emma's heart thumped. Did Brisbane have her phone bugged? "Not yet," she lied. "I'll try to talk to him next week, too."

"Have any other tenants shown hostility to the buy-out?"

"No."

"Good. That means it's likely everyone will move out early if the price is right. Send out another letter raising the stakes by three thousand dollars. And keep me posted if anyone balks. The prospective buyer is very anxious to empty the building."

"Okay," Emma said brightly.

"Thank you again for your help on this, Emma. I do appreciate it."

"No problem," Emma said.

She got up hurriedly and walked out to Lorraine's desk. "I have to run an errand," she said. "I'm not sure when I'll be back."

"Have fun." Lorraine gave a little wave.

On the short drive to see Oak's old friend, Emma found herself continually checking her rearview mirror to see if she was being followed. She didn't relax until she was inside the building's parking garage.

Lucille Adina's spacious condominium was full of fresh flowers, well-worn furniture and family photos. "This was taken at a family reunion last year," Lucille, a spry octogenarian, said proudly as she took a large picture off of the mantel. "Everyone was there. All my children, their spouses, their children, and these are my two great-grandchildren."

"They're a lovely group. You must be very proud," Emma said.

"I am proud of them," Lucille said. "I never worked outside the home like all young women seem to do nowadays, but I do feel a real sense of accomplishment in steering my children down the right path. None of them was ever in trouble, even once."

"That's very impressive," Emma said.

"Come sit down here on the couch," Lucille said, "and we'll have a nice chat about Oak. Would you like something to drink?"

Before Emma could request either water or iced tea, Lucille continued, "I generally have a gin and tonic this time of day. How would that suit you?"

"Well—" Emma hesitated. She wasn't accustomed to drinking in the middle of a work day, but she didn't want to risk offending Lucille. "That's very nice of you," she said. "But make mine light on the gin and heavy on the tonic. I have to go back to work, so I need to keep a clear head."

As they sipped their drinks, Lucille waxed eloquent about her former neighbor.

"Oak Greythorne was such a dear. I truly miss him. It's still hard to believe he's gone."

"Frank Marsden said you and Mr. Greythorne were quite close."

"Oh, yes. You can probably tell that I'm sort of a mother hen, and I took him under my wing when he first moved into the building. He was a very private man, didn't seem to take to people too easily. I respected that, but over time I wore him down. I love to cook and I'd bring over fresh baked bread or cookies or sometimes a pan of lasagna. I don't think Oak got homemade cooking too often, and he seemed to really appreciate it."

"Did he ever talk to you about his past?" Emma asked.

"Not too much," Lucille said. "I gathered he'd had a rather unhappy childhood. I'd heard rumors about mental problems and alcohol abuse but we never discussed it."

"Did he ever mention a woman named Janice Hall?"

Lucille shook her head. "No, he didn't. Who was she?"

"According to a boyhood friend, she was someone Oak almost married when they were in college."

"What a shame it didn't work out. Oak should

have had a family. I think he would have been an excellent father. He truly seemed to love children. Anytime any of my grandbabies visited me, he was always so pleased to talk to them."

"Tell me about some of your more recent recollections of Mr. Greythorne," Emma said. In order to make her story about the trust's brochure seem credible, she had brought along a legal pad. She set it in her lap and scrawled a few cryptic notes as Lucille talked.

"To tell you the truth, in the last six months of his life he seemed happier than I'd ever seen him," Lucille said.

"In what way?"

"It's hard to put a finger on it, but I guess in every way. He seemed less tense, less mopey, more outgoing."

"Do you have any idea what could have caused this change in his personality?" Emma asked.

"I'm not sure, but one day, about a month before he died, he did say something to me about possibly going back to work."

"Really? Doing what?"

"Running his own business, I guess. We were down in the lobby getting our mail. He subscribed to all these business journals and magazines about finance and commerce. I made some remark about him being a regular Alan Greenspan, and he laughed and said he didn't want to be Alan Greenspan, but he was thinking about starting up a new company."

"Did you ask any details about what he had in mind?"

"No. I never had a head for business, so I doubt I would have understood it anyway."

"And he never mentioned it again?"

Lucille shook her head. "Would you like me to freshen your drink?"

"No, thanks," Emma said, "but you go right ahead."

Lucille nimbly got up and went to the kitchen. She returned in short order. "There's nothing like a tall refreshing drink on a warm day," she said, settling back into her chair. "Now, let's see. Where were we? Oh, yes. My most recent recollections of Oak. Well, as I said, it appeared to me that he was finally at peace with himself. That's what makes it so hard to accept his passing."

"Did he ever talk to you about going to AA?" Emma asked.

"No. He was too much of a gentleman to discuss personal matters with an old woman like me."

"How long before he passed away did you last see him?"

"Three days."

"You have an excellent memory to be able to pin-point it that exactly," Emma said.

"It was a Monday night," Lucille said. "I remember because two of my grandchildren had come over for dinner and their father came to get them. He was in a hurry and didn't want to take the time to park

191

the car and come up, so I brought the children down to the street and saw that they got in the car. I was just going to come back inside when I heard Oak's voice."

"Where was he?" Emma asked.

"A little ways up the block, talking to a man in a parked vehicle. They were talking very loudly. Arguing."

Emma's pulse began to race. "Could you tell what they were arguing about?"

"No, but I could tell they were angry at each other. Some swear words were exchanged."

"You couldn't make out anything that was being said?"

Lucille shook her head. "I didn't linger down there long enough to try. It was a chilly night and I hadn't bothered to put on a sweater to see the children to their car, so I wanted to get back inside where it was warm. But I'll always feel bad that my last memory of Oak will be of him arguing with someone."

"You never saw him or talked to him again after that?"

"No. And by Thursday he was gone."

"Had you ever seen the man Oak was arguing with before that evening?"

"I really didn't see him—or at least not all of him. He was sort of leaning out the window, so I saw his arm. It looked like he was wearing a suit jacket."

"What kind of car was he driving?" Emma asked.

"It wasn't a car, and he wasn't driving. He was sitting in the front passenger's seat."

"What kind of vehicle was it?" Emma asked, almost afraid to hear the answer.

"One of those huge sports utility things. A great big shiny black one."

Just like Tommy Corona drove, Emma thought, her stomach churning.

"Could you see the driver?" Emma asked.

"No. I've told you everything I remember about that incident. Now if you'd like, I'd be happy to tell you a few anecdotes that you might be able to use for your brochure."

"That'd be great," Emma said, taking a deep breath to remain calm. "I don't want to take up your whole afternoon, and I do need to get back to the office."

After Lucille launched into a lengthy recollection about Oak, Emma finally found a break in which to make her escape. "I really have to go," Emma said, pumping the old woman's hand. "Thank you so much for seeing me. You've been very helpful."

"If you need any other quotes, let me know. I'm sure I could come up with a few more."

Emma raced to her car and headed back to the office. By the time she arrived, it was after five and the support staff had all left. Barricading herself in her office, Emma called Kansas City and relayed the afternoon's events to Coleen.

"So you think the guy who assaulted you in the partner's office was driving the SUV with the passenger who was arguing with your client a few days before he died?" Coleen said.

"That's what it sounds like," Emma agreed. "And I'm afraid to think about who the passenger might have been."

"I agree that it sounds too fishy to be a coincidence," Coleen said. "What are you going to do now?"

"I'm not sure. I guess try to find the other person who witnessed the will, to see if she was aware of any coercion. But she was an associate who was only here a few months, so I have no idea where to start looking."

"What's her name?" Coleen asked.

"Julia Boswell."

"I can maybe help you out by running the name through various criminal databases. Of course that would only help you if she'd run afoul of the law, but at least it's a start."

"I'm willing to try anything," Emma said.

"Okay. Let me see what I can find. And I know this is stating the obvious but please, Emma, be very, very careful. There's something rotten in the state of Franklin and Holland."

"I'm beginning to agree with you on that," Emma said. "Thanks for your help. I'll talk to you soon."

After Emma disconnected the call, she looked at her desk. She had six phone calls to return and a seemingly endless supply of work to do. She'd only managed to bill five hours that day. She knew she should stay a couple of hours, but she was too skittish to accomplish anything.

She was meeting Flynn at his place at eight. She

needed some time to regroup before then. One thing she knew for certain was that she didn't want to spend another minute in that office. She grabbed her purse and bolted for the elevator. When she reached the parking garage, she ran to her car and didn't relax until she was safely inside with the doors locked and was speeding out to the street.

CHAPTER 19

That evening, Emma discovered another one of Flynn's talents: he loved to cook. While giving her a glass of wine, Flynn casually asked if Emma would like to stay in that evening.

"Sure," Emma replied, thinking they'd order pizza or Chinese takeout.

"Great," Flynn said. "I've been wanting to make dinner for you."

"You cook?" Emma asked.

"Why do you look so surprised?" Flynn asked. "Don't tell me you believe that old wives' tale that men can't even boil water."

"No, it's just that I've never been lucky enough to date anyone who cooked."

"I'm a real Renaissance man," Flynn joked, tousling her hair. "So, what are you in the mood for?"

"You mean, you know how to make more than one or two things? I am impressed." Emma thought for a moment. "Ah, how about pasta with seafood?"

"Good idea. We can have Caesar salad. I make it

from scratch. I hate that stuff you get in the bag with the tasteless dressing. And for dessert how about key lime pie?''

''I'm hungry already,'' Emma said. ''What time do we eat?''

''Give me about forty minutes,'' Flynn said. ''And I've got an idea how you can spend the time.''

Thirty minutes later, Emma called Kathy. ''Guess where I am?'' she asked when her friend answered the phone. ''I'm in Flynn's Jacuzzi drinking a glass of pinot noir.''

''Is Flynn there with you?'' Kathy asked in a chipper tone. ''And if so, get off the phone at once and devote your full attention to him.''

''No, he's in the kitchen making dinner.''

''You mean he's making dinner reservations or he's ordering dinner?''

''He's cooking the dinner!'' Emma exclaimed triumphantly. ''He loves to cook. He's making pasta with seafood and key lime pie, and he told me I should just soak in the tub and relax and he'd call me when it was time to eat.''

''Unbelievable!'' Kathy exclaimed. ''Does he do windows? And more importantly, can we have him cloned so I can get in on some of the fun you're having?''

''I think he's one of a kind,'' Emma said, sinking back into the tub and sipping her wine. ''And he's all mine.''

''Damn! Some people have all the luck. As soon as

we hang up I'm going to take Pepper outside and let him off his leash and see if he can scrounge up a guy for me."

There was a knock on the bathroom door. "Dinner is served," Flynn called out.

"Gotta go," Emma said. "The butler just announced that dinner is ready."

Although the meal was wonderful, as the evening went on Emma found herself more and more distracted by thoughts of her conversation with Lucille Adina.

"You're awfully quiet," Flynn said gently. "Is there anything you'd care to share with me?"

Emma hesitated. Of course she wanted to share her concerns with him, but she was afraid his reaction might not be too positive. "I decided to pursue an investigation into Oak Greythorne's death," she said carefully. "Some discrepancies have come up, and I'd like to straighten them out."

Flynn nodded. "Go on."

"I got a list of Oak's neighbors and last night I started calling them to see if anybody could fill in any details about his life or if anyone noticed anything unusual or different about him shortly before he died."

"I take it you found someone who did notice something."

"Yes. One of the people in the building told me that Oak was fairly close to an old woman named Lucille Adina. I spoke with her this morning and she insisted that I come over so we could chat in person.

I drove over there this afternoon. She's over eighty but really sharp and observant. We talked for quite a while. She was very fond of Oak, sort of treated him like a son. She told me that the last time she saw Oak was three days before he died. He was arguing with a male passenger in a black SUV."

"Could she hear what they were arguing about?"

"No."

"Does she know who Oak was arguing with?"

"No," Emma said, "but I'm afraid I might know who was driving the SUV. And that's what has me spooked, because Tommy Corona drives a black SUV."

Flynn slammed his fist down on the table. "Jesus Christ!" he exclaimed. "I warned you that Corona was a slimeball. Now you're telling me he's somehow involved with the *Greythorne* estate? How can that be?"

"I don't know," Emma said. "That's what I'd like to find out. Louis Brisbane was a lifelong friend of Oak Greythorne. I have no idea how Tommy Corona fits into the picture."

Flynn thought a moment, then said, "Wait a minute. Didn't you tell me the reason you're supposed to try to buy out all the leases in Lee Hennick's building was because the prospective buyer wants to gut the place and turn it into more upscale housing?"

"That's right."

"I never thought to ask you where the building is. Do you remember the address?"

"Sure." Emma rattled it off.

"And how much is the buyer paying for the property?"

"Around four million."

"Four!" Flynn exclaimed disbelievingly. "I'll bet that's where Corona comes in."

"You've completely lost me," Emma said.

"There's no way you'd be aware of this, but there are plans in the works for a major—and I mean with a capital M—development just a few blocks away from that apartment building. We're talking a huge new shopping center with anchor tenants like Nordstrom and Bloomingdale's. A hotel, a water park, restaurants. It'll really give what's been an almost blighted area an enormous boost. The project was first proposed about two years ago and it's been stalled at the Plan Commission level, but the word is, it's going to be approved before the end of the year, with construction likely to start early next spring. And once it gets the green light, property values in that whole area will skyrocket."

"So you're saying Oak's building will be worth more than four million."

"Try fifteen or twenty."

"I'm still confused," Emma said. "Why would Brisbane, as Oak's executor and trustee, allow the property to be sold for a fraction of its true value?"

Flynn walked over behind Emma and put his hands on her shoulders. "Because, my dear, he's probably in cahoots with the buyer and knows they can turn around and resell it and make a mint."

Emma gasped and turned around to face him. "Do you think Brisbane and Corona are the buyers?"

"It wouldn't surprise me a bit. Have you seen the buyer's name mentioned anywhere?"

Emma thought hard. "I think I did. It's a corporation. Something like Mustang Enterprises. That's not it, but I seem to remember the name reminded me of a car. I think I can find it. If I do, is there a way to check out who the principals are?"

Flynn nodded. "I've got contacts at city hall and the secretary of state's office. If you get me the corporate name, I'll put them on the case. I'd bet anything that Tommy Corona's name will show up prominently." He walked back to his chair and sat down.

"Assuming the people in the black SUV that Lucille saw were Corona and Brisbane, I wonder what the argument with Oak was about," Emma said. "Do you suppose they were trying to talk him into selling his building?"

"I doubt we'll ever know the answer to that," Flynn said.

"Maybe they tried to buy the building and Oak refused to sell and they killed him," Emma said. "Maybe Lee was right after all."

"I still think the murder angle is pretty far-fetched," Flynn said, "although I have to admit that now that I know Tommy Corona is part of the equation, murder no longer sounds totally preposterous."

"Follow the money," Emma said.

"What?"

"My friend Coleen said that whenever you're investigating any kind of foul play, you should always follow the money because the odds are that's where you'll find the bad guy."

"That makes sense to me."

"I have to find out more about the relationship between Brisbane and Greythorne," Emma said. "It sounds like they enjoyed sort of a love/hate relationship their entire lives. I have to wonder if Brisbane was truly Oak's first choice to act as executor and trustee or if Brisbane somehow forced him into that."

"How do you propose to find that out?" Flynn asked.

"Oak's will was witnessed by two people. One of them is Brisbane's secretary, J. Devereaux Braxton, a woman who makes Cruella De Vil look like a stand-up comic. The other witness was an associate named Julia Boswell. She was at the firm only a few months and left under somewhat mysterious circumstances. If I could track her down, she might be able to fill in some of the gaps."

"How do you plan to unearth this mystery woman?"

"I don't know," Emma admitted. "If she was an employee of Franklin and Holland, even for a short time, there must be a personnel file on her. If I could find it, there should be some information in it that would help me determine her present whereabouts."

"How are you going to get access to an old personnel file?"

"You ask too many practical questions," Emma

grumbled. "There must be a way. I just haven't figured it out yet." She leaned back in her chair. "The more I learn about Oak Greythorne, the more of an enigma he becomes. It's too bad that someone with so much to offer had so much sadness in his life."

"Didn't anyone ever tell you life's not fair?"

"Oak's life was more than just unfair. It sounds like it was almost cursed." Emma ran her finger around the rim of her wine glass. "Everyone who knew Oak well says that he was intelligent, kind and giving. What a shame that he not only never married, he left no heirs. No close relatives even. Let's say that I'm able to find evidence that someone—whether Brisbane or someone else—used undue influence to get Oak to draft that will. The remedy in undue influence cases is to throw out the will and allow the estate to pass by intestate succession. But if Oak has no relatives, where would his money go?"

Flynn shrugged. "I don't know. You're the lawyer. You tell me."

"Brisbane made a point of reminding me that the purpose of probate is to carry out the testator's intentions. I wonder what Oak's true intentions were. And I also wonder if Corona and Brisbane maybe had their own intentions for Oak's money—deadly intentions."

The mention of Corona's name made Flynn turn somber. He reached over and took Emma's hand. "I meant what I said earlier. Tommy Corona is a bad man and he's dangerous. I know I can't dissuade you from trying to get to the bottom of the *Greythorne*

203

case but you have to give me your word that you'll stay away from Corona."

Recalling how the mere sound of Corona's voice had caused Emma to take shelter between two parked cars, she nodded. "I promise."

Flynn kissed Emma's hand. "Good girl. Tommy Corona is not someone to take lightly, and I don't want anything to happen to you."

CHAPTER 20

"Come on, Kathy, I know you're in there." Emma pounded on her friend's door. "It's time to get up. I promised Flynn we'd be at the construction site at eight."

It was Sunday morning, and Emma had spent the last ten minutes trying to rouse Kathy by telephone. She had gotten no answer, so she decided to try a more direct approach.

"Get up now!" Emma increased both the timbre of her voice and her level of pounding. "Or you're going to have to explain to Flynn why we were late."

Just as Emma was about to start kicking the door, it flew open and she found herself facing a very tired and grumpy-looking Kathy, dressed in an oversized T-shirt. "Will you please keep your voice down? Some people in this building are trying to sleep. Namely me." She started to close the door again, but Emma wedged her foot inside.

"You promised me you'd help at the Habitat for Humanity site today, and you're going to keep your word if I have to drag you there."

Kathy shoved her hair behind her ears. "What time is it?"

"Ten after seven."

"Oh, God. No wonder I feel like shit. I didn't get to bed until three."

"That's your problem. Go take a shower and get dressed. I'll make you some coffee and take Pepper out for a quick walk. Then we're heading out."

"You're mean. Do you know that?"

"Of course I'm mean. I'm a lawyer. I'm paid to be mean. Now get going."

"All right," Kathy sputtered. "But if I get injured because of my weakened condition, I'm going to sue Flynn Fielding and Habitat for Humanity and anybody else I can think of."

"Great." Emma gave her friend a shove. "Now get a move on. You've got exactly thirty minutes."

By the time the two women were in Emma's car heading toward the work site, Kathy's mood had mellowed somewhat although she was less than thrilled with the loose-fitting jeans and T-shirt Emma had lent her for the occasion. "This looks like something my mother would wear to garden," she complained. "Don't tell me you actually wear this."

"I do wear it to clean and to exercise," Emma replied.

"No wonder I don't own anything like this. I never willingly engage in either of those activities."

"By the end of the day you'll be thanking me for insisting that you dressed comfortably," Emma said.

"I'll bet you a dinner at Charlie Trotter's that you're wrong."

"You're on," Emma said.

They arrived at the work site precisely at eight. "That's what I like to see," Flynn said, walking up to them. "Crew members who believe in punctuality. How are you today, Kathy?"

"Just great," Kathy said, flashing him a big smile. "We would have been here earlier but Emma overslept."

Emma coughed loudly, then said to Flynn, "What would you like us to do?"

"Have you ever used a nail gun?"

Kathy gave him a blank look. "Unless you're referring to some sort of device that's used on fingernails, the answer is most definitely no."

Flynn laughed. "No problem. We have jobs for people of all skill levels. Emma, you go over there and talk to the guy in the blue shirt. His name is Nick Amhaus. He'll get you started. Kathy, you come with me. You can work with Ed Bubert on landscaping."

"See you later," Emma said, giving them a little wave.

After minimal instruction, Emma settled comfortably into assisting the master carpenter. Yet the manual work didn't occupy all of her attention. Her thoughts continually returned to Oak Greythorne.

Emma had remembered the name of the entity interested in purchasing Oak's apartment building:

Regal Enterprises, Ltd. Flynn had made a few calls
and discovered that the corporation's principals were
in fact Corona and Brisbane.

Emma had a strong feeling that Brisbane and Corona had been trying to force Oak into doing something against his will and he had resisted. And it no
longer seemed outside the realm of possibility that
his resistance might have led to his death.

But at the moment that was mere speculation.
What Emma needed was some proof. And she
couldn't help but wonder if Julia Boswell might be
the one person able to provide it. The problem was,
Emma had no idea where Julia went after leaving
Franklin & Holland and, so far, her efforts to find
the former associate had yielded no results. As Emma
continued nailing, she thought about the leads she'd
pursued to date in her search for the elusive Ms.
Boswell.

Coleen Kennedy had called the day before to let
Emma know that she had exhausted her resources and
turned up no information about Julia. "I found no one
with that name between the ages of twenty-eight and
thirty-five in the law enforcement databanks," Coleen
said. "There was also no missing persons report filed
on anyone with that name in the last six years, so
she must be out there someplace."

"Do you have any other suggestions?" Emma
asked.

"I did have one thought," Coleen said. "Do you
know what happened to the contents of Greythorne's

home? If the bad guys were trying to pull something, Greythorne might very well have had some kind of written evidence."

"That's a great idea," Emma said. "I'll see if I can find out what happened to his personal belongings."

"It's a real long shot," Coleen said. "If somebody was clever enough to do him in and make it look like an accident, I'm sure they would've also thought to sanitize the apartment."

"It's something to look into," Emma said. "I'll take any suggestions I can get."

"If I think of any others, I'll let you know. In the meantime, keep watching your back."

"Believe me, I'm keeping a close watch on all my body parts," Emma assured her.

As soon as she had finished talking to Coleen, Emma called Lucille Adina. After a few minutes of friendly chatter, Emma zoomed in on the reason for her call. "I was thinking it might be a nice touch if we included some photos of Oak Greythorne in our brochure," she said. "We don't seem to have any in our files here. Do you happen to know if his belongings are still in his apartment? There might be some photos there we could use."

"Oak's place was completely cleaned out shortly after he died," Lucille said. "Everything was loaded into a truck and hauled away. I assumed someone from your law firm probably arranged it."

"I didn't know that," Emma said, wondering what Brisbane had done with the evidence of Oak Greythorne's earthly existence. "I wasn't assigned to the case until somewhat later. I'm sorry to have bothered you."

"No bother at all, dear," Lucille said. "Call me anytime."

As she stopped to reload the nail gun, Emma wracked her brain to come up with a way to discreetly locate the firm's old personnel files but nothing sprang to mind. She was afraid she had already made Lorraine suspicious with all of her half-truths and skulking around.

Emma paused to get a drink of water. Her mind drifted back to the first time she'd met with Brisbane about the estate. He had said the reason for secrecy was that other associates might be jealous if they knew she had gotten this plum assignment. Emma groaned, thinking how naïve she had been to believe him.

Brisbane was a managing partner. He didn't give a damn if a few associates' noses got out of joint. The reason he didn't want anyone else at the firm to know was because he was unethically profiting from his client's estate. As Oak's executor and trustee, Brisbane had a fiduciary duty to sell Oak's property at fair market value. Instead he was selling it to himself at a fraction of its true worth. This was not only an ethical violation, it was a criminal offense.

"You look kind of flushed." Flynn's voice interrupted Emma's internal dialogue. "Do you want to take a break?"

Emma shook her head. "No, I'm fine. I was just

thinking about something. I'll get back to work now."

"Don't push yourself too much," Flynn said. "It's getting hot out here, and I know you're not accustomed to manual labor."

"Kansas girls are from tough stock," Emma said. "I'll be fine. How's Kathy holding up?"

"I'm afraid upper-class Chicago girls aren't quite so tough," Flynn said with a chuckle. "She threw a wad of dirt at me and said she'd never worked so hard in her life. I said we'd all go out for margaritas if she stuck it out until at least three o'clock."

"She'll stick it out," Emma said. "She knows I'll never let her live it down if she doesn't."

Someone called, and Flynn looked up. "There's a problem with the staircase I need to take a look at," he said. "I'll see you later."

As Emma watched him walk away, she realized that this was the first time she'd seen Flynn's professional side. And what she saw made her proud. Flynn was clearly a born leader. He took charge. He solved problems. He had organized a group of disparate workers into a cohesive band. He kept things humming and people looked up to him. Emma threw herself back into her work, temporarily forgetting about Oak Greythorne and company.

That afternoon, as Emma was taking a short break, Kathy stormed over. Her clothes were dirty and drenched with sweat. Her face was splotched with dirt. "I have had it!" she said. "I kept my end of the bargain. I lasted until three o'clock. I'm not staying a minute longer. I'm going to get the hell out of here. Are you going to take me home or do I have to call Lenny, my favorite limo driver?"

"I'll take you home," Emma said.

Kathy's eyes narrowed. "Don't tell me you intend to come back."

"I planned to work until at least six," Emma said.

"You're insane! How can you stand to work like a common laborer? If they made prisoners work like this, they'd call it cruel and unusual punishment."

Before Emma could reply, Flynn and a tall blond man walked up to them.

"Good afternoon, ladies," Flynn said cordially. "How are things going?"

Expecting Kathy to unleash a tirade of expletives, Emma turned toward her friend and saw that her gaze was fixed on the good-looking stranger. "Things are going just fine," Kathy said, wiping her dirty hands on her pants and giving the stranger a big smile.

"Glad to hear it," Flynn said. "Emma Davis, Kathy Flood, this is my friend Graham Reedsburg."

"Hi, Graham," Emma said.

"A pleasure to meet you, Graham," Kathy said, shaking his hand.

"Nice to meet you, too," Graham said.

"Graham is a late arrival," Flynn explained. "But he's got a good excuse. He's a vascular surgeon and he was in the OR until about an hour ago."

At the sound of the word "surgeon," Kathy's perkiness level increased even more. "How wonderful that, after saving someone's life, you'd take the time to come here and build this house," she gushed. "You must be a true humanitarian."

"I believe those of us who have been given a lot of benefits in life have a duty to share with others," he said.

"What a wonderful philosophy," Kathy said.

"You've been a real trooper today, Kathy," Flynn said. "Thanks so much for coming."

"I'm not leaving yet," Kathy said. "I'm staying until six o'clock."

"I'm going to install windows," Graham said. "Would you like to help me out?"

"I'd love to," Kathy said.

"You know, it's so refreshing to see a woman who isn't afraid to get dirty for a good cause," Graham said. "I get so tired of all these snotty socialites strutting around all over the city."

Kathy flashed him a brilliant smile. "I agree with you completely," she said. "I hate pretension. With me, what you see is what you get."

Emma had to fight the impulse to laugh out loud.

"Did you say something?" Graham asked.

Emma shook her head. "No. I just had something in my throat. You two run along and work on windows. I'm going to get a drink of water."

Graham and Kathy started to walk away, then Kathy turned back. "Oh, Emma, I almost forgot. You know that dinner at Charlie Trotter's—the one that's going to be my treat—well, any night in the next few weeks would be good for me. Why don't you check your calendar and pick out a date."

"Will do," Emma said.

"What was that all about?" Flynn asked as Kathy and Graham drifted out of earshot.

"Let me put it this way," Emma said, smiling at him. "If my intuition is correct, I don't think Kathy will need to invite Mr. Mediocre to the zoo benefit."

CHAPTER 21

On Monday morning, Emma was forced to temporarily put aside her plan to locate Julia Boswell when Tom Cane asked her and Jill Bedner to meet with a client about a new case.

"The client's name is Mike Laskis," Tom explained as the three lawyers met in Emma's office. "I've done some other work for him over the years. He's an interesting character. I think you'll like him."

"What kind of case is it?" Emma asked.

"First Amendment issues," Tom replied. "Mike owns a gentleman's club called Big Louie's. It's located in a small town that recently adopted an ordinance prohibiting some of the activities that go on at the club. Mike wants us to challenge the constitutionality of the ordinance."

"A gentleman's club?" Jill repeated. "You mean a strip joint?"

Tom laughed. "It's a legitimate business that happens to feature exotic dancers. You do support the First Amendment, don't you, Jill?"

"Within limits," Jill said.

"If this client can pay our fees, we support the First Amendment all the way," Emma assured the partner.

"That's the spirit," Tom said. "Mike will fill you in on the details of the case, and we'll get together this afternoon to decide how best to mount our attack."

"You mean you're not going to sit in on the meeting with the client?" Emma asked.

"I have depositions," Tom explained. "You two can handle it. I think once you get into the issues, you might even find the case somewhat entertaining. I promise it won't be as dull as looking at paint chips." He stood up and walked to the door. "I'll talk to you later. Don't be too hard on Mike."

Emma and Jill looked at each other. "Have you ever done any First Amendment work?" Emma asked.

Jill shook her head. "No. How about you?"

"No. I suppose this case might be more fun than your run-of-the-mill commercial lawsuit, but why couldn't we get a client who did something a little more respectable in the exercise of his First Amendment rights, like burning an American flag?"

"What time is this guy coming in?" Jill asked.

"In a half hour," Emma replied. "I need to send some e-mails. I'll meet you in conference room four in twenty-five minutes."

Jill got out of her chair. "Okay. In the meantime I'll try to do some rudimentary research about First Amendment law as it pertains to exotic dancers."

Tom Cane had not been exaggerating when he described Mike Laskis as a character. The club owner was in his late forties, with graying curly hair and a beard. He was dressed in khaki pants and a Hawaiian shirt. "It's nice to meet you both," Mike said after Emma and Jill had introduced themselves. "I can tell this case is off to a good start. You're both a hell of a lot prettier than Tom Cane."

"Do you have a copy of the ordinance?" Emma asked, ignoring his remark.

"Got it right here." Mike reached into his shirt pocket and took out several folded sheets of paper. He set them down on the conference room table and pointed at the first page. "Here's where they say that clubs that feature all nude dancing are prohibited from selling alcohol."

"Big Louie's has all nude dancing?" Emma asked.

"No, it doesn't," Mike replied.

"Then why are you concerned that this part of the ordinance is going to affect your business?"

"Because the town and I don't exactly see eye to eye on what 'all nude' means."

Jill frowned. "What is there not to see eye to eye on? Either the dancers are completely nude or they're not."

"They're definitely not all nude," Mike said.

"You mean, they wear pasties or G-strings," Emma said.

"No, they wear shoes," Mike said.

Emma and Jill exchanged a puzzled look.

"Shoes?" Emma repeated.

"Yeah, all the dancers wear those high-heeled shoes. You know, stilettos."

"They don't wear anything on the upper parts of their body?" Emma asked.

"No, but somebody wearing shoes is not 'all nude.'"

Jill picked up the copy of the ordinance and quickly skimmed through it. "He might have a point," she said reluctantly. "It doesn't define what constitutes clothing, so we might be able to make an argument that shoes are enough to take a person out of the realm of total nudity."

"All right," Emma said, wanting to bring this meeting to an end as quickly as possible. "What other parts of the ordinance do you want to challenge?"

Mike took the papers out of Jill's hand and flipped to the second page. "Here," he said pointing. "They're prohibiting the dancers from having any physical contact with club patrons while the performance is going on."

"How will this affect your business?" Emma asked.

"They're outlawing lap dancing," Mike said. "Can you believe that? It's one of our biggest moneymakers— and the biggest source of the dancers' tips."

Emma didn't know if she should laugh or cry. Little had she known that when she went to law school she might one day have to use her knowledge of constitutional law to defend lap dancing. "I suppose our argument here would be that the ordinance stifles freedom of expression," she said to Jill.

Jill nodded. "Definitely stifles it."

"Do you have any other problems with the ordinance?" Emma asked.

"No, that pretty much covers it," Mike said.

"Great," Emma said. "We'll do some research and talk to Tom Cane about strategy and let you know how we intend to proceed."

"Sounds good." Mike stood up and the two lawyers did likewise, thrilled that the meeting had been so brief. Mike reached into his pants pocket and pulled out two business cards. He handed one to each of the women. "Here's the address and phone number for Big Louie's," he said. "You two should come over sometime. We serve good food and strong drinks."

"We'll keep that in mind," Emma said.

"Every Thursday is Hawaiian night," Mike said. "Mai tais and piña coladas are half price, and I personally lei every woman who walks in the door."

His remark was met with stony silence.

"Lei," Mike repeated. "L—E—I. Get it?"

"Oh, we get it," Jill said.

"The first Tuesday of every month we have a wet T-shirt contest. You girls might want to check that out. I guarantee you'd win a prize."

"We'll keep that in mind," Emma said, moving over to the door of the conference room to give the client a hint that it was time for him to leave.

"Nice meeting you," Mike said, giving them a little

wave as he walked out. "Hope to see you again real soon."

"Ta ta," Jill said, waving back.

"Aloha," Emma called after him.

As soon as the conference room door closed, the two women burst into uncontrolled peals of laughter. "This has to be Tom's idea of a joke," Jill said. "That guy can't be for real. He looks like something that crawled out of South L.A. in the sixties."

"If we have to make any court appearances, we'll either have to pick out clothes for him or leave him home. If a judge took one look at him, he'd immediately grant summary judgment in favor of the town."

"Especially if the case were assigned to a woman judge," Jill said. "She'd not only throw his case out, she'd find him in contempt the minute he opened his mouth."

"Maybe he could make some points by trying to lei her," Emma said. "Wait till we talk to Tom about this. I am really going to give him the business."

To Emma and Jill's surprise, Tom assured them that Mike was in fact a legitimate client. "I've handled a number of cases for him over the past ten years," he said when he met with the two women that afternoon.

"What kinds of cases?" Emma asked. "Sexual harassment?"

"Various business litigation matters," Tom replied. "Mike is a real entrepreneur. He has a knack for buying down-and-out businesses and then turning them around. He's been very successful."

"Well, if confidence counts for anything, he's got

that in spades," Emma said. "What do you want us to do next, draft a complaint?"

"Right," Tom said, "but you don't need to reinvent the wheel. I handled a similar case for another client about five or six years ago. *Manthey v. City of Antioch.* That file should give you a good background on the law, and you might even be able to make use of some parts of the complaint."

"Can we get the file from your secretary?" Emma asked.

Tom shook his head. "Files that old are in the morgue."

Emma gave him a blank look.

"You've never heard of the morgue?" Tom asked.

"No. Have you?" Emma asked Jill.

"I've heard of it, but I've never been there," Jill said.

"The morgue is how we affectionately refer to the warehouse where the firm's old files are kept," Tom explained. "It's a rather dark, cavernous place. Associates and support staff complain loudly when they are forced to go there to retrieve files. The two of you can draw straws for the honors."

"I'll go," Emma said at once. She hoped she didn't sound too eager, but the prospect of having access to Franklin & Holland's old files—dare she hope personnel files?—was not something she was about to pass up.

"Great, a volunteer," Tom said. "Get one of the messengers to go with you. Tell them to take a cart along to haul the file out. As I recall, it filled several boxes."

"I might as well get on that right away," Emma said. "I'll see if a messenger is available now."

"Very good," Tom said. "We'll talk again after you've had a chance to review the *Manthey* file."

"Why do you look so enthusiastic about digging around in an old dingy warehouse?" Jill asked after Tom left.

"Mike was so smarmy, I just want to finish this project as quickly as possible," Emma said.

"Let me know when you get back with the file so we can split it up and each review half of it," Jill said.

"Sounds good," Emma said. "I'll see you later."

Emma located one of the messengers in the copy center on the thirty-fifth floor. "You want to go to the morgue right now?" the messenger, a young man named Bill, asked. "All right. I have to get the key and then we'll go."

Emma followed him around the corner to a supply room. He opened a cabinet on the wall, revealing several rows of keys. Emma watched closely as he removed a key from a peg labeled "9."

"I'm ready if you are," Bill said, holding up the key.

"Let's go," Emma said.

The morgue was a two-story cement building located a couple of miles south of the Loop. Bill opened the door with the key, reached inside and flipped a switch, turning on a low level of lights.

"Here's an index to the locations of the files in here," Bill explained, taking a black notebook out of a Plexiglas holder on the inside wall. "Whenever new files are brought here, this index is updated. You want *Manthey*?" He flipped through the folder until he came to the Ms. "Here it is, row twelve, shelf D. Piece of cake."

Emma followed him to the designated location. "Here it is. *Manthey v. City of Antioch.* Hot damn, the system does work. Let's see, how many boxes do we have here? Looks like four. I'll run out to the car and get the cart. Be right back."

As soon as Bill was out the door, Emma raced back to the entrance and pulled the black notebook back out of its holder. Her hands shaking, she turned to the Ps.

Patrick, Penson, Personnel. There it was. Row twenty-one, shelves A through T. Emma put the notebook back in its proper location. As she was debating whether she had time to attempt to search for Julia Boswell's file, the door opened and Bill stepped inside, pulling the hand cart.

"Okey-dokey," he said brightly. "We'll get those babies loaded up and back to the office in a flash."

"Wonderful," Emma said. She looked at her watch. It was three thirty. She took a deep breath and tried to calm her jittery nerves. It didn't matter if she were frightened. She was now on a mission. In about six hours she was going to return to this site and locate the file that would enable her to find Julia Boswell.

CHAPTER 22

At seven that evening Emma sat in her living room trying to read through part of the file the messenger had retrieved from the morgue, but her nervous anticipation made it impossible to concentrate. She was anxiously waiting for another two hours to pass so that she could go back to the office, retrieve the key to the morgue and find Julia Boswell's personnel file.

Flynn was at a two-day conference in Indianapolis. Emma was almost glad that he was out of town since there was no doubt he would have strongly disapproved of her plan. As she tried for the third time to force herself to read through a brief Tom Cane had written, there was a knock at the door. "It's me," Kathy's voice called out. "Open up. It's an emergency."

Grateful to have an excuse to stop pretending that she was accomplishing anything, Emma got up and went to the door. "What's the emergency?" she asked as Kathy and Pepper swept into the apartment.

"I need to borrow a dress," Kathy said, making a beeline for Emma's bedroom.

"What did you say?" Emma asked, following her friend.

Kathy had already opened one of Emma's closets and was peering intently inside. "I need to borrow a dress," she repeated.

"Why do you need to borrow a dress from me?" Emma asked. "Did all of your clothes spontaneously combust while you were at work today?"

"I did such a good job with Graham pretending that I was an unpretentious, natural girl," Kathy lamented as she pawed through Emma's garments. "Now we're going out tomorrow night and I have no clothing that could be called either unpretentious or natural. My entire wardrobe is best described as high-class call girl chic. So I need to borrow something from you. I was thinking about a simple black dress with a high neck. I know you have at least eight of those."

"I think you're getting a little carried away," Emma said as Kathy searched through the rack of clothes. "So what if unpretentious isn't exactly the first word that comes to mind when describing you? You shouldn't try to pretend to be somebody you're not. It doesn't work. You're a wonderful person, and I'm sure Graham will adore the real you."

"I think I'll get a lot further with him if he doesn't discover the real me just yet. Where are you hiding those damn black dresses? Oh, here's one that'd be perfect. Can I borrow it?"

Emma stared at her friend holding a sedate black sleeveless dress up to her body. "To quote a famous unnamed personage, you'd look like a Pilgrim or a nun in that."

"No, I wouldn't," Kathy insisted. "I'd look like a well-dressed Chicago working woman. It's understated, sedate, classy."

"It's dull," Emma said. "It's an outfit a lawyer would wear. In short, it's me, not you."

"It's the temporary new me," Kathy said. "What kind of accessories do you wear with this? Would my Judith Leiber bag that looks like Pepper totally destroy the sedate image?"

Emma burst out laughing. "Trust me, you can't possibly look unpretentious while carrying a three-thousand-dollar minaudière."

"All right," Kathy said crossly. "I'll tone down the accessories. But I *am* wearing this dress tomorrow. If Graham asks me out a second time, I'll wear something a little jazzier. Then I'll gradually build up to my usual wardrobe."

"Fine," Emma said. "I must say I do enjoy this role reversal. I never in my wildest dreams thought you'd be borrowing clothing from me."

"I really like this guy," Kathy said. "I don't want to blow it by coming on too strong."

"Then wear the dress with my blessings," Emma said. "But he's going to care about you, not what you're wearing."

"I'm so excited!" Kathy said, hugging the dress to her and spinning around. "I haven't been this enthusiastic about a date in eons. Graham might not have been on my wish list like Flynn, but that's only because I'd never heard of him. He is definitely wish list material. Can you believe it? Now both of us have great guys—or at least I have the potential of having one, depending on how things go tomorrow—and now that you're lending me this dress I'm sure they're going to go fine. So, let's go have a drink and celebrate our good fortune." She looked at Emma expectantly.

"I can't," Emma said.

"Why not? It's my treat. We can go anywhere you want."

"I have to go back to work later."

"What for? Is Franklin and Holland starting a night shift?"

"No. I think I may have found a way to track the woman associate who witnessed Oak Greythorne's will." Emma briefly explained about her visit to the morgue. "So, my plan is to go back to the office around nine, 'borrow' the key, go to the morgue and find Julia's file, then return the key to the office before anyone misses it."

"That's a great idea," Kathy said. "I'm going with you."

Emma looked at her in alarm. "You can't go with me. It might be dangerous."

"All the more reason for you not to go alone. There's safety in numbers. Plus, if I go with you we should be able to find the file twice as fast."

Emma hesitated a moment, then nodded. "How can I argue with that logic? All right. Let's leave here at quarter to nine."

"We'll take my car," Kathy said. "Less chance of recognition." She headed for the door, with Pepper trailing behind. "I've never done breaking and entering before. What should I wear?"

"For God's sake, who cares what you wear? And it's not breaking and entering. We're going to have a key."

"Oh, that's right. Well then, I'll see you in a little while."

At five minutes after nine, Kathy pulled her car into a fifteen-minute parking space half a block from Emma's office. Kathy looked at the austere building. "I'll wait right here," Kathy said. "If anything goes wrong, call me on my cell phone."

Emma nodded, took a deep breath, and got out of the car. She walked briskly to the building, punched in the security code to gain after-hours entrance, and rode the elevator to the thirty-fifth floor. In case she ran into anyone she knew, she would simply say that she had come back to the office to retrieve another portion of the file in Tom Cane's old case.

Franklin & Holland, like most big law firms, had its share of workaholic-associates, and it was not uncommon for lawyers to be roaming the halls all hours of the day and night. No one would think it unusual for Emma to be working at nine in the evening.

Emma hoped it would be a fairly simple matter to retrieve the key, but as she approached the supply room she heard voices. She stopped in her tracks and peeked inside. Two of the night secretaries were in there chatting. Emma ducked into the conference room across the hall and waited for them to finish their conversation.

"So then I told him flat out," one of the women said, "either we get married or I'm moving on. We've lived together for two years and I'm getting tired of helping support him. I want kids. If he isn't willing to commit, then I'm going to find somebody who is."

"Good for you," the other woman said. "What did he say to that?"

"He says he can't live without me and that we'll definitely get married by the end of the year, but I won't believe it until I see a ring."

Emma shifted nervously from foot to foot. How long were those damn women going to stand there and jabber? If someone saw her, she would be hard pressed to explain what she was doing standing around in the dark.

The chit-chat continued. "Make sure he buys you a decent ring, not something with a crappy little diamond. You're a high quality person. You deserve a high quality ring."

"That's exactly what I told him. He bitched at first and said he couldn't afford it but now he's been working overtime to earn some extra money. I figure I should have a ring by Fourth of July."

"You call me the minute you get it. We'll have a little party after work."

"That'd be nice."

"Oh, geez, look at the time. My break's over. I better get back to work or I'll get fired."

Emma breathed a sigh of relief.

"I know. These lawyers are such slave drivers. Nice talkin' to you, and good luck."

Emma counted to sixty after the voices stopped, then quickly walked across the hall into the supply room. She opened the cabinet, removed the key from peg nine, and slipped it in her pocket. The whole process took perhaps thirty seconds.

Five minutes later, Emma was back in Kathy's car. "I got it," she said. "Let's get going."

As Kathy pulled out of her parking place, she said, "There's a twenty-four-hour Walgreens a few blocks from here. Why don't we stop and have a copy of the key made?"

"What for?" Emma asked.

"For insurance purposes. In case you need to go back to the warehouse again, you won't need to keep swiping the key from the office and returning it."

"I plan on this being my only trip there."

"You never know what's going to happen," Kathy said. "Why not be prepared?"

"You have a criminal mind," Emma said. "You should have been a lawyer. All right. Let's stop at Walgreens and get a key made. But step on it. I want to get this project over with."

After a brief detour to Walgreens, Kathy soon pulled up in front of the warehouse. In the daytime the building had simply looked nondescript. At night it looked downright foreboding. There were no street lights in the vicinity, and when Kathy turned off her headlights the entire area was plunged into darkness.

"This place is creepy," Kathy said. "And it's not

exactly in the best neighborhood. You were nuts to think of coming here alone."

"I do appreciate the company," Emma agreed. She opened the car door. "Well, let's get started. I don't want to hang around here any longer than I have to."

"Try out the Walgreens key," Kathy suggested. "So you're sure it works."

The new key worked fine. The women stepped inside, and Emma turned on the light. "What a depressing place," Kathy said. "I'd hate to spend much time in here."

"I'm hoping we won't be here long," Emma said. She pulled a flashlight out of her bag and switched it on. "I'm glad I thought to bring this. The lighting in here is really bad. Come on, I think row twenty-one is over here."

The women found the shelves containing the law firm's old personnel files with no problem. Locating Julia Boswell's file was another matter.

"I swear there is no rhyme or reason to this filing system," Kathy grumbled an hour later as the women had methodically made their way through eight shelves. "The firm doesn't need to worry about anything being stolen. It'll be a miracle if we ever find what we're looking for."

"The personnel office must have its own index showing individual file sites," Emma said.

"Maybe we should go back to the office and try to steal that," Kathy said. "Whoever set up this system must be schizophrenic. It's not chronological or alphabetical."

"It must be here somewhere," Emma said. She paused a moment as a depressing thought flashed through her head. "Unless someone wanted to make sure Julia Boswell would never be found and purged her file."

"Don't even think that," Kathy said. "It's got to be here. Keep looking."

Thirty minutes later, Kathy pulled a slim file out of a box, squinted at the name on the label and let out a whoop. "Eureka!" she shouted, holding the file in the air. "I have found it. Julia Boswell."

Emma, who was working several shelves away, hurried over and took the file out of her friend's hand. "Julia Boswell," she murmured. "I was beginning to think she never existed." Emma opened the file and saw the questionnaire that all new employees were asked to complete. Julia Boswell. Corporate department. Next of kin: Gail Boswell, mother. Minneapolis, Minnesota. A phone number was listed.

"It lists her mother's name and phone number," Emma said. "That should be a good start."

"Read it off and I'll write it down," Kathy said, reaching into her bag for paper and a pen.

Emma shook her head. "I'm taking the whole file with me."

"Do you think that's such a good idea?" Kathy asked.

"Who's going to miss it? Besides, now that I have a spare key, I can bring it back some other time. I'd planned to read through it here and make notes, but I didn't realize it would take us so long to unearth it. I don't want to spend another minute in this creepy place tonight. Besides, if I take the whole file along, I can make a copy."

"That plan works for me," Kathy said. "I was beginning to feel like a mushroom in here. Help me put this box back up on the shelf and then let's split."

It was eleven when Emma walked into the supply room and slipped the key back onto peg nine. Within minutes she was back in Kathy's car and they were speeding toward home.

"Thanks for coming with me," Emma said. "It did make the job a lot easier. If I'd gone by myself, I would have been there all night."

"I'll be happy to join you in criminal activity anytime," Kathy replied. "Except tomorrow night, of course, when the unpretentious me will be dining with Dr. Graham Reedsburg."

"I've got to hand it to you," Kathy continued as she pulled into the building's underground parking garage. "When you first started talking about this conspiracy stuff, I thought you were nuts. But now you've got me convinced that there is something to it and you're doing a damn good job of getting to the bottom of it. If you get tired of being a lawyer, you could probably have a successful career as a private investigator."

"Believe me, I don't have plans to take on any cases after this one," Emma said.

Upon their return from the morgue, Emma and Kathy toasted their success with a beer at Kathy's place. As they drank, Emma paged through Julia Boswell's file.

"There's not much here," Emma commented. "Julia started working at the firm six years ago in June and she left in October."

"Does it say why she left?" Kathy asked.

"The personnel department exit interview form says 'terminated employment October 13. Personal reasons.' "

"Did Julia give an exit interview?"

Emma shook her head. "It says 'not available for interview.' Apparently she left abruptly. There's no indication where she went."

"What if the mother has moved or if she won't talk to you?" Kathy asked.

Emma took a sip of beer. "Then at least I'll know I tried."

"And what if the mother gives you Julia's phone number and you call Julia and she confirms that Brisbane, the putative head of your firm, is a crook? Then what are you planning to do?" Kathy asked.

"To be honest, I haven't thought that far ahead," Emma admitted. "I just want to find out the truth, whatever that might be. If I can accomplish that, then I'll have to figure out the best course of action."

"Your job could be on the line here," Kathy said.

"I know that, but this is just something I have to do."

"Kind of like the people who try to climb Mount Everest because it's there."

"I suppose so." Emma finished her beer. "It's getting late. I'd better get some sleep. I'm going to try to call Julia's mother before I go to work tomorrow." She got up and walked to the door. Kathy followed her.

"Good luck," Kathy said. "Let me know what you find out."

"I will. Good luck to you on your date with Graham. Where's he taking you for dinner?"

"Spiaggia."

Emma let out a low whistle. "Pretty classy for a first date. The guy's certainly no piker." She reached out and gave her friend a hug. "Thanks so much for coming with me tonight. It meant a lot to me."

"My pleasure," Kathy said, hugging her back. "It was kind of fun. When I was a kid, I used to pretend I was Kathy Flood, secret agent. Thanks to you I got to live out another one of my fantasies."

"Your whole life is one big fantasy," Emma joked. "But I say more power to you. Talk to you tomorrow, kiddo."

"Sleep tight," Kathy called as Emma headed down the hall to her own apartment.

Even though she was exhausted, Emma found that sleep eluded her. She tossed and turned most of the night and kept looking at the clock, waiting until she could call Julia Boswell's mother. She was out of bed at six. At seven, after showering, dressing, drinking three cups of coffee and skimming through the morning paper, she finally decided it was time. With a trembling hand she picked up the phone and dialed Mrs. Boswell's number.

The phone rang five times, and Emma was starting to think no one was home when a woman answered.

"Gail Boswell?" Emma asked.

"Yes," a guarded voice replied.

"My name is Emma Davis. I'm an attorney in Chicago with Franklin and Holland. I'm calling about your daughter Julia."

Emma heard a sharp intake of breath and a lengthy silence.

"Mrs. Boswell? Are you still there?"

"I have nothing to say to anyone at Franklin and Holland," Gail Boswell said in an icy tone. "Please don't call here again."

"Wait. Please, don't hang up," Emma implored. "Let me give you some background on why I'm calling."

Another silence followed on the other end of the line. Emma pressed forward with her story.

"I've been with the firm only three months. I transferred here from Kansas City after Franklin and Holland merged with my old firm. A few weeks ago I was asked to help one of the senior partners with an estate. At first it seemed like a routine matter, but the more I got into it, the more it seemed that there was something fishy going on. Julia was one of the people who witnessed the deceased's will. I was hoping she might be able to shed some light on the situation."

"Who is the senior partner you referred to?" Gail Boswell asked.

"Louis Brisbane."

Emma's response was met with another sharp intake of breath.

"I take it Julia talked to you about Brisbane," Emma said.

"What do you want from my daughter?" Gail Boswell demanded.

"Just some information," Emma said. "I have some hunches about what's going on with the estate, but I can't pin them down."

Afraid the woman might hang up, Emma took a leap of faith and said, "I have no proof of this, but there's a chance the deceased was either murdered or driven to commit suicide. Louis Brisbane may have been responsible. I'm desperate to get to the bottom of this, and I can't do it without Julia's help. Please tell me how to get in touch with her."

"I can't do that," Gail Boswell said.

"Then someone may get away with murder," Emma said.

"I can't tell you how to get in touch with Julia," Gail Boswell repeated, "but I will relay your message to her. She can make up her mind whether or not she wants to speak to you."

"Thank you so much," Emma said.

"I can't make any promises," Gail Boswell said. "Julia has not had contact with anyone from Franklin and Holland since she left the firm. I'm not sure she'll want to break that silence now."

"Just tell her that it's very important and that I

won't take up more than a few minutes of her time,"
Emma said. "Have her call me at home. I don't trust
the phones at the office." She gave the number.

"I'll see that my daughter gets the message," Gail
Boswell said. "I can promise no more than that."

"That's plenty," Emma said. "I really appreciate
your help."

"You sound like a bright young woman, Ms.
Davis," Gail Boswell said. "Be very careful. You
could be in grave danger."

Before Emma could form a response, Gail Boswell
had hung up. Emma sat there with the phone in her
hand, pondering Mrs. Boswell's last remark.

"You could be in grave danger." Had Julia left the
firm six years earlier because she had been in grave
danger? If so, from whom?

Emma shuddered and put the phone down. Now
that she was one step closer to knowing the truth
about Oak Greythorne's estate, she was almost afraid
to find out what it was. "I will find out the whole
story," she murmured, "no matter how bad it is or
how many people at the firm are implicated." Forti-
fied with that resolve, she headed off to work.

She certainly had enough to do. She turned to Tom
Cane's First Amendment file and jotted down some
notes on points to incorporate into the complaint she
and Jill Bedner were drafting for Mike Laskis.

Emma worked straight through lunch and all afternoon without a break. It was quarter to five when
she finally got up from her desk and stretched out

her aching back muscles. She walked over to the window and looked out at the skyline. She was pleased to note that she felt no twinges of fear at all. Flynn's conditioning treatments were truly working miracles. By the end of the summer she'd be ready for the Ferris wheel at Navy Pier.

Emma was so engrossed in the lovely summer city panorama spread out in front of her that she didn't hear a visitor step into her office. Not until she felt a hand on her arm did she realize someone had entered.

"Lovely afternoon, isn't it, Emma?"

Louis Brisbane's voice made her jump a full six inches. She wheeled around to face the managing partner.

Brisbane chuckled. "Still afraid of heights, I see," he said. "It's such a shame. One of the great pleasures of working in this building is being able to gaze out over the city. You truly don't know what you're missing."

Emma nodded, trying to catch her breath. She was grateful that Brisbane attributed her skittishness to a fear of heights.

"What can I do for you?" she asked, walking back to her desk.

"I had other business on this floor so I thought I'd stop in," Brisbane said. "I was wondering if the second letter to the tenants in Greythorne's apartment building was ready to be sent out."

"I have it dated for Thursday," Emma replied.

"Redate it and send it out tomorrow," Brisbane instructed. "The buyer is quite anxious to clear the building and begin renovations. Every day counts."

Emma nodded. "I'll take care of it."

"Splendid." Brisbane smiled at her. "And what progress have you made with Mr. Hennick? Has he returned his signed lease termination form?"

"He called earlier today and said he was putting it in the mail," Emma lied. "I should have it in a day or two."

"Excellent. Keep up the good work, Emma. It's a pleasure to have you on my team."

"Likewise," Emma said lamely. You murdering, conniving bastard, she added silently.

CHAPTER 23

By Wednesday, Emma and Jill Bedner had drafted a complaint in Mike Laskis's lawsuit challenging the constitutionality of the town's ordinance regulating various types of activities at Big Louie's gentleman's club. That afternoon Emma, Jill, and Tom Cane met with Mike to go over the complaint and discuss strategy for handling the case.

For this meeting Mike had dressed in Bermuda shorts and a Harley-Davidson shirt. "You girls really work fast," Mike said appreciatively as he read through the complaint. "You've got a couple of winners here, Tom."

Tom smiled as Emma and Jill glared at him. "I agree with you completely. They are both winners. That's why I put them on your case."

"You haven't forgotten about Hawaiian night, have you?" Mike asked the women.

"Oh, no," Jill said. "We've been practicing the hula."

"We don't do the hula," Mike said. "But we do have a hula hoop contest."

241

"Then we'll start practicing that," Emma said as she gave Tom's shin a little kick under the table.

"And don't forget I lei all the ladies on Hawaiian night."

"We can't wait," Jill said.

"We're just tingly with anticipation," Emma added.

"Do you have any comments or questions about the complaint?" Tom asked, deciding it was time to put an end to his associates' not-so-veiled sarcasm.

"No, this looks pretty good," Mike said. "I don't quite understand all this legal stuff, but that's what I pay you the big bucks for."

"That's the Franklin and Holland motto," Emma said. "Big bucks gets you good legal stuff."

Mike laughed. "These two are a riot. You've got to make sure they come down to the club, Tom. Why don't you bring them? You can have free drinks all night."

"That's a tempting offer," Tom said. "We'll check our calendars and see what we can do. Now, getting back to your lawsuit, we plan to file the complaint tomorrow and ask for a temporary restraining order barring the ordinance from going into effect before a judge rules on its constitutionality. There will be a hearing on the TRO request, probably early next week. You'll need to come to that, and you'll need to give testimony."

"No problem," Mike said. "I've been in court lots of times."

"As soon as we get a time for the hearing, we'll

let you know," Tom said. "We'll want you to come in about ninety minutes early so we can go over the questions you'll be asked."

"Okay," Mike said.

Emma looked at their client's attire, hesitated a moment, and then said, "I know a lot of places have done away with dress codes, but as a general rule shorts and loud shirts are not considered appropriate courtroom attire."

"Are you saying I should wear a suit?" Mike asked.

"Do you have a suit?" Emma asked.

Mike turned to Tom and laughed. "She's a riot. I love her." Turning back to Emma, he said, "Of course I have a suit. I have a whole closet full of suits. Which one would you like me to wear?"

Emma shrugged. "I don't care. Something dark and conservative is always good. With a white shirt and simple striped tie. Do you have something like that?"

"You betcha. You let me know the time and I'll be here with bells on."

"Great," Tom said. "I think we're all set. Thanks for coming in today, Mike. We'll get this baby filed and see if we can strike a blow for the First Amendment."

"Don't forget lap dancing," Mike reminded him.

"How could I forget that?" Tom asked. "Good seeing you again, Mike."

As soon as their client was out of the room, Jill turned to Tom. "That guy is smarmy. I don't care if he is our client. I wish they would shut his stupid club down."

"Now, now," Tom said. "It's just harmless banter. He doesn't mean anything by it."

"Strip club owners probably have to talk like that," Emma said. "I'll bet it says so in the official club owner instruction manual."

"Well, I think he's a sexist pig," Jill said. "You should bill our time at double the usual rate for making us put up with all his smart remarks."

Tom rubbed his chin. "Charge him double. I like the way you think. You've got a real future here, Jill."

Jill threw a legal pad at the partner.

Tom deftly caught the missile in his left hand. "All right, girls," he joked. "That's enough fun and frivolity for one day. I've made a few changes on my copy of the complaint. Have the secretary incorporate them. Then draft a standard motion requesting a TRO and we'll get the case on file tomorrow. Good work, both of you." He stood up and walked toward the door.

"Are you coming to the hearing on the TRO request?" Emma asked.

"No, I think you two can handle it," Tom replied.

"We'll handle it," Emma said, "but so help me if our client shows up in court dressed in a polyester leisure suit, I'm withdrawing from the case."

"And if he shows up carrying a hula hoop, I'm going to bash him over the head with it," Jill added.

"Battering a client is not a good idea," Tom said. "And I'm sure it won't be necessary. Mike will be dressed appropriately. Trust me."

"That's what Jack the Ripper told his victims," Jill muttered.

"Before or after he 'leid' them?" Emma laughed.

Emma went to bed early and was sound asleep when the telephone next to her rang, instantly jolting her awake. What time is it? she wondered. It felt like the middle of the night. She blinked a couple times and looked at the clock. It was only eleven. The phone rang again. She picked it up.

"Hello," she said, her voice hoarse from sleep.

"Is this Emma Davis?" a woman's voice asked.

"Yes. Who is calling?"

"This is Julia Boswell."

Emma's heart thumped. She sat up straight in bed and turned on a light. "Julia, thank you so much for calling."

"My mom gave me the message," Julia said. "I don't know if I can help you—or if I even want to help you. But Mom said you sounded sincere so I decided to take a chance and call. What kind of information are you looking for?"

"I'm working on the estate of a man named Oak Greythorne. You witnessed his will."

There was a pause. "Greythorne. It really doesn't ring a bell. I witnessed a lot of wills in the short time I was at the firm."

"Oak Greythorne would have been in his early fifties at the time. He was a childhood friend of Louis Brisbane."

"My mother said you mentioned something about suicide or murder," Julia said.

"The official cause of Greythorne's death was an accidental overdose of liquor and prescription drugs," Emma said. "But a couple of people who knew him well said he was in the best shape, mentally, of his life and that he was even thinking of going back into business. At least one person thinks he might have been driven to commit suicide—or possibly even murdered."

"Who do you think could have been responsible for that?" Julia asked.

"I don't know. That's why I wanted to talk to you," Emma said.

"I don't think I want to get involved in this," Julia said.

"I'm not asking you to get involved in anything," Emma said. "I'd just like to talk to you about your experience at the firm."

"For what purpose?"

"To help me understand what or who I might be up against here."

Julia chortled. "You could be up against a monster."

"Are you talking about Louis Brisbane?"

"I have never spoken to or about anyone at Franklin and Holland since I left there," Julia said, avoiding Emma's question. "Why should I start now?"

"Because a man is dead and I want to find out why he died."

"How did you find my mother?"

"I got her number out of your personnel file."

"The personnel department just gave you that information?" Julia asked.

"Let's just say I had to engage in a little self-help. I don't mean to intrude on your life. I promise that I won't tell anyone we spoke. I just need to find out the truth about Greythorne and Brisbane."

"As I told you, I really don't remember Greythorne. I could, however, tell you volumes about Louis Brisbane—none of it good."

"I'd love to hear it," Emma said.

"Not over the phone," Julia said. "If you want to talk, we'll have to do it in person."

"All right. Where are you?"

"California. In the Napa Valley."

"Can you give me an address or phone number?"

"I'd rather not do that. I know a place we could meet. The Vineyard Country Inn. It's a bed and breakfast in St. Helena."

Emma had not expected that her investigation into Oak Greythorne's death would entail a cross-country trip, but she badly wanted to speak to this young woman. Plus, Memorial Day weekend was coming up, so the draining flights to California and back would not be as bad. "All right. I'll try to arrange something quickly. How can I reach you to let you know my plans?"

"I'll call you back," Julia said. "Same time tomorrow night?"

"Fine," Emma said.

"All right. I'll talk to you then. Oh, one more thing. I'm using my mother's maiden name. Julia Cutillo."

"Thank you, Julia. I know how hard it must have been for you to call me. I really appreciate what you're doing."

"You might have a different view after you hear what I have to say," Julia said cryptically. Before Emma could respond, she had hung up.

Emma replayed her brief conversation with the woman who had witnessed Oak Greythorne's will. "I really don't remember Oak Greythorne . . . but I could tell you volumes about Louis Brisbane—none of it good."

Was Emma crazy to traipse off to California to meet Julia? What if she had been fired from Franklin & Holland for cause and simply had a personal vendetta against Louis Brisbane? Emma shook her head. She was a pretty good judge of character and Julia Cutillo-Boswell had sounded like an intelligent, level-headed young woman. Whatever information she wished to share, Emma was certain it would be useful.

Now all she had to do was make arrangements to go to California. Emma had been to the Napa Valley once before and had loved it. It was such a romantic place. It would be a shame to go out there by herself.

She smiled. There was no law against mixing business with pleasure. She picked up the phone and dialed Flynn's number.

"Hi, it's me," she said when he answered. "What are you doing this weekend?"

"I don't know. What do you want to do?"

"I was thinking of going to the Napa Valley. Would you care to join me? Our tour will include a country inn, good wine and food and a bit of intrigue on the side."

"Wine, intrigue and you?" Flynn repeated. "Count me in."

CHAPTER 24

Emma and Flynn caught a Saturday morning flight to San Francisco. Although Flynn was still not thrilled about Emma delving into Oak Greythorne's past, he jumped at the chance to spend Memorial Day weekend in a romantic venue with her. Flynn traveled a lot for business and had immediately volunteered to make all their arrangements. They picked up their rental car, a black Mercedes convertible, shortly after lunch, then drove north into the heart of California's wine country.

The Napa Valley was hot and dry. As Flynn drove, Emma tried to quell the feelings of trepidation over what Julia Boswell might reveal and, worse, what Louis Brisbane's reaction would be if he knew that Emma was investigating him. She sat back and enjoyed the scenery, mile after mile of well-manicured vineyards and picturesque wineries. "I love the Midwest, but it's nice to get away once in a while," she said. "Isn't it beautiful here? It's just like France."

"The French wine country is one of my favorite

places," Flynn said. "We'll have to go there some-time."

Emma reached over and put her hand on his leg. "I'd love that."

Flynn flashed her a sexy smile. "I'd love going anywhere with you."

They checked into their suite at the Vineyard Country Inn by mid-afternoon. Emma had made arrangements to meet Julia Boswell on Sunday morning, so she and Flynn had the rest of the day to themselves. They headed north to Sterling Vineyards, where they took the aerial tramway to the top of the hill.

After spending an hour admiring the panoramic view of the valley below and sampling the wine, they returned to the quaint village of St. Helena and browsed in some of the shops. They had dinner and, exhausted from their flight and the time change, went to bed early.

On Sunday morning, after a continental breakfast, they awaited Julia's arrival.

Emma's first impression of the former Franklin & Holland associate was of her size. Petite and trim, with short dark hair, Julia Boswell-Cutillo could have passed for a college student rather than a woman in her early thirties. "It's nice to meet you," Emma said as they met in the inn's lobby. "I really appreciate your agreeing to talk to me."

Julia's handshake was firm. "Nice meeting you, too."

"My boyfriend came along with me," Emma said. "He's waiting out by the pool. Would you mind if he joined us? He's been helping me track down some information about Brisbane's real estate holdings."

Julia frowned. "Is he with Franklin and Holland?"

"No, he's an architect. I promise he's completely trustworthy."

Julia paused a moment to consider the request. "All right. Let's go out by the pool and talk. It'll be more private out there."

"This is a beautiful inn," Emma commented as they made their way to the pool area.

"The owners are friends of mine," Julia replied. "Two women who were former litigators in San Francisco and decided they were completely burned out on law and in need of a calmer lifestyle."

"I can understand that," Emma said.

Emma introduced Flynn, and he and Julia shook hands.

Once seated under a huge umbrella at a poolside table, Emma reached into her bag and pulled out a copy of Oak Greythorne's obituary. "This is Oak Greythorne, the man whose will you witnessed. Do you remember him at all?"

Julia took the paper and looked at it closely, then shook her head. "He looks vaguely familiar, but I really can't place him."

"How did you happen to be assigned to work with Louis Brisbane?" Emma asked.

"At the time I thought it was a dream come true,"

Julia replied. "Now I realize it was all a setup. I have an undergraduate degree in accounting, so working for a trusts and estates partner seemed perfectly natural. Brisbane latched onto me almost from the day I arrived at the firm. I was thrilled that a management committee member actually wanted to work with me, so of course I jumped at the chance. In the four months I was there, I worked almost exclusively for him. I barely had a chance to even meet any of the other attorneys, let alone work with them. I'm sure that was part of Brisbane's plan—to keep me isolated from the pack."

"What type of projects did you do for Brisbane?" Emma asked.

"Mostly estate planning and probate," Julia said. "While I don't remember Greythorne specifically, I did witness a lot of wills."

"Was Brisbane's secretary always the other witness?"

Julia nodded. "Good old J. Devereaux Braxton. That woman scared the hell out of me."

"She scares me, too," Emma admitted. "I'm glad to hear I'm not the only one who's affected that way."

"She's so loyal to Brisbane, she almost reminded me of a robot—or maybe a Stepford wife," Julia said. "I swear if he told her to jump out the window she'd do it."

"Were you involved in drafting the wills, or were you simply called on to witness them?"

"I just witnessed them," Julia said. "Brisbane or Devereaux did the actual drafting."

"Did anything strike you as peculiar about the wills?"

"Yes. It didn't take me long to notice that the majority of Brisbane's clients seemed to give him a great deal of authority in handling their affairs. Most of them named him executor and trustee. Some also gave him power of attorney. This struck me as odd because most of these people had family members who would have been more natural designees."

"Did you mention that to Brisbane or the clients?"

"I never mentioned that to him. But I did mention that I noticed in two estates where he was the executor, he had entered into a contract to sell real estate for substantially less than its assessed value. The numbers just jumped out at me, so I pointed it out to him. I was sure there must be a mistake."

"What was his reaction?" Flynn asked.

"He was furious," Julia said. "Read me the riot act, asked how dare I question his business judgment, that he knew what was best for the estate and that it was my job to draft the instruments of conveyance, not challenge his methods. By the time he finished reaming me out, I was shaking. He looked positively menacing."

"So you drafted the instruments of conveyance?" Emma asked.

"Yes."

"Meaning the properties were sold for less than they were really worth?"

"Yes."

"Do you happen to remember who the buyers were?"

Julia nodded. "That struck me as odd, too. It was the same buyer in both cases. Regal Enterprises, Ltd."

Flynn and Emma exchanged a knowing look. "Did you know who the principals of Regal Enterprises were?" Emma asked.

"Not at the time," Julia said. "But later on it occurred to me that Brisbane must be one of them."

Flynn nodded. "That's right. Regal Enterprises is also the prospective buyer of an apartment building owned by Oak Greythorne. Regal proposes to pay only about one-quarter of the property's true value."

"So he's still up to his old tricks," Julia said.

"Why did you leave the firm so abruptly?" Emma asked.

"The final nail was pounded in my coffin in early October," Julia explained. "Brisbane came into my office one morning and said he had a special project for me. I was to go to a building site owned by Regal at noon and deliver an envelope to a building inspector. I thought it was a strange assignment for an associate. I mean, why not send a messenger? But I didn't argue. I went to the site and gave the man the envelope. I had no idea what was in it, but the inspector opened it in my presence and I saw it was filled with cash. Hundred-dollar bills. Then I understood. It was a bribe."

Julia paused and took a deep breath. "That took things to a whole new level. Not only was Brisbane cheating his clients, he was now using me to do illegal things. My law license was on the line. I could go to jail. And of course he was doing it to box me in. If I refused to do his bidding, he'd have grounds to fire me for insubordination. If I did what he asked and got caught, he'd disavow any knowledge of the bribe and I'd take the fall. I was in a lose-lose situation."

"What did you do?" Flynn asked.

"I was so mad that I didn't stop to think things through. I raced back to the office and confronted Brisbane. I told him I was onto him and I was going to go to the police."

"What was his reaction?" Emma asked.

"He gave me the most sinister look I'd ever seen in my life and said he was very sorry that I wasn't a team player. Then he went back to whatever he was working on and acted as if I weren't even there. I was so stunned that I stood there about thirty seconds with my mouth hanging open. Then I turned around and left."

"Then what happened?" Flynn asked.

"That's when things got really nasty," Julia said. She took a couple of deep breaths to prepare herself to disclose the rest of the story. "I stormed out of Brisbane's office and went back to my apartment. I was still so upset and so confused that I was almost numb. I had a couple of drinks and tried to figure out what to do. I was still pondering my options around nine o'clock when the doorbell rang." Julia paused and swallowed hard.

"I went over to the door and peered out. It was a man I'd never seen before. I had no intention of letting him in. I was just going to ignore him, but as I turned around he broke the door latch—and it was a sturdy one—and burst into my living room."

Emma gasped.

Julia's breath was coming quicker as she recalled her horror. "I tried to scream, but he was too quick. He kicked the door shut, grabbed me and put his hand over my mouth. He said if I made even the slightest noise he'd kill me. I believed him. Then he shoved me into a chair and told me to keep quiet and listen." Julia's lower lip began to quiver.

"What did he say?" Emma asked gently.

Julia swallowed hard. "He told me I shouldn't have been shooting my mouth off at work, that I'd gotten myself into a lot of trouble. He said it was obvious to everyone that I had no future at Franklin and Holland. Then he started talking about my family. He knew details about my life, where my mother and sister lived. The implication was clear: if I didn't do what he said they would all be in grave danger."

Julia took another deep breath. "Then he told me to get out of Chicago right away and never come back. At that point I finally managed to recover enough to say something. I told him I couldn't just quit my job, that I needed to work."

"What did he say to that?" Flynn asked.

"He reached into his pocket, took out an envelope, and dropped it into my lap. I just sat there staring at it for a minute. He told me to open it, so I did. It was a passbook in my name at Chase Manhattan Bank. It showed a balance of $250,000."

Emma's mouth dropped open. "They paid you a quarter of million dollars hush money?"

Julia nodded.

"Did the man say anything else to you?"

"No. I looked at the passbook, then I looked at him, and in that instant I guess he could see that I'd agreed with him that a change of scenery was in order. He left without saying another word. After I'd calmed down a bit, I called my mother and told her I'd be coming to stay with her for a while. I left Chicago the next day and I haven't been back since."

"And you never went to the police or told anyone what happened?" Emma asked.

"How could I?" Julia asked. "I was afraid for my own life and for my family's. And once I left town with the money, I felt as though I were no better than that building inspector who took a bribe."

"How did you end up out here?" Emma inquired.

"I always liked the area and I had some contacts out here."

"Are you practicing law?" Flynn asked.

Julia shook her head. "No, Franklin and Holland cured me of that. I'm using my accounting background," she said vaguely, obviously not wanting to reveal too much about her new life.

"The man who came to your apartment," Emma said. "What did he look like?"

"He was about fifty. Big and burly, with a big

258

square face and arms like a gorilla. He was the scariest looking person I've ever seen in my life."

Flynn and Emma looked at each other. "Tommy Corona," Emma said.

"You know him?" Julia asked.

Emma nodded. "I'm afraid I had my own close encounter with him. He and Brisbane are partners in Regal Enterprises."

Julia put her head in her hands. For the first time the young woman appeared close to breaking down. "I've relived the time I spent at Franklin and Holland over and over," she said. "I keep asking myself if I could have done something differently to stay out of Brisbane's clutches, but I just don't see how."

Emma reached over and put her hand on Julia's shoulder. "Louis Brisbane is a powerful man. You couldn't have beaten him. You did the right thing by getting out and saving yourself and your family."

Julia put her hands down and looked squarely at Emma. "But apparently you must think you can beat him."

Emma's stomach lurched as the cold truth of Julia's statement struck home. "I don't know if I can or not," Emma admitted, "but I'm going to try."

Julia nodded. "What can I do to help?"

"Do you remember the names of the two estates where Brisbane sold property for less than fair market value?"

"Yes. One was Kenneth Bartelt and the other Daniel Loichinger."

Flynn pulled a small pad of paper out of his shirt pocket and recorded the names.

"And what can you tell us about the incident where you delivered the bribe to the building inspector?"

"The inspector's name was Lawrence Marconi. The address of the property was 3940 Lincoln."

Flynn recorded that information as well.

"Thank you so much for talking to us," Emma said. "I know how hard this must have been for you."

"Actually, it's been a relief to get it out in the open," Julia said. "I've kept it repressed for so long. When my mother called to tell me she'd spoken to you, I was shocked at first but then I felt almost happy. It's been rather cathartic to finally be able to talk about it."

Julia stood up and Emma and Flynn followed suit.

"Is there a way I can get in touch with you if I think of any more questions?" Emma asked.

Julia hesitated, then said, "I'll give you a cell phone number." She recited the number and Flynn took it down. "It's not mine. It's a friend's, but she'll know how to reach me. I'm sorry if I sound paranoid, but I don't want Brisbane or his henchman to be able to trace me."

"I understand," Emma said. She reached out and gave Julia a hug. "Thanks so much. With the information you've just given us I think we might be able to put an end to Brisbane's crimes against his clients."

"I hope so," Julia said. "Let me know what happens."

"I will," Emma promised.

"And please be very, very careful. I firmly believe that if I hadn't left Chicago when I did, Corona would have killed me and maybe my mother and sister, too. I have no reason to doubt that he'd do the same to you if he knew what you were up to."

"I hear you," Emma said. "Thanks again."

Julia gave a little wave, then walked out toward the lobby. Flynn moved close to Emma and put his arm around her. "What a story," he said. "I'm sorry that I pooh-poohed your concerns about Brisbane. You were obviously right all along."

Emma suddenly felt dizzy as she began to realize the gravity of the task before her. She was actually contemplating actions that could topple the head of her law firm. How would that bode for Emma's career? For her life? She leaned her head against Flynn's shoulder. "Oh, God," she murmured. "Why did I have to be right? Now what am I going to do?"

"We are going to enjoy the rest of our time in the Napa Valley," Flynn said. "Then we are going back to Chicago and we'll do whatever you decide is best."

Emma lifted her head. As she gazed into Flynn's eyes, she suddenly felt much stronger. "Yes, *we* will."

That evening, Flynn and Emma had dinner at Auberge du Soleil in nearby Rutherford. As they enjoyed a delectable meal and a bottle of local cabernet sauvignon, they discussed what they had learned from Julia Boswell-Cutillo.

"Why would someone like Louis Brisbane, who seemingly has everything a man could want, resort to stealing from his clients?" Emma asked.

"The desire to have more," Flynn replied, taking a bite of his venison.

"More what? Money? I'm certain he takes home well over a million dollars a year from his practice. How much money does a person really need?"

"Then maybe he does it to see if he can get away with it," Flynn said. "For the same reason kleptomaniacs are driven to steal. Some people find risk to be an aphrodisiac."

Emma pushed the remains of her dinner around her plate. "And why would Brisbane team up with a lowlife like Tommy Corona?"

"For the same reason, I suppose. The secret thrill of knowing he's doing something forbidden. A lot of people almost deify bad guys and think it's cool to hang out with them. John Gotti had a fan club, for God's sake. Plus, if Brisbane's main goal in life is to acquire more money at other people's expense, Tommy Corona would be a natural partner. He's spent his entire life preying on those less fortunate than himself."

Emma sipped her wine. "For all my suspicions about Brisbane and Corona, I'll have to admit I never really thought I was right. Julia's revelations have left me almost in shock."

"Assuming we can find written documentation for

what Julia said, what do you intend to do?" Flynn asked gently.

Emma had been thinking about nothing else for the past few hours, but now she had made up her mind. "Once we get proof positive that Brisbane cheated clients, I intend to expose him."

"You mean go to the police?"

"I guess I'd tell the police and the bar association," Emma said, "but I think I'd start by telling Tom Cane. He's one of the lead litigation partners. He's an ethical man, and he's also well respected at the firm. I have a very good working relationship with him. I know if I had evidence of Brisbane's wrongdoing, Tom would take me seriously and would know how to handle things."

"It's interesting how we came out here hoping to find evidence that Brisbane somehow coerced Oak Greythorne into drafting his will a certain way," Flynn said. "And while Julia had some dynamite information about what a scoundrel Brisbane is, she couldn't help us with the *Greythorne* case—other than to confirm that Brisbane has a pattern of buying real estate out of clients' estates for a song and then turning it for a quick profit."

Emma pushed her plate away and took another sip of wine. "Maybe Brisbane didn't do anything underhanded with Greythorne's will and maybe he didn't contribute in any way to the man's demise, but it's still wrong for him to be cheating the estate, just as it was wrong for him to cheat the *Bartelt* and *Loichinger* estates. And if I don't try to stop him, he'll

go right on cheating more heirs out of what's right-
fully theirs."

Flynn finished his venison, and an attentive waiter
immediately removed their plates. "Do you really
think the files at the morgue will contain proof of
what Brisbane did?" Flynn asked.

"I won't know that until I look," Emma said.

"I'm going with you," Flynn said. "It's not safe for
you to go there alone."

"I'd welcome the company," Emma said gratefully.

"I'll also try to get some information on the corrupt
building inspector Julia mentioned. I've got a number
of contacts at city hall. I can find out if the guy is
still working and if anybody has any dirt on him."

"That'd be great," Emma said.

"And I'll see if I can get a list of other properties
owned by Regal Enterprises in the past five or six
years. I should be able to track how much they paid
for each and how much they were sold for. Who
knows, we might be able to connect some more properties to your law firm."

As Flynn paid the check, Emma fought hard to
quiet the feelings of anxiety that swept over her. Did
she really think she was up to the task of investigating her boss, the managing partner of a national law
firm, behind his back? And even if she did find proof
that Brisbane had done something illegal, what were
the odds she could get to the authorities before Brisbane and Corona stopped her, maybe permanently?

As Emma's nervousness escalated, she thought of

Oak Greythorne. Whether Brisbane caused his old friend to self-destruct or actually participated in his death, it was becoming increasingly clear that Oak's life had been cut short because of Brisbane. The senior partner had ruined Julia Boswell's life, driving her out of the legal profession and virtually causing her to become a fugitive. Thinking about all the people Brisbane had hurt gave Emma the resolve she needed. Regardless of the consequences, she would proceed with her investigation. She was not about to let Brisbane and Corona claim any more victims.

CHAPTER 25

The moment Emma stepped off of the elevator on Tuesday morning, she felt a chill creep up the back of her neck. As she walked down the hall, her feeling of unease grew stronger. She said a brief good morning to Lorraine, then went in her office and shut the door. She sat down at her desk and tried to ignore how nervous she was. But she couldn't help being afraid of what might happen to her if Brisbane and Corona knew she was onto them.

To distract herself, Emma switched on her computer. Jill Bedner had left an e-mail message. The hearing on their request for a temporary restraining order in the Laskis case had been scheduled for the following morning. Jill had phoned their client and reminded him to come to the office in advance of the hearing to prepare for his testimony. Jill suggested that she and Emma meet later in the day to do their own preparation.

Emma sent Jill a reply, confirming that a late afternoon meeting was agreeable. Then she turned her attention to a brief she was drafting for one of the litigation partners. It took all her powers of concentration to stay focused on her writing. Every few minutes she would glance at her watch. This was clearly not going to be a productive day. The only thing on her mind was counting down the hours until nine o'clock, when she and Flynn would sneak into the morgue and try to locate the case files Julia had mentioned.

Happily, once Emma got past the first hour or so of work on the brief, she found that her interest in the project did pick up and the rest of the morning passed quickly. She grabbed a bite of lunch, came back to her office and continued work on the brief. She then spent ninety minutes with Jill discussing strategy for the Laskis hearing. Emma worked until six, then drove straight to Flynn's place.

"I found out the sale prices of the real estate in the two estates Julia mentioned," Flynn said as they ate dinner.

"Thanks," Emma said, picking at her food. "That should really be helpful."

"You're looking awfully pale," Flynn observed. "Maybe you should stay here. There's no reason I can't liberate those files by myself."

"You'll do no such thing!" Emma said, sitting up straighter in her chair. "I'm fine. I'll admit I'm feeling a little stressed out from the whirlwind weekend and realizing how big the stakes are here, but there's no way I'm going to let you do this without me. We're a team."

He took her hand and kissed it. "I'm glad I'm able to help you with this. It is a noble cause."

"I just hope it works out," Emma said.

"Oh, and my source also came through with some info on the crooked building inspector that Julia encountered. Lawrence Marconi is still very much on the job and on the take."

"Can we prove that?" Emma asked.

"I'm still working on that," Flynn said. "My guy is making some discreet inquiries to see if he can find someone willing to speak on the record about Marconi's habit of accepting bribes. He's got one person that he thinks will do it. He'll know more by the end of the week."

Flynn took a final bite of his food. "It's eight thirty. What do you say we clear the table and then head out?"

Emma nodded. "Let's do it. Having to wait around all day has been sheer agony."

They took Flynn's car. As Emma directed him to the gloomy warehouse, he commented, "We're only a few blocks from one of Tommy Corona's big construction projects. I'll take you by there on the way home."

"Okay," Emma said without enthusiasm. She just wanted to get in and out of the morgue as quickly as possible.

As during the visit Emma had made with Kathy, the Walgreens key worked smoothly. Once inside, Emma switched on the lights and Flynn locked the door behind them. Emma rapidly paged through the file index and recited the locations of the two probate files Julia had identified.

"You look for *Bartelt* and I'll get *Loichinger*," Emma said. "But first I'm going to return Julia's personnel file to its proper location."

"Gotcha," Flynn said, heading into the depths of the building to find his designated row.

Emma slipped Julia's file back in place and carefully rearranged the files around it to lessen the chances anyone would notice that shelf had been disturbed. Satisfied that nothing looked out of place, she headed off to locate the *Loichinger* estate records.

"I've got mine," Flynn said. "How are you doing?"

"I'm working on it," Emma said. As she reached the proper row, there was suddenly a loud crash outside. In spite of herself, Emma let out a little shriek. Flynn rushed to her side.

"What was that?" Emma whispered. She looked anxiously toward the door.

"Probably some kid threw something at the side of the building," Flynn said. "This place looks like a prime target for vandalism. You'd think your law firm could afford a little better lighting outside." Flynn motioned toward the row of shelves. "Which one is it?"

Emma pointed to a large box. Flynn eased it down from the shelf, then removed the lid and peered inside. "This is it," he said. "Let's get out of here."

Minutes later Flynn's powerful car engine roared

to life and he pulled away from the building. "Mission accomplished," he said. "And, if I do say so myself, in record time. We make a good team."

Emma was still recovering from the fear that had overwhelmed her when she'd heard the noise outside the morgue, so she simply grunted in response. Not until Flynn turned south rather than heading for home did she find her voice. "You made a wrong turn."

"No, I didn't," Flynn said. "I told you I'd take you past Tommy Corona's building site."

"Oh." Emma didn't want to let on that the mere thought of Tommy Corona made her physically ill, so she remained silent.

Two blocks later, Flynn pulled over to the curb and pointed across the street. "There it is. It's a handsome project, though I don't like the company that's building it."

Emma peered over at the construction site where several enormous towers were taking shape. Two huge cranes towered over the landscape. Emma felt her stomach lurch. "I'm feeling kind of queasy," she said. "Can we please go home now?"

"Sure thing," Flynn said, patting her knee. "I just thought you might like to see Corona's work. I didn't mean to upset you."

"I'm just sort of on overload," Emma said. "It's not your fault."

Back at Flynn's place, they each paged through one of the files they had retrieved from the morgue. "Put a Post-it note on anything that refers to real estate values," Emma said.

Less than an hour later they had finished looking through the two files. "Now I'm confused," Emma said. "Julia clearly said these properties were sold for far less than they were worth. But according to these records, the assessed value for each property was exactly the same as the price it was sold for. So where's the fraud?"

"I don't know," Flynn said. He took out the sheet of paper on which he had written down the two estate names Julia had mentioned. "I'm positive I wrote the names down correctly. These have to be the estates she meant. You don't think she could have been mistaken about what Brisbane and Corona did?"

Emma shook her head. "Julia's story is completely consistent with what Brisbane and Corona are doing in the *Greythorne* estate. I'm sure she knew what she was talking about." She thought a moment. "When I get to work tomorrow, I'm going to find the names of some other estates Brisbane handled in the last few years. Then when we take these files back, we can check out a few others and see if anything is out of kilter."

Flynn stacked the files on top of each other. "I'll make copies of these documents tomorrow so we can get the files back to the morgue as quickly as possible."

"There's probably no hurry," Emma said. "After all, who would be looking for these old files?"

"We've come too far to get careless now," Flynn said. "These files need to go back ASAP."

"If you say so," Emma said.

"You don't need to go," Flynn said, sensing her reticence. "I can handle it."

Emma shook her head. "No. I've put my foot into this mess. I'm going to see it through."

CHAPTER 26

The following morning, Emma and Jill Bedner waited in one of the firm's conference rooms for the arrival of their client, the gentleman's club owner. "Let's make bets on what he's wearing," Jill suggested. "I'll bet it's a green leisure suit with a floral shirt."

"I'll put my money on plaid," Emma said. "He looks like the kind of guy who'd think plaid is appropriate for formal occasions."

Lorraine stuck her head in the conference room. "Mr. Laskis is here," she said.

Emma and Jill looked at each other. "Oh, joy," Jill said. "Should I go get him?"

"Be my guest," Emma said.

Jill walked back into the conference room a short time later with a dazed expression on her face. Emma was just about to ask what was wrong when she saw the source of Jill's confusion. Mike Laskis, following closely on Jill's heels, looked as if he had just stepped out of the pages of *GQ*.

Big Louie's owner sported a deep charcoal suit, a white shirt with French cuffs nicely complemented by attractive gold cuff links, a conservative tie and black wing tip shoes. "You look terrific," Emma exclaimed. "That's a gorgeous suit."

"It's Hugo Boss," Mike said. "I'm glad you like it. You told me to dress up. I was hoping this would be okay."

"It's better than okay," Jill said. "Did you go out and buy a new suit just for your court appearance?"

"Of course not," Mike said, taking a seat at the table. "I told you, I have a whole closet full of suits. Now, shouldn't we be getting down to business? We have to be in court in an hour."

The temporary injunction motion was held in front of Judge Lucy Neuenschwander. The judge had a reputation for having a keen legal mind and moving cases along expeditiously. While most jurists took cases under advisement so they could do the research and render a decision at their leisure, Emma and Jill hoped that Judge Neuenschwander would make her ruling at the close of the hearing rather than keeping everyone in suspense.

"Motion for temporary injunction filed by Michael Laskis, d/b/a Big Louie's," the judge read from the morning's docket. "Ms. Davis, Ms. Bedner, please proceed."

Emma stood up. "I'd like to call Michael Laskis to the stand."

After Mike had affirmed to tell nothing but the truth, Emma led him through a somewhat sanitized description of the activities that took place at Big Louie's.

"Are the dancers allowed to engage in sexual acts with customers?" Emma asked.

"Absolutely not," Mike said. "The first thing I tell them at their interview is no hanky-panky with the customers. If I find out that any dancer is fraternizing with a customer, she is fired on the spot."

"What about the activity known as lap dancing?" Emma asked. "Doesn't that, by its very nature, involve intimate contact with customers?"

"No, it does not," Mike said. "The primary difference between a lap dance and the other dancing that takes place at the club is that it is done in an area where the dancer and the customer are secluded from the rest of the crowd. The exact nature of the dance is up to the participants. While it does typically involve physical contact between the dancer and the customer, the dancer totally controls the nature of the touching. At the time the customer pays for the dance, he is told he is not allowed to touch the dancer with his hands or any other body parts."

As Emma caught a glimpse of the judge's mouth dropping open, she fought hard to keep a straight face. "How can you ensure that no overt sexual activity occurs between the dancer and the customer?"

"The lap dancing areas are continually monitored by a member of my staff," Mike said. "Both the dancers and the patrons know they are under surveillance at all times. I assure you there is no illegal activity at Big Louie's."

"I have no further questions," Emma said.

The municipality was represented by a gray-haired

attorney named Bryce Neild. "Mr. Laskis, Big Louie's dancers perform in the nude, do they not?" Neild asked.

"No," Mike said.

Neild frowned. "I have been to your establishment on a number of occasions, sir, and all of the dancers I saw were completely nude."

"Then you weren't looking very closely," Mike said. "Big Louie's has never had completely nude dancers. All of our performers wear shoes."

Neild chortled. "All right. They wear shoes. Do they wear any other type of garment or G-string or even a postage stamp on any part of their bodies besides their feet?"

"Just the shoes," Mike confirmed. "Except on Hawaiian nights, of course. Then they wear leis and hula hoops."

"Just shoes," Neild said, returning to his seat. "No further questions, your honor."

"Thank you, counsel," the judge said. "Mr. Laskis, you may return to your seat. Ms. Davis, would you care to summarize why I should grant a TRO preventing the town's new ordinance from taking effect?"

Emma stood up again. "Your honor, as Mr. Laskis explained, the dancers at Big Louie's are closely monitored and are strictly prohibited from engaging in sexual activities with customers. While lap dancing may not be everyone's idea of a good way to spend money, it is no less a form of creative expression than the ballet and so long as it does not involve sex between the dancer and the customer, local governmental bodies have no legitimate basis to prohibit it. The ordinance would stifle creative expression. It should not be allowed to take effect." Emma took her seat.

The judge nodded. "Mr. Neild?"

Neild stood up. "Shoes do not a costume make, nor does lap dancing qualify as a legitimate form of creative expression. There's an old saying that if it looks like a duck and quacks like a duck, it probably is a duck. Well, if you're running a business that deals in pure, unadulterated sex, the mere fact that one of the participants is wearing a pair of shoes doesn't turn the activity into a Sunday school picnic. The ordinance is clearly directed toward protecting public morals and is narrowly tailored. It should be allowed to take effect."

The judge scribbled some notes on a legal pad, then looked up. "All right. I'm ready to rule on the motion. I can't quite believe I'm doing this, but I find the plaintiff's arguments convincing enough to warrant closer scrutiny. I hereby grant the TRO. The municipality may not enforce the new ordinance until there has been a full hearing and decision on the merits of the case. Because both parties have an interest in finality and because the case implicates public health and safety concerns, I will expedite the matter. Thank you, counsel. Case adjourned." The judge slammed her gavel down on the bench.

Mike Laskis was ecstatic about the result. "This is great," he exclaimed as he walked out of the courtroom with Jill and Emma. "Super job, ladies. You know, I have to admit that at our first meeting I was a little skeptical as to whether you'd be able to handle this case, but obviously Tom Cane knew what he was doing when he assigned you two. So you tell Tom that as a little expression of my thanks, I'm going to send him a case of Cohibas. They're fresh off the boat from Havana."

"I'm sure he'll be thrilled," Emma said, thinking how much she hated the smell of cigar smoke and hoping Tom would not feel compelled to light up in the office.

"And as for you two," Mike said, putting one hand on each woman's shoulder. "I'll need a little more time, but I promise I'll come up with something appropriate." They had reached the elevators. "As long as I'm in the building, I have to pay a couple fines," Mike said. "I'll catch you later."

"This whole morning has been surreal," Emma said as she and Jill got on the elevator.

"The important thing is, we won," Jill said.

"We wouldn't have won if Mike had come to court dressed in khakis and a Big Kahuna shirt. I think the judge was rather smitten with him."

"He cleaned up very nicely," Jill agreed. "And I'm sure Tom will be tickled with his cigars."

Emma nodded. "I wonder what Mike will decide is an appropriate gift for us."

"Probably the three video set of 'Lap Dancing Made Easy,'" Jill said. "Or else a gold lamé hula hoop."

Around four that afternoon, Lorraine walked into Emma's office carrying a shopping bag from Cyn's, Kathy's employer. "Special delivery for you," Lorraine said, setting the bag on Emma's desk.

"What's this?" Emma asked.

"It's from Mike Laskis," Lorraine replied.

"Mike bought something from Cyn's?" Emma reached into the bag and pulled out a beautifully gift wrapped box. Emma ripped off the wrapping and opened the box. Inside was a pair of black Manolo Blahnik strappy sandals, size seven and a half.

"Oh, my God!" Emma exclaimed. "These are four-hundred-dollar shoes!"

At the bottom of the box was a handwritten card. "All beautiful women should have at least one pair of beautiful shoes. Hope you enjoy them. Thanks again. Mike."

As Emma was staring dumbstruck at the shoes, Jill burst in the door carrying an identical box. "They're even the right size," Jill said.

Emma nodded. "Mine, too. Is he a mind reader or does he have a foot fetish that we didn't notice?"

"You can thank me for the size information," Lorraine said. "Mike called me around noon and asked if I could find out your shoe size and Jill's. I knew you keep an extra pair of black pumps in your desk, so, while you were at lunch, I came in and peeked. Then I called Jill's secretary and found out her size. I hope you don't mind."

"Mind?" Emma said, slipping the shoes on her feet and standing up to appreciate the effect.

"This is a wonderful gift. And it couldn't have come at a more appropriate time. I'm going to a formal dinner on Saturday, and I've been wondering what shoes to wear with my gown. These will be just perfect."

Jill had also slipped into her shoes. "I take back all the bad things I said about him," she said. "Any man who has good taste in women's shoes can't be all bad."

"You know what this means?" Emma said, looking Jill in the eye.

Jill nodded. "We're going to have to go to Hawaiian night at the club."

"And let him lei us," Emma added. "For shoes like this, it'll be worth it."

An hour later, Emma was finishing some correspondence when the phone rang. It was Lee Hennick.

"I haven't heard from you," Lee said. He sounded agitated. "What's going on?"

"I'm sorry I haven't called," Emma said, swiveling her chair around so that she was facing the wall. "Things have been really hectic here, but I am making progress."

"What does that mean?" Lee asked. "You have proof that Oak was murdered?"

"No, but I do have proof that what happened to him might not have been an isolated incident."

"You have proof that other people were murdered?" Lee asked excitedly.

"No. I have proof of irregularities and mishandling in other estates," Emma said in a hushed tone.

"How does that help explain what happened to Oak?"

"I'm not sure yet. I'm still working on that."

"How long is this going to take? Oak's been dead for more than a month. The trail is getting cold."

"I'm working as fast as I can," Emma said, trying to calm the man down. "Believe me, I want to get to the bottom of what happened to Oak just as much as you do. And as soon as I have more information, I'll let you know."

"That's what you said the last time and you never called me. I'm just going to keep calling you."

"That's fine," Emma said, "but I think it would be best if you didn't call me here. I'll give you my home number. Do you have a pencil?" She recited the number. "I know the waiting is tough, but just hang in there. I expect something to break soon."

"All right," Lee said. "But I'm going to keep bugging you until we get this solved."

"That's fair enough. Talk to you soon. Bye."

As Emma hung up the phone and turned back toward the door, she gasped. Louis Brisbane was standing in her doorway.

"Hello, Emma," Brisbane said, giving her a small grin. "How are you?"

"Fine," Emma squeaked. How long had he been standing there? Had he heard part of her conversation? Had he heard her utter the word Oak?

Brisbane walked over to Emma's desk. "I was just wondering if any more tenants had responded to your most recent letter," he said.

"I got one more response from someone who is willing to accept the buyout," Emma said. "I sent that up to Devereaux this afternoon. The tenant's name was Menendez."

"That's fine. What about Mr. Hennick? Has he returned his acceptance form yet?"

"Not yet," Emma said, trying not to betray her nervousness. "Maybe he was gone over the holiday weekend. I'm sure it will arrive in the next day or so."

"Keep on him," Brisbane directed. "And then I'd like you to send out a third letter a week from now upping the ante once more."

"Fine," Emma said, feeling more uncomfortable by the moment.

Brisbane made no move to leave. It felt to Emma as though he were looming over her desk and that his eyes were boring through to her very core.

Emma started to panic. She had to get out of there. Feigning complete calm, she switched off her computer, pulled her purse out of a desk drawer, grabbed her briefcase and stood up. "Thanks for stopping in," she said, coming around her desk. "If you'll excuse me, I'm late for an appointment."

As Emma started to walk past Brisbane, he, too, moved toward the door, partially blocking her path. "I have really enjoyed working with you on this project, Emma," he said, giving her an enigmatic look. "You are every bit as intelligent and resourceful as I thought you'd be."

"Thanks," Emma said, using her briefcase to push

past him and gain the doorway. "If I get any more tenant responses, I'll be in touch." She rapidly walked out the door, past Lorraine's desk and raced down the hallway toward the elevator. Her heart did not stop pounding until she was safely locked in her car speeding out of the parking garage to the street.

CHAPTER 27

Emma was still shaken from her encounter with Brisbane when she and Flynn returned to the morgue later that night to replace the files they had purloined the previous evening and to pick up two additional files that Emma's computer search had identified.

"Do you think he suspects something?" Flynn asked as he sped south on their mission.

"Not really," Emma said. "It's like when you're a kid and you do something you shouldn't. You're feeling guilty about it, so you assume everyone around you, especially your parents, are on to you even though they're not."

"You have nothing to feel guilty about," Flynn said. "You're not the one cheating your clients."

"You know what I mean," Emma said, sinking back in her seat. "I'm not exactly helping my chances of advancement at the firm by doing this."

"Then stop doing it."

"I can't. I certainly don't think of myself as a white knight, but now that I believe Brisbane's been cheating clients I have to do something to stop him. On the other hand, when I think what his reaction will be—" Her voice trailed off.

Flynn looked over at her. "If you think there's any chance Brisbane knows you're onto him, maybe you should go to Tom Cane right now."

Emma shook her head. "I don't have proof."

Flynn put his hand on her knee. "This isn't a game, Emma. Julia left Chicago because she feared for her life. Tommy Corona isn't somebody you mess with. If there's the slightest chance he and Brisbane know what you've found out, you've got to call in reinforcements."

"When do you think you'll be able to get me a full list of properties Regal has owned in the last five years and who they acquired them from?"

"Probably tomorrow. The next day at the latest."

"I'd like to wait and see what they show. I need hard proof that Brisbane's company has been buying real estate from its clients' estates for less than fair market value and that he proposes to do the same thing in the *Greythorne* estate."

"All right, but if Brisbane says or does anything the least bit weird or if you so much as see Tommy Corona drive by your apartment building, all bets are off and we have to go with what we've got immediately. Is that a deal?"

"It's a deal," Emma said, grimacing at the thought of Tommy Corona stalking her.

"Don't worry about your future," Flynn said,

seeing the look on her face. "I'll be there for you, no matter what happens." He reached over and squeezed her hand.

For the first time since she'd discovered Brisbane in her office that afternoon, Emma relaxed. She closed her eyes, and images of California popped into her head. There were other careers besides law. Even Brisbane had admitted she was resourceful. No matter how this played out she'd land on her feet— unless, of course, Tommy Corona got hold of her and stuffed her into cement overshoes.

Emma's eyes flew open at the thought of Corona and she was horrified to see the shadows of the two enormous cranes looming over the construction site just as Flynn pulled into the morgue's parking lot.

Sensing Emma's unease, Flynn said, "There's really no reason for you to come in. Why don't you give me the key and I'll put these files away and pick up the new ones?"

This time Emma didn't argue. She handed him the key. "Hurry back," she said.

"Don't worry, I will." Flynn lifted the files out of the car, hurried up to the door and let himself into the building.

Within ten minutes he was back. "Piece of cake," he said, sliding back into his seat and handing her the new files.

"I hope we won't have to come back," Emma murmured.

Flynn patted her leg. "I'll take you home. You've

had a rough day. I can look through these files myself and let you know what I find."

Emma nodded gratefully.

Later that night Emma was sitting on the sofa in her living room, trying to read through some briefs while Kathy admired the shoes Mike Laskis had picked out.

"These are great shoes," Kathy said. "I have them in four colors."

"I'm going to wear them to the zoo gala," Emma said.

"Perfect," Kathy exclaimed. "They're very sexy. Your client might run a strip joint, but he obviously has good taste. You don't suppose he'd like to set up an account at the store so he could buy shoes for his dancers? I could get him a nice discount."

"I don't think he buys four-hundred-dollar shoes for his dancers," Emma said.

"He should. Expensive shoes are much better for the feet and the back. The right footwear could extend a dancer's working life by years."

"I'll mention that the next time I see him," Emma said.

Kathy put the shoes back in their box and sat down next to Emma. "Graham has officially accepted my invitation to the zoo benefit. I am no longer dateless."

"That's great. I'm so happy that things are working out with him. He seems like a great guy."

"He is," Kathy said. "I can hardly believe my good luck. After all the bad dates I've endured over the years, this one is almost too good to be true. He's smart. He's sexy. He's funny. The only negative thing I can say about him is that he's so damn practical."

Emma looked up from her reading. "Since when is being practical a bad quality?"

"It's not a bad quality. It's just not exactly a quality that I share. Do you know that Graham actually takes public transportation?"

"That's smart," Emma said. "The traffic in this city is horrendous, and parking is impossible."

"I know," Kathy said, "but since he thinks I'm a down-to-earth girl, he automatically assumed that I take public transit, too."

Emma burst out laughing. "You? Taking public transit? I'd pay to see that."

Kathy got up and started pacing in front of the sofa. "Well, then, you should have seen me yesterday after lunch. I met Graham at his office. I took a cab to get there. His office is very near Old Orchard. How perfect for me to be dating a wonderful man with an office two blocks from my favorite shopping center. Anyway, after lunch he walked me over to a bus stop. And of course I didn't want to admit that I've never been on a city bus in my entire life, so I hopped on the first bus that came, sat down and waved to him out the window."

"Let me guess," Emma said. "You got off at the very first stop and took a cab back to work."

"No. I stayed on the bus and it kept going and going and eventually I ended up in Rolling Meadows."

"How in the world did you end up way out there?" Emma demanded. "Didn't you look at the sign on the front of the bus that says where it's going?"

"No, I told you I just got on the first one that came along."

"Then why didn't you ask someone where the bus was headed? Or why didn't you just look out the window at which point you would have seen that you were going in the wrong direction?"

"I wasn't paying attention," Kathy said. "I told you I'd never been on a bus before. I just assumed all buses went to the Loop. By the time I started looking out the window, it was way too late."

"You are hopeless," Emma said. "So you got off the bus in Rolling Meadows and took a cab back downtown."

"No, I called my limo guy, Lenny Berkowitz." Seeing Emma's chastising look, Kathy said, "I was worn out from the long bus ride, and I was pissed that I was umpteen miles from civilization. I needed pampering, and nobody does that better than Lenny. He was thrilled to hear from me. I haven't used him once since I started dating Graham. He thought I was either angry at him and found another driver or that I'd left town."

"So Lenny brought you back to the real world of Michigan Avenue, where you lived happily ever after." Emma smiled.

"Don't make fun of me," Kathy said. "I adore Graham, but pretending to be somebody I'm not is hard work. I'm beginning to think I should sign up for acting lessons."

"Why do you insist on pretending?" Emma asked. "I'm sure Graham wouldn't think any less of you if he knew that you had an upper-class upbringing and that you are accustomed to the perks that go along with that lifestyle, including the occasional limo ride. I mean, what are you going to tell him if he meets your grandmother? That she's the caretaker of that mansion?"

"It's too soon to spring any of that on him," Kathy said. "I have to work up to it slowly."

"Well, then, I have another suggestion," Emma said.

"What's that?"

"Get a bus map and memorize the routes you need to take. It's all well and good to want to look like you're a working-class girl, but if Graham ever sees you hopping on a bus bound for Gary, he's going to think you've lost your mind."

CHAPTER 28

Around ten o'clock the following morning, Emma got a phone call from Flynn. "What are you doing for lunch?" he asked.

Flynn had called her late the previous night with the frustrating news that the two latest estate files, like the first two they had reviewed, contained no proof that Brisbane was cheating his clients. Emma hoped that he now had something more promising to report.

"I've got a deadline on a brief, so I thought I'd work through lunch today," Emma replied. "Why? What do you have in mind?"

"Can you spare about fifteen minutes?" Flynn asked. "I think it'll be worth your time."

"Sure. What's up?"

"Meet me at the Chinese takeout around the corner from your office at twelve fifteen. We'll talk then."

As Emma hung up the phone, she fought to control a churning sensation in the pit of her stomach. She hoped this meant that Flynn's contact had been able to come up with a list of Regal's properties. She realized that her investigation had a very narrow time frame before Brisbane discovered what she was doing. If she wasn't able to find solid proof of his wrongdoing in the next few days, she might be forced to admit defeat.

As Emma approached the rendezvous point two hours later, Flynn came out of the Chinese takeout holding a brown bag. "I got us each a shrimp egg roll," he said. As he reached inside the bag and handed one to Emma, he added, "Well, my buddy at city hall came through."

"You got a list of Regal-owned properties?" Emma asked eagerly, biting into her egg roll.

Flynn nodded and pulled a folded piece of paper out of his coat pocket. "This is a partial list detailing what Regal owned four and five years ago. My source is swamped with other work, but he's going to get me the listings from the last four years as soon as he can."

Emma took the paper and scanned it. "There are twelve names here," she commented.

"Will you have a chance to check them against the firm's client database sometime today?" Flynn asked.

"I'm on a really tight deadline with this brief, so I won't be able to do it until the end of the work day," Emma replied. "But once I get started it shouldn't take long. If I get any matches, are you up for another run to the morgue tonight?"

"Absolutely," Flynn replied. "I want to wrap this case up. Every day that goes by with Brisbane on the loose, I worry about you more and more."

"I'll be fine," Emma assured him, wishing she felt a little more confident of that statement. "He has no reason to suspect we're onto him."

"Just be careful at work," Flynn said.

"I will." Emma finished her egg roll and wiped her hands on the napkin. "Speaking of work, I'd better be getting back. Tell your friend thanks for the info. I'll come over to your place as soon as I've searched the client database. It'll probably be around six thirty."

"I'll be waiting." Flynn leaned down and kissed her.

"See you later."

Back at work, Emma forced herself to concentrate on the brief. Her mind kept wandering back to Brisbane, Corona, and the list Flynn had given her. She breathed a huge sigh of relief when she finished the brief and delivered it to Mike Hoover, the lead partner on the case, shortly after five o'clock. After taking a short break for a bottle of diet soda from the kitchen, she went back to her office.

Lorraine had left for the day, and the floor was relatively quiet. Emma closed her office door, sat down at her computer and accessed the firm's client database. She retrieved Flynn's list from her bag, then typed in the name of the person from whom Regal had acquired the first property.

"No records were found matching your search," came the prompt reply.

Emma moved on to the second seller. After striking out four times in a row, she hit pay dirt with seller number five, Linda Pils. "Pils, Linda. Executor of the Estate of Sarah Pils."

"Bingo," Emma said aloud. She circled Pils's name and wrote "Sarah Pils estate" next to it. Ten minutes later she had four more matches. She hoped that would be enough.

As she shoved Flynn's list back into her bag and shut down her computer, Emma briefly wondered if there was a way for someone to tell that she had been searching the client database and, if so, whether they could tell what she had been searching for.

Although Emma was reasonably proficient in using a computer, she knew virtually nothing about technical or security issues. She knew a skilled technician could track virtually every keystroke that had ever been made on a computer. She just had to hope that Louis Brisbane didn't have someone in the firm's computer department keeping watch over the associates' computer activities.

"Don't get paranoid," Emma muttered to herself as she headed for the door. The odds that anyone was monitoring her computer were about the same as the odds she would be struck by lightning on the way home.

The phone rang just once before it was picked up.

"Hello, Mr. Brisbane? This is Josh Wilson in the IT department. I was calling to report some more activity on that computer you asked me to monitor."

"Was the client database accessed again?" Brisbane asked.

"Yes, sir. She spent about twenty minutes executing twelve searches."

"Give me the clients' names."

Josh Wilson relayed the information.

"Is she running more searches now?"

"No, sir. She logged off her computer about ten minutes ago."

"Thank you, Josh," Brisbane said. "That was good work. Be sure to keep me posted on any additional activity on that computer."

"Sure thing, Mr. Brisbane. Good night."

"Good night."

At nine o'clock that night, Emma and Flynn were back inside the morgue. They made short work of returning the files they'd picked up the previous night and finding the new ones Emma had identified from Flynn's list.

"I hate to keep making return trips back here to replace the files, particularly when we haven't found anything useful so far," Emma said. "Why don't we take a quick look at these right now? That way, if we do find something we can take it away and have it copied and if we don't find anything, we can just leave the files here."

"Are you sure you want to hang around in here?" Flynn asked. "This place gives me the creeps."

"It's the most efficient way," Emma said. "Here, you take these two files and I'll take the other two. It shouldn't take us over an hour to go through them."

"You're the boss," Flynn said. "I think there are

some empty shelves in the back corner of the building where we can spread the files out. They're not the best working conditions, but I guess they'll do."

"Let's get cracking," Emma said, picking up her two files and heading toward the area Flynn had indicated. "I agree that I don't want to stay here any longer than we have to."

The first two files, like the others they had looked at, showed no evidence of fraud. An extremely frustrated Emma picked up the third file and began paging through it. She soon noticed something curious.

The *Pils* estate file indicated that a medium-sized commercial building on the city's south side had been assessed at two million dollars a year before Mrs. Pils died. Yet the price Regal had paid to purchase it from the estate was missing. More curious still was the fact that the last file Flynn perused was also missing all data on the sales price of the real estate.

"What's going on here?" Emma wondered as she and Flynn compared notes. "First we go through a number of files where everything looks on the up-and-up, even though Julia clearly said Brisbane's company bought real estate at criminally low prices. Now we find files where there's no sales data at all. From everything I've seen, Brisbane is a meticulous record keeper. There's no way his files wouldn't be complete."

"Unless he purged them of the incriminating information," Flynn said.

Emma nodded. "That's just what I was thinking."

As she contemplated the situation, she also began to wonder if perhaps the sales data in the earlier files they'd reviewed was bogus. It made sense that Brisbane, in an effort to cover his tracks, had removed the real documents from the files and replaced them with phony ones. If this is what happened, Emma wondered if the real data still existed and, if so, where it was.

"We might as well put these files back and get out of here," Flynn said, interrupting her musings. "There's nothing more we can do here tonight."

"I'm with you," Emma said.

They had just reshelved the files and were heading for the door when they heard a noise. "What was that?" Emma whispered.

"It sounded like car doors slamming," Flynn said. They looked at each other for a fraction of a second, then Flynn flicked off the lights and grabbed Emma's hand. "Come on," he said. "Let's try to get back to where we were looking at the files."

Feeling their way cautiously in the dark, they had almost reached their destination when the door opened. Flynn pushed Emma to a crouching position on the floor behind a tall shelf stacked with boxes, then folded his own body over hers. Emma held her breath.

The light went on, and a booming voice said, "This would be a great place for a Halloween party. Nice and spooky."

Emma's heart raced. It was Tommy Corona.

"Yeah, my kids would like it in here," a second,

unfamiliar voice said. "Good place for hide and seek."

"You're right," Corona said. "You don't suppose there's anybody hiding in here right now, do you? Let me check. Come out, come out, wherever you are!" There was a pause, then he said, "I guess there's nobody here." He laughed raucously.

"You want me to look around and make sure there's no intruders in here, boss?" Corona's hench-man asked.

Emma's whole body began to shake. Flynn hugged her tightly.

"No need to do that," Corona said. "I'm sure there's nobody here. Why would anybody want to be prowling around in this dark old warehouse? There's nothing here but a bunch of old papers. Nothing that would appeal to anybody. Now if I were some young Tom, Dick or Emma—"

Emma felt the bile rising in her throat as she heard him say her name.

"—why, I'm sure I could find lots more entertain-ing things to do than hang around some musty old warehouse."

"It is musty in here," the henchman agreed. "Smells really damp and moldy. Kind of dis-gusting, really."

"It's always dark and damp in here, even in the summertime," Corona said. "Hey, I've got an idea what would help air it out. Go get me a couple files."

"Which ones?"

"Doesn't matter. Just pick a couple files off a shelf and bring 'em over here."

There were footsteps, then the sound of files sliding off a shelf, then more footsteps.

"That's good," Corona said. "Dump the papers out right here."

Emma heard the sound of the files' contents hitting the floor.

"Perfect," Corona said. "Now we'll freshen the air a little bit."

The distinctive sound of a match being struck filled the air, followed by a crackling noise.

Emma gasped. Corona was setting the building on fire!

"There, doesn't it smell less musty already?" Corona asked.

"Much better," the henchman agreed.

"Let's hit the road," Corona said. "We've got some other stops to make."

The lights went out and the door to the morgue opened and closed. After thirty seconds, two car doors slammed and an engine roared to life.

Flynn leapt to his feet, then helped Emma up. "Come on," he said, pulling her toward the front of the building. "We've got to get out of here."

The fire had taken a firm hold on the papers strewn about the floor. "See if they barricaded the door," Flynn urged. "I'll try to put the fire out." As he beat at the fire with one of the heavy folders that had housed the burning papers, Emma raced over to the door and anxiously turned the handle. The door opened normally.

"We're not locked in!" she said as relief swept over her. "Do you want me to call 911?"

"I've got it under control." Flynn beat on the papers for another sixty seconds, then stomped on the charred remains for good measure. "There. It's all out."

"Thank God," Emma murmured. She walked over to Flynn, and he put his arms around her.

"That was a very close call," he said.

Emma nodded.

"What do you want to do now?" Flynn asked.

"You mean should we call the police?"

"Yeah. Should we call the police? Brisbane is obviously onto you."

Emma looked up at him. "And we still don't have any proof that he's been cheating clients."

"We have clear proof that Corona committed arson—and threatened you."

"Let me talk to Tom Cane tomorrow," Emma said. "I'd feel a lot better waiting to go to the police until after I've told Tom what's going on. The whole story is going to have a lot more credibility if I have another partner's backing."

Flynn frowned. "I don't like it."

"It'll be okay," Emma said.

"All right, but you've got to promise me that you'll go to the police as soon as you've talked to Tom."

"I promise."

Flynn looked at the mess on the floor. "What should we do about this?"

"Leave it," Emma said. "One of the messengers can deal with it the next time they come. Let's get the hell out of here. This place is way too creepy for me."

CHAPTER 29

When Emma arrived at work Friday morning, she was a nervous wreck. She had scarcely slept at all. Every time she dozed off, memories of Tommy Corona's cruel laughter and the smell of burning paper came flooding back and jolted her awake. She could not continue living with this level of stress. She had to put an end to it.

Her first order of business was to call Tom Cane. It would be such a relief to confide in someone she trusted who was also in a position of authority at the firm. Unfortunately, Tom's secretary was the bearer of bad news.

"I'm sorry, but Tom's elderly mother had emergency heart surgery yesterday," the secretary said. "He flew out to Boston to be with her. I don't expect him back until sometime next week. He will be calling in today. Would you like me to give him a message?"

Emma hesitated, then said, "I do need to talk to him about something, but he obviously has more important things on his mind right now. I'll wait and talk to him early next week."

"Damn," she muttered as she hung up the phone. So much for her hope that the situation could be resolved that day. She would just have to try to channel her nervous energy into her work and hope she could stay clear of Brisbane until she was able to speak to Tom Cane.

Emma and Jill Bedner spent a good part of the morning methodically looking through numerous boxes of materials that had been produced as the result of a discovery request in the lead paint case. Around twelve thirty Jill suggested a break. "I'm going stir-crazy in here," she said. "It's beautiful outside. Let's go grab a hot dog and get some fresh air."

"Sounds good to me," Emma said.

As the two women walked around eating their hot dogs and sipping lemonade, Jill said, "On beautiful days like this, when I'm cooped up inside looking at boring documents, I try to remember why I went to law school in the first place. And you know what? No good reasons spring to mind."

"What about prestige, glamour, a nice paycheck?" Emma suggested.

"Who cares about any of that? On a day like this I'd rather be penniless and out windsurfing than reading about paint."

"I can't argue with you there," Emma said. "Well, should we head back? If we push it, we might be able to finish by three and still have part of the day left for less tedious work."

"Let's go," Jill said.

They dropped their garbage in a trash container

and started the short walk back to their building. As they rounded the corner, Emma saw something that made her stop dead in her tracks. Louis Brisbane and Tommy Corona were standing a few steps from the building's entrance.

Noticing that Emma was no longer beside her, Jill turned back. "What's the matter?" she asked.

Emma grabbed Jill by the arm and pulled her around the side of the building. "What's wrong?" Jill repeated. "You look like you've seen a ghost."

Emma peered around the corner. Brisbane and Corona appeared to be engaged in an intense conversation. Their heads were close together, and even from a distance Emma could tell they were conversing in low tones.

Jill stuck her head out to see what had attracted Emma's attention. "Isn't that Louis Brisbane?" Jill asked.

"Yes."

"Who's that other guy?"

"Nobody you'd want to meet in a dark warehouse," Emma replied in a low voice.

"I'm obviously missing something here," Jill said. "Is there some reason you don't want Brisbane to see you?"

Emma nodded.

"Anything you'd care to share with me?"

Emma looked at her colleague. "I really can't explain it right now, but would you do me a favor?"

"Sure, if I can. As long as it doesn't involve meeting that other guy in a dark warehouse."

"I'd like you to walk by them and see if you can hear what they're talking about. But you can't be too obvious about it. I don't want them to know anyone is paying attention. Can you do that?"

"Piece of cake," Jill said. "I'm from a large family. We were always eavesdropping on each other. I'll stroll by them and see what I can find out and then I'll double back."

"Great," Emma said. "I'll wait right here."

Brisbane and Corona were standing near a popcorn wagon, so Jill sauntered over and got in line to buy popcorn. The two men were so engrossed in their conversation that they didn't notice Jill at all. After a few moments Jill bought her popcorn, took her time putting her change in her wallet, and nonchalantly walked back over to Emma.

"Well?" Emma asked eagerly.

"They obviously want to keep whatever they're talking about really hush-hush," Jill reported. "I had to strain to make out anything at all. But I did hear them repeat one word several times."

"What was that?"

"Greythorne."

Emma's stomach lurched, and for a moment she was afraid her hot dog was going to come back up.

"Are you all right?" Jill asked. "Did I say something wrong?"

Emma shook her head. "Could you hear anything else?"

"Not really, but I got the impression they are mad at each other over something."

Emma peeked around the corner and saw that Brisbane and Corona were walking away from the building in the other direction. She breathed a small sigh of relief. At least she didn't need to worry about running into them.

"Are you all right?" Jill repeated. "Do you want to go sit down or something?"

"No, let's go back in and finish going over the documents." She patted her friend on the arm. "Thanks a lot for doing that for me. I'm sorry I'm being so secretive about it. I'd appreciate it if you didn't mention this incident to anyone."

"No problem," Jill said, though she was still curious. "Let's get back to the paint."

As the women walked back into the building, Emma kept checking to make sure Brisbane and Corona weren't coming back. She pushed through the revolving doors so hard Jill nearly stumbled into the lobby. She hurried toward their bank of elevators, her heels echoing loudly in the large lobby.

On the elevator ride to the thirty-fourth floor, Emma couldn't stop wondering why Brisbane and Corona had been talking so intently about Oak Greythorne. She feared that they might have also been talking about her.

As Emma reached Lorraine's desk, she stopped in her tracks. Her secretary's entire working area was filled with large helium balloons. What was going on?

"What's the occasion?" Emma asked. "Did you win the lottery?"

"Much better," Lorraine said happily. "Barrie Holman, the anti-scent queen, has been fired!"

Emma felt a wave of relief wash over her. "What was her offense, failure to use deodorant?" she quipped.

"Stealing computer equipment," Lorraine answered. "The office manager found two of the firm's laptops and a printer in her apartment."

"Why would she do that? I thought you said her uncle was a retired partner here."

"He is, and Barrie appealed loudly to him to rescue her, but apparently Uncle Art has some scruples, because he told the office manager he could not countenance having a thief on the firm's payroll, even if she was a blood relative. In return for her resignation, the firm agreed not to have her criminally prosecuted."

"Congratulations," Emma said. "I know she's been a real thorn in your side."

"I must admit I was hoping to force her into taking a medical leave of absence by spraying scent all over her side of the floor, but as long as she's gone I guess I can't quibble over how it happened."

"This just goes to show that the good guys usually do come out on top," Emma said. As she walked into her office she hoped that the same axiom would hold true when it came to her and Louis Brisbane.

Late that afternoon, after she and Jill had completed their work and just as the knot in Emma's stomach was starting to relax, her phone rang.

"Emma Davis."

"Emma, Louis Brisbane here." The voice sounded curt.

The knot in Emma's stomach yanked hard. "Hi, how are you?" she said lamely.

"Fine. I was wondering if you could come up to my office. There's something I would like to discuss with you."

"Sure," Emma said, trying to keep her voice from shaking. "I'll be right there."

She hung up the phone stiffly. Every muscle in her body seemed wooden and sluggish. "Keep calm," she told herself. He couldn't do anything to her in his office during working hours. He might just want to discuss the *Greythorne* estate. So why was her entire body shaking uncontrollably?

Emma walked out to Lorraine's desk. "I'm going up to see Louis Brisbane."

Lorraine looked up from her computer. "Another recruiting meeting?"

"I'm not sure," Emma replied. "Would you do me a big favor?"

"Sure."

"If I'm not back in fifteen minutes, would you call up there and remind me that I'm late for a meeting with Mike Hoover?"

Lorraine frowned. "Do you have a meeting with Mike Hoover today?"

Emma shook her head. "No, but I need you to call and say that I do. I can't explain right now, but it's important."

"All right," Lorraine said agreeably. "I've had far

stranger requests from lawyers I've worked for over the years."

"Thanks. You're a lifesaver." Maybe literally, Emma thought to herself as she walked resolutely toward the elevator.

When she reached Brisbane's office, Devereaux was even more unfriendly than ever. She spoke not a word, simply jerked her head toward her boss's office as a signal that Emma should enter. As Emma walked inside, she found Brisbane standing at the window.

"Emma, how good to see you. I was just admiring the progress that's been made on this new building. Come take a look at it."

Emma took a deep breath and walked toward him. She stopped about two feet away.

"You need to get right up close to really appreciate the workmanship." Brisbane put his arm around Emma's shoulders and forcibly pushed her toward the window. The conditioning exercises she had done with Flynn had helped dispel her fear of heights, but the proximity to Brisbane and the rough familiarity of his contact with her caused her to break out in a cold sweat.

"Take a look at that," Brisbane said, pushing her closer still to the window. "Isn't it amazing the way that crane can lift those enormous blocks into place?"

Emma tried to say something, but all that came out was a feeble squeaking sound.

"We are really living in a marvelous age," Brisbane said, tightening his grip on her. "Still afraid of heights?'' he asked as he felt Emma trembling. "What a shame. We'll have to do something about that." He leaned close and whispered in her ear. "I can think of several methods that would rid you of that phobia."

As Emma felt her stomach lurch, Brisbane finally released her, walked over to his desk and sat down. Emma gratefully scurried around the front of the desk and took a seat. "Isn't this lovely weather?" the partner asked conversationally, as if the encounter by the window never happened. "Do you have any special plans for the weekend?"

"Not really," Emma replied, wishing he would come to the point so she could get out of there. "How about you?"

"I'm going to my cottage in Door County. In fact, I was just getting ready to leave when it occurred to me that we had an item of unfinished business. Do you have any idea what that might be?" He stared straight at her.

Emma shook her head dumbly.

"Well, then, let me tell you. I want to expedite the final letter to the remaining holdouts in the Greythorne apartment building. The new buyer is so eager to gain possession of the building that I've been authorized to pay ten thousand dollars to induce them to vacate. Would you please draft such a letter and send it out next week?"

"No problem," Emma said, trying to keep her voice from quavering. She looked at him warily, wondering what he would say or do next.

"That's all," Brisbane said brightly.

Emma fairly leapt out of her seat and headed for the door. "I'll send you a copy of the letter and keep you posted on the tenants' responses," she said.

"Keep up the good work, Emma," Brisbane said. "Oh, one more thing," he said just as she reached the door.

She swallowed hard and turned back.

"Is there some particular reason for your interest in the *Pils* estate?"

Emma fought to control her breathing and put on her best poker face. "What estate?"

"*Pils*," Brisbane replied.

Emma looked him in the eye. "I've never heard of it."

Brisbane raised an eyebrow. "Really? Someone had mentioned that you were trying to locate the closed file but perhaps they were mistaken."

"It must have been someone else. What would I want with a closed estate file?"

"My sentiments exactly," Brisbane said. "That file would be completely useless. Well, that finishes our discussion, Emma. You may go."

As she turned back toward the door, Emma suddenly found herself staring at the ornate file cabinet in the corner of Brisbane's office. It was a very unusual piece of furniture. She recalled that when she first saw it, she had wondered what sort of valuable documents it might house. Now, as she looked at it, she thought she might know the answer. It would be the perfect place to hide incriminating documents that had been removed from client files.

"Is something wrong?" Brisbane asked.

"No, I just had a little dizzy spell and needed a moment to get my bearings," Emma said, moving quickly toward the door, and hoping Brisbane had not noticed her interest in the cabinet. "I'll send the letter to the tenants early next week."

As she headed for the elevator, Emma's head was spinning. Perhaps her hopes of finding evidence of Brisbane's wrongdoing weren't dashed just yet. That file cabinet might contain the proof she'd been looking for. Now all she had to do was find a way to check it out.

When Emma pulled up in front of her building ninety minutes later, Flynn was already there, waiting in his car.

"I'm sorry I'm running late," she said as they both exited their vehicles and met on the sidewalk. "I got roped into helping with an emergency project."

"No need to apologize," Flynn said. "I'm a little early. Actually, the reason I'm early is because I was worried about you. I wanted to call you but I was tied up in meetings all day. How did things go?"

"It was a very stressful day, but not as bad as I thought it might be."

"Did you talk to Tom Cane?"

Emma shook her head. "Let's go inside, and I'll tell you about it."

Flynn put his arm around her. They were heading for the building's entrance when they heard the squeal of tires behind them. They looked back and saw a black SUV speeding toward them. As Flynn instinctively jumped back onto the grass, pulling Emma with him, Tommy Corona brought his vehicle to a screeching halt only inches away from where they were standing.

"What the hell do you want?" Flynn demanded, protectively stepping in front of Emma.

"I was in the neighborhood so I thought I'd stop by," Corona said through his rolled-down window. "There's no law against that, is there?"

"There is a law against arson," Flynn said brashly.

"You shouldn't go sticking your nose into things that don't concern you, Mr. Fancy Architect. Or haven't you heard the story about how curiosity killed the cat?"

"This is private property, and you're trespassing," Flynn said. "Get out of here or I'll call the cops."

"Fuck you," Corona said. Then he leered at Emma. "Come to think of it, I'd rather fuck her, but I'll save that pleasure for another time. Have a good evening, you two. And better keep your feet on the ground. I heard the little lady is afraid of heights, and it could be a really bad scene if she doesn't stay close to terra firma." He stepped on the accelerator and squealed off.

CHAPTER 30

On Saturday morning, in preparation for the zoo gala, Emma and Kathy spent several hours pampering themselves at the spa at Cyn's. After a massage, facial, manicure, leg wax, pedicure and light lunch, they went back to Kathy's apartment. Kathy wanted to have a glass of wine to celebrate their physical improvement and their good fortune in finding great men, but Emma begged off. "I have something I need to do this afternoon," she said vaguely. "Then I think I'll take a little nap before I get dressed."

"What time is Flynn picking you up?"

"He was supposed to come at seven thirty," Emma replied, "but he could be a little late. He got a call this morning about a crisis at his big Converse Towers project. Something about the wrong flooring being delivered for a high-powered law firm's suite. They're threatening to pull out of their lease unless Flynn agrees to correct the error immediately. He's over there now trying to work things out. He said if he's not here by seven forty that I should head over to the Ritz by myself and he'd meet me there."

"You'd better not be late for dinner," Kathy scolded.

"We won't. What time is Graham calling for you? Or are you taking the bus to the gala?" Emma asked with a grin.

"No, we're driving, thank God," Kathy said. "He's supposed to be here at seven fifteen."

"That's good." Emma stood up and walked toward the door. "Well, I'll see you tonight at the Ritz."

Back in her own apartment, Emma paced the floor, contemplating what she was going to do next. Ever since leaving Brisbane's office the previous afternoon, she had not been able to let loose of the idea that the expensive file cabinet might contain just the proof she'd been seeking about his underhanded dealings with client estates.

Even though she knew it was both foolhardy and dangerous, the prospect of sneaking into Brisbane's office and getting her hands on that proof had been haunting her for nearly twenty-four hours. She had not breathed a word of the idea to Flynn, knowing full well that he would go ballistic and refuse to let her out of his sight, thereby quashing any hope she might have of seeing Brisbane brought to justice.

As the afternoon wore on, Emma found herself rationalizing why a search of Brisbane's office would not be an act of utter lunacy. Although someone was toiling away at Franklin & Holland virtually twenty-four seven, in her experience, by late Saturday afternoon, the number of live bodies on the premises normally dwindled to a mere handful of workaholics. Since this was a beautiful spring weekend, it was likely that even the most die-hard attorneys were enjoying outdoor activities rather than spending the day cooped up in their offices. So Emma reasoned that the chance of running into anyone was remote.

The fact that Brisbane himself was over two hundred miles away at his Wisconsin cottage also made her feel somewhat less apprehensive about snooping around his office. Once inside, it shouldn't take her more than twenty or thirty minutes to search for the documents. If she found them, she'd take them with her and talk to Tom Cane about what to do next. If she didn't find anything, she wouldn't be any worse off than she was now and at least she'd know she had done everything within her power to expose Brisbane's criminality.

By mid-afternoon, she had made up her mind. At four forty-five she would make a quick run to the office and see what she could find. If everything went according to plan, she should be home again shortly after six, giving her plenty of time to dress for the zoo gala. She already had her dress and all her accessories laid out on her bed. She sat down in a chair and tried to concentrate on a fashion magazine, willing time to pass quickly.

Emma checked her watch as the elevator doors opened on the fortieth floor. It was five minutes past five. There had been no one in the lobby when she'd entered the building, and she'd had the elevator to herself. So far, so good. Now came the risky—and stressful—part of the operation.

She took a deep breath and stepped out of the elevator. The hallway was dark and quiet. So quiet that it reminded her of a tomb. She shuddered. Very bad analogy.

Emma walked toward Brisbane's office at a normal pace. It was important to appear as if she belonged there. She was carrying a manilla folder containing a few more responses from tenants in Oak's building accepting the offer to buy out their leases. In the unlikely event she did run into someone, she would say that she had come into the office to catch up on some work and thought she would drop the letters off in Brisbane's office so that he could issue the checks promptly. After all, he had repeatedly impressed upon her the need to empty the apartment building as quickly as possible so the new buyer could renovate.

When Emma reached Devereaux's desk, she paused and fought back the urge to abandon her plan and rush back to the elevator. No, damn it, she had come this far and she was going to see it through. She squared her shoulders and stepped up to Brisbane's closed door. She knocked briefly on the door, just for appearances, then opened it and stepped inside.

Quietly closing the door behind her, she set the manilla folder down on a chair and immediately went over to the file cabinet. She had expected it to be locked and had feared she might not be able to find the key, but to her delight the top drawer slid open invitingly. Emma felt a bit of the tension draining out of her body. Maybe this wasn't going to be so tough after all.

She had committed to memory the names of the files she was seeking. She quickly thumbed through the contents of the top drawer. The files all had unfamiliar names. Just to be sure that the contents matched the file label, Emma briefly pulled out every third one and peeked inside. Everything looked on the up-and-up. Trying not to feel too disappointed, she closed that drawer and moved on to the next one.

She had examined about half of the files in the second drawer when she thought she heard a noise out in the hallway. Her heart began to pound wildly and her whole body shook from fright. Oh, my God, she thought. Was that the elevator? Was someone coming? She glanced over at the door, then looked around for a hiding place.

Sliding the drawer shut as quietly as she could, she scurried into Brisbane's restroom. She left the door open just enough to see out into the office. Leaning against the marble wall, she slowly counted to one hundred and listened intently. There was no sound, only dead silence. Her pulse rate began to return to normal. There was no one there. Her imagination and nerves must have been playing tricks on her. She left the restroom and returned to the file cabinet.

As she opened the second drawer, a chill went ran through her. This was almost too easy, with the entire floor seemingly deserted, Brisbane's office and the file cabinet both wide open and beckoning. What if this were a trap? Emma looked back toward the door, giving brief thought to getting the hell out of there. Then she shook her head. There was no one there. It wasn't a trap, and she was going to finish what she started. She steeled her resolve and resumed her methodical inspection of the files.

Exactly fifteen minutes into her search, she hit pay dirt in the third drawer. Just when she had been wondering if her hopes of finding something useful had merely been a pipe dream, a familiar name leapt out at her. Pils. Her hands trembling, Emma pulled out the slim file and scanned its contents. She drew in her breath. There it was in black and white. Proof positive of Louis Brisbane's unethical and criminal behavior.

The *Pils* file contained an appraisal showing that a piece of real estate was valued at five million dollars. It also contained documents showing that the property had been sold to Regal Enterprises, the company owned by Brisbane and Tommy Corona, for only two million.

"Now I've got you, you bastard," Emma murmured aloud. She set the *Pils* file on Brisbane's desk and continued looking through the rest of the drawer's contents. Ten minutes later the stack on the desk included *Bartelt* and *Loichinger*, the two estates Julia Boswell had mentioned, as well as three others from the list Flynn had provided.

Each file told them the same story: Brisbane had

systematically cheated his clients out of millions of dollars. Emma's suspicions, as confirmed by Julia Boswell, had been right and now Emma had the proof to prevent Brisbane from ever cheating another client. Not a bad afternoon's work.

Emma scooped up the files and the manilla envelope. She glanced around to make sure that nothing had been disturbed, then looked at her watch. It was five thirty-six. She was right on schedule. She would be home by six o'clock and would have plenty of time to primp for the gala at the Ritz. She could hardly wait to show Flynn what she had found. She knew he would be angry with her for not telling him what she was going to do but once he saw the files he would forgive her.

Balancing the files on her left arm, Emma reached out with her right hand to open the door and let herself out. As she turned the knob and began to pull the door toward her, it suddenly swung in with such violence that she was knocked to the floor. The files flew out of her hands, papers scattering everywhere. As Emma fought to catch her breath, she looked up, then swallowed hard.

Standing over her were Louis Brisbane and Tommy Corona.

CHAPTER 31

As Brisbane closed the door behind him, Corona pulled Emma to her feet and roughly twisted both arms behind her back. She bit down on the inside of her lip to keep from crying out in pain.

"Well, well," Brisbane said, as he walked over to Emma. "What do we have here?" He got down on the floor and picked up the strewn files. "Bartelt and Loichinger," he said aloud. "Two of our more lucrative deals, eh, Tommy?"

"What should we do with this lousy cunt?" Corona asked, twisting Emma's arm even harder.

"That's a very good question." Brisbane set the files down on the floor and approached Emma. "You seem to have turned into quite the little detective. What would you do if you were in our position?"

Emma did not respond.

"What's the matter? Cat got your tongue?" Brisbane slapped Emma hard across the face. She cried out in pain.

"You can scream all you want to," Brisbane said with a sneer. "There's no one to hear you."

"I'm sure you thought you were rather clever," Brisbane said, pacing back and forth in front of Emma, "but you underestimated your enemy." Seeing Emma's confused expression, he said, "I've had logs of your computer requests made ever since you began assisting me with the *Greythorne* estate. Still, for a hick from Kansas City, you proved yourself to be quite resourceful. I can see where you'd have the potential to be a damn good lawyer. It's a shame your career is going to be cut short."

Corona broke into a loud guffaw.

Emma was shaking with fright. She had no idea what to do to save herself other than stall for time. "Did you wait around all day to see if I'd come?" she asked Brisbane in what she hoped sounded like a defiant tone.

"No, Tommy had someone following you all day. Nice nail polish, by the way."

"Did you have something to do with Oak Greythorne's death?" Emma asked.

Brisbane was silent.

Emma twisted her head around and addressed Corona. "Or was it you who did him in?"

"It wasn't me," Corona said, chuckling. "Louis was the one who helped him overindulge his bad habits for drugs and booze."

"Shut the fuck up, Tommy!" Brisbane shouted. "You always did have a big mouth."

"Who gives a shit what I say now?" Corona countered. "She ain't gonna be around to tell anybody."

"I already have told people," Emma said, her voice

rising. "I wrote everything down and sent it to people at the firm. I told them about what you did and gave them documentation. Names of the people you cheated. By Monday they'll all be onto you. You can't get away with this."

Brisbane laughed. "I don't believe you. You're bluffing. And you're quite wrong, my dear Emma. I will get away with this, just as I've gotten away with so many other things."

"My boyfriend and some other friends know where I am right now," Emma said. "I'm supposed to meet them in thirty minutes. If I don't show up, they'll come here looking for me."

"I happen to know your boyfriend is busy taking care of a little problem at Converse Towers," Corona said. "So he won't be riding to your rescue right away."

"By the time your friends arrive," Brisbane said, "you will no longer be here." He started walking toward the door, then turned back. "I am truly sorry that it has to end this way. We could have made a good team, you and I, if only you weren't so damn ethical."

"What are you going to do with me?" Emma asked, not wanting to hear the answer.

"I'm afraid you're going to be the victim of a most unfortunate accident," Brisbane replied. "That is, after I follow up on my promise to cure you of that wretched fear of heights."

As Emma's mind tried to process what he meant, Corona loosened his grip on her arms. She was about to try to make a run for it when she felt the big man's hands go around her neck. She clawed at him and tried to make him let go, but he kept squeezing methodically, tighter and tighter, and soon everything went black.

Tommy Corona opened the back door of his SUV and scooped Emma's motionless body into his arms as easily as if he were lifting a small child. "Make yourself useful and shut the door," he directed Brisbane. "Then come with me. I might need some help rigging her up."

Brisbane did as he was told and followed Corona into the heart of the construction site, a few blocks from the morgue. When Corona reached one of the cranes towering over the project, he unceremoniously deposited Emma on the ground.

Corona removed a roll of heavy tape and a Swiss Army knife from his pocket and handed them to Brisbane. "Here. Wrap the tape around her mouth and then bind her ankles and tie her hands behind her back. Use plenty of tape. We don't want her to get loose. While you're doing that, I'll go up in the crane and lower the hoist."

Brisbane looked skeptically at his compatriot. "I know I was originally in favor of this idea but now I'm having a change of heart. Why don't we just put her back in the SUV, drive her out to the country and dispose of her? Maybe there is no need for these theatrics."

"Yes, there is," Corona shot back. "We tried to get her to back off and she wouldn't do it. Now the little cunt needs to be taught a lesson. And I can't think of a better way to deal with someone who gets scared shitless whenever she's above the fifth floor. Now get busy with that tape. I want to get her in position before she wakes up."

Brisbane wound the sticky tape over Emma's mouth and around her head half a dozen times. He used the knife to cut the tape, then bound Emma's ankles. He was just finishing with that job when Corona returned.

"Jesus, you're slow," Corona said. "Give me that." He grabbed the tape and knife away from Brisbane, then roughly rolled Emma onto her side so he could bind her hands. "Good," he said. "Now for the final touch."

Corona walked over to a nearby trailer and returned with a sheet and a length of rope. He spread the sheet on the ground and wrapped Emma's body from her neck to her feet. Then he pushed Emma into a sitting position. "Hold her right there so I can get this rope around her." Within minutes Emma was trussed up like a chicken.

"Looks good," Corona said, throwing Emma over his shoulder. "If anyone sees her, they won't realize it's a body, but if she wakes up she'll be able to see exactly where she is. Now comes the fun part: it's time to string her up."

Corona carried Emma over to where he had lowered the crane's hoist. He slipped the hook on the end of the hoist through the rope between Emma's shoulder blades. "Perfect," he said.

"I still think we should just smash her in the head with a tire iron and be done with it," Brisbane said.

"Where's your sense of humor?" Corona asked. "A tire iron is too quick. It's much better to prolong her agony." He took out the Swiss Army knife and made a few shallow cuts in the rope near where the hook was fastened. "If she wakes up, she'll discover she's dangling helplessly two hundred feet off the ground. Then, after an hour or so the rope will probably let go and she'll do a nice free fall into the sub-basement."

"What do you mean the rope will probably let go?" Brisbane asked. "We have to make sure she doesn't make it out of here."

"The only way she's gonna make it out of her is if she sprouts wings and flies out," Corona said. "I'll check back in about ninety minutes. If she hasn't fallen by then, I'll bring her down and finish her off."

Brisbane nodded.

Emma moaned softly.

"She's starting to wake up," Corona said. He hurried back toward the crane. "It's time for Emma to do her Peter Pan act."

CHAPTER 32

When Emma regained consciousness, her first sensation was of a breeze rippling around her face. Her eyes fluttered open, and she felt completely disoriented. She blinked hard and tried to figure out where she was, but she couldn't. Nothing looked familiar. It seemed as if she were staring into outer space.

She blinked again, forcing herself to focus on some nearby object. But the closest object was a tall building, which Emma seemed to be viewing at eye level. Nothing made any sense. Maybe she had suffered a brain injury. Then, suddenly, panic more extreme than she had ever experienced in her life gripped her. She knew exactly where she was. She was bound and gagged and suspended from one of the giant cranes towering nearly two hundred feet over Tommy Corona's construction site!

She tried to scream but discovered that her mouth was taped shut. She could breathe only through her nose, and she had difficulty swallowing. Corona must have bruised her windpipe when he choked her into unconsciousness. Her heart pounded wildly in her ears, and as she fought to get her breath, she felt a pain in her chest. Whatever material was wrapped around her midsection was crushing her ribs.

She wondered how long she had been unconscious. She forced herself to remember the confrontation with Brisbane and Corona at the office. The last time she had looked at her watch it had been around five thirty. She wished she could see her watch now. Although the sun was moving toward the horizon, it was not yet ready to set.

She guessed it must be around seven o'clock, or maybe a bit later. Seven o'clock. Flynn was supposed to pick her up at seven thirty, that is unless he was running late, in which case he would go directly to the Ritz. As thoughts of Flynn flooded over her, her eyes welled up with tears. Brave, resourceful Flynn would rescue her if he could, but it could be an hour or more before anyone even realized she was missing. And in an hour she would surely have either expired from fright or suffocated.

Emma tried not to look down, but even looking straight ahead caused waves of nausea to rise in her stomach. She squeezed her eyes tightly shut, thinking that would help calm her but it only made her dizzy. She opened her eyes again and could feel her body swaying ever so slightly at the end of the cable.

She tried to remain perfectly still and breathe shallowly through her nose, willing herself to stay calm. Then she felt a ripping sensation at her back and an even more intense horror gripped her. She didn't need to worry about hanging there for an hour and dying of fright or suffocation. Whatever was holding her on to the cable was starting to give way. She was going to fall twenty stories to her death. Again, she tried to scream but only a muffled sound came out.

At seven forty, Kathy and Graham were enjoying a pre-dinner glass of wine in the Ritz-Carlton's ballroom when Flynn walked up to them. "I'm sorry I'm late," Flynn said. "This is a great turnout. Where's Emma?"

Kathy stared at him blankly. "You mean, you haven't seen her? I thought you were picking her up."

Flynn shook his head. "When I talked to her this morning, I told her that if I was running late she should go without me. I tried to call her from the car a half hour ago and didn't get an answer so I figured she came on ahead. You haven't seen her?"

The color drained out of Kathy's face. "No, we haven't seen her," she said.

"Oh, my God," Flynn said, remembering the previous afternoon's encounter with Corona. "I've got to find her." He headed for the door.

"Wait for us," Kathy said, setting her wine glass on a table and grabbing Graham by the arm. "We're coming with you."

Within minutes, the three of them had piled into Graham's car and were speeding south toward the morgue, with Flynn at the wheel since he knew the way. "I'm so sorry," Kathy said. "I should have kept an eye on her."

"It's not your fault. Damn it, her car's not here," he said as he squealed around a corner and pulled into the morgue's parking lot. They all barreled out.

"Emma, are you in there?" Flynn yelled as he pounded on the door to the warehouse.

There was no response.

"Emma!" Graham screamed. "If you're in there, make some noise."

There was only silence.

Kathy frantically looked around the area. "Where else might she be, at the office?"

As Flynn racked his brain for possibilities, Corona's thinly veiled threat came rushing back. "I heard the little lady is afraid of heights, and it could be a really bad scene if she doesn't stay close to terra firma." Then, with mounting horror, Flynn recalled an even more ominous remark Corona had made. "Don't mess with me, Fielding, or I'll hang you from a crane and leave you thre until the crows devour your lousy carcass."

"What's the matter?" Kathy asked, seeing his face.

"Get back in the car," Flynn ordered.

"Where are we going?" Graham asked.

"A few blocks from here," Flynn replied. As he fired up the engine, he said to Graham, "Call 911 and tell them to meet us at Tommy Corona's Southside construction site ASAP."

"Do you really think that's where they took Emma?" Graham asked as he pulled out his cell phone.

"I'm banking on it," Flynn said as he zoomed out of the morgue's parking lot. "Because if she's not there, I have absolutely no idea where they might have taken her and we may never find her."

Within minutes Flynn had parked the car at the construction site and raced off in the direction of the twin cranes. Graham followed closely behind him.

"Emma?" Kathy yelled as she struggled over the rough terrain in her high heels. "Can you hear us?"

"She's over here," Flynn called back.

"Where?" Kathy asked, panting heavily as she arrived at their side.

"She's hanging from that crane," Graham said, pointing skyward. "Look."

Emma's heart was pounding so hard she felt as if it were going to explode. This had no doubt been what Brisbane had meant when he'd said she was going to be the victim of an unfortunate accident. Of all the possible ways she might meet her death, this had to be the most horrifying.

"No!" her mind screamed. It simply couldn't end like this. She held her breath and prayed for a rescue. Then, suddenly, she heard voices.

"Oh, my God!" Kathy screamed. "She's hanging up there. Flynn, do something!"

Emma's heart leapt. Her friends had found her. She had a chance after all.

"Emma, if you can hear me, stay perfectly still," Flynn yelled. "I'm going to get you down."

"Are you sure you know what you're doing?" Graham asked. "You could make things worse."

"I grew up around cranes," Flynn said. "I'll get her down."

"Emma, I'm going to climb up and get you down," Flynn called. "Try not to move at all."

Emma held her breath and tried to remain calm, but then she felt another ripping sensation at her back. Hurry! she exhorted Flynn silently.

"Hold on!" Flynn's voice was closer now.

Emma could hear the wailing of police sirens.

"Hurry, Flynn!" Kathy shouted. "Before she falls."

"Okay, Emma." Flynn's voice was closer still. "I'm getting into the operator's cab now. I'm going to start this thing up, and then I'm going to slowly lower you to the ground. It's very important that you stay perfectly still."

The police sirens were directly under Emma now. She heard car doors slam. "What's going on?" a new voice called.

"A woman is hanging up there," Graham explained. "We're trying to get her down."

"Jesus Christ!" another policeman exclaimed. "Does that guy know what he's doing?"

"Yes, he knows what he's doing," Graham said. "Just leave him alone."

Emma heard a motor whir to life. "Stay calm and don't move," Flynn yelled. "Here we go."

Emma held her breath and all at once felt herself

descending toward the ground. Tears of joy filled her eyes. Maybe she wasn't going to die after all!

"She's coming down!" a jubilant Kathy screamed. "He's bringing her down!"

Slowly and steadily, down she came. The journey seemed to last for an eternity.

"You're halfway there!" Graham shouted. "Hang on, kiddo. You're doing great!"

Emma didn't feel so great. Even though she was now only ten stories above the ground, she was still in an extremely precarious position and both falling and dying of fright seemed like real possibilities.

"Another fifty feet and you're home free!" Graham said encouragingly.

Just then Emma felt another jolt at her back. Her harness had separated even more from the cable. She was still high enough to fall to her death. She bit at the tape and tried to scream but made no sound.

"Twenty-five more feet," Graham called out the remaining altitude.

Emma's harness ripped again. She sent a silent entreaty out to Flynn: Please hurry. I can't last much longer.

Then she felt the most wonderful sensation in the world: many hands on her legs. And then she was on the ground and Kathy was hugging her and Graham and the policemen were cutting off the tape and removing her makeshift harness.

"Are you all right?" Kathy asked anxiously.

Emma nodded and croaked out a response. "I'm fine now, thanks to all of you."

"This rope had been cut, and it was just about ready to let go," one of the policemen said as Emma pulled her hands free of her bonds. "I don't think it would have held up for another minute. You are one very lucky lady."

Graham gently ran his fingers over Emma's bruised neck. "Does it hurt when you swallow?" he asked.

"It's not too bad."

"Maybe you should go to the emergency room to be checked out," Graham suggested.

Emma shook her head. "I'll be okay once I stop shaking."

"Emma!" Flynn jumped the last few feet off the crane rigging and ran over to embrace her. "I was so worried about you." He kissed her, then nuzzled his face in her hair. "As soon as I got to the zoo gala and saw you weren't there, I knew you must be in trouble. We headed down to the morgue right away and when we couldn't get in, we called the police and came here looking for you. I don't know what I would have done if we hadn't found you in time."

"But you did find me," Emma said, beaming.

"Could you tell us what happened here, ma'am?" one of the policeman asked. "Do you know who did this to you?"

Emma nodded. "I certainly do. It was Louis Brisbane, a senior partner at Franklin and Holland, and Tommy Corona, the general contractor on this construction project."

"Do you have any idea where they are now?" the policeman asked.

"I'm not sure," Emma said. "But Corona drives a black Cadillac SUV."

"We'll put out an APB," the policeman said. "They won't get far."

Just then a white stretch limousine pulled up next to the squad cars. Its rear bumper sported a "Just Married" sign. The driver's door opened and a short, bespectacled man with dark curly hair got out. "Miss Kathy!" he called. "I'm here."

"Who's that?" Graham asked.

"Lenny Berkowitz," Kathy replied. "We sometimes use his company's services at the store. You know how some of those society dames are. They wouldn't be caught dead on public transit, so we have to call people like Lenny to haul them around."

"What's he doing here?" Graham asked, bewildered.

"Ah—" Kathy stammered, thinking fast. "Well, you see, I thought it would be a nice treat to give Emma and Flynn a surprise limo ride to the gala. And then when Flynn was delayed, I had to call Lenny to tell him we wouldn't need him until later, and then when we all headed down here I decided, why not have him come here and pick Flynn and Emma up? After Flynn had rescued Emma, of course."

Graham gave Kathy a perplexed look, then he and Flynn walked over to talk to one of the policemen.

Lenny came trotting up. "I got here as soon as I could, Miss Kathy," he said. "I just finished taking a bridal couple to O'Hare."

"That's great, Lenny," Kathy praised. "You certainly made good time. I called you only fifteen minutes ago."

Emma tapped Kathy on the arm. "I thought you said you had him lined up to take Flynn and me to the gala."

"Shhh!" Kathy scolded. "That story was for Graham's benefit. I didn't think of calling Lenny until we got down here, but I didn't want Graham to know that I've got a limo driver on speed dial."

Emma laughed. "You're a good friend."

"Nothing but the best for you," Kathy said, hugging her.

One of the policemen walked over to Emma. "We're going to need you to come to the station and give a formal statement, ma'am," he said politely.

"Does she have to ride in a squad car?" Kathy asked. "Would it be all right if she came to the station in the limo?"

The policeman looked from Kathy to Emma to Lenny and back again. "It's a bit irregular, but I guess it'd be okay."

"Great!" Kathy said, as Flynn and Graham walked back over. Kathy patted Flynn's and Emma's arms and motioned toward the limo. "You kids go with Lenny."

"Aren't you and Graham going to join us?" Flynn asked.

"Oh, no," Kathy demurred. "Limos are so pretentious."

"Oh, come on with us," Emma said.

Graham put his arm around Kathy. "I think this occasion calls for a little over-the-top pampering for all of us," he said. "Let's go with them."

"Well, okay," Kathy said. "I guess just this once."

Emma and Flynn looked at each other and started to laugh.

EPILOGUE

The following day, Emma and Flynn had brunch at the Omni Hotel.

Brisbane and Corona were in the Cook County jail, having been arrested within an hour after Emma's dramatic rescue. Franklin & Holland had placed Brisbane on unpaid administrative leave. He had hired one of the city's top criminal defense attorneys and refused to make a statement to police.

With his prior criminal record, Tommy Corona was much less reticent about speaking to the authorities. Hoping to get a break in return for his cooperation, he had spilled his guts in a lengthy interview.

According to Corona, Brisbane had made a great deal of money over the years manipulating property into various shady investment ventures. Knowing that Oak Greythorne's apartment building was in a location primed for a major upscale development, Brisbane had thought it would be child's play to convince his old friend to sell the building for a song.

Unfortunately for him, Brisbane had not reckoned on the fact that, for the first time in his life, Oak was finally able to maintain his sobriety. A clean and sober Oak Greythorne spurned Brisbane's offer and bluntly told his erstwhile friend to take a hike.

Brisbane had never been one to admit defeat, so Oak's refusal to sell spurred the senior partner into action. He tried to browbeat Oak into changing his mind, but all he succeeded in doing was further alienating his old classmate. Things came to a head in late April when Brisbane and Corona paid Oak a visit. Oak happened to be outside when the two henchmen pulled up and a loud public exchange, which had been overheard by Lucille Adina, ensued.

A few days later, Brisbane returned to Oak's apartment, ostensibly to make amends. He was the picture of contrition and friendship. He started talking about old times.

Oak had always been an emotional man and before long the reminiscences had caused him to become almost maudlin. Brisbane suggested they have a drink for old time's sake. Oak protested that he had no liquor in the apartment. No problem. Brisbane just happened to have several bottles in the car. He went to get them. The men started to drink.

Oak tried to protest that he didn't want any more to drink but Brisbane kept insisting. Just one more drink between friends. Soon Oak was suffering a full-scale panic attack. Brisbane came to the rescue and retrieved Oak's pills. More liquor and more pills followed. Before long, Louis Brisbane's lifelong rivalry with Oak Greythorne was finally over.

"Would you like dessert or coffee?" Flynn asked.

Emma shook her head. "I'm stuffed," she said. "Besides, I told Lee Hennick we'd meet him at one o'clock. We don't want to be late."

"Are you sure you want to do this?" Flynn asked. "You've had more than your share of excitement lately. This might be a little too much. You have every right to take it easy for a while."

"I'm ready." Emma looked across the table at Flynn and smiled. "I am going to ride on the Ferris wheel at Navy Pier with you and Lee Hennick. And believe me, I've been waiting a very long time for that ride."

New York Times Bestselling Author

JOHN MARTEL

BILLY STROBE   0-451-20668-1
Billy Strobe had always dreamed of becoming a lawyer like
his father, the best criminal defense attorney in Oklahoma,
until alcoholism, allegations of fraud, and a suicide on the
eve of his imprisonment ended Joe Strobe's life. But not
Billy's dream. Haunted by his belief in his father's
innocence, Billy is determined to become a lawyer, to
uncover the truth, and to clear his father's name.

THE ALTERNATE   0-451-19996-0
Elliot Ashford, a millionaire congressman, is forced to
resign because of a sex scandal. When he's charged with the
brutal murder of his wife, Lara, assistant district
attorney Grace Harris seems to have everything she needs to
make a strong case for the prosecution. She also has
ambitions that could propel her career up several notches.

CONFLICTS OF INTEREST   0-451-41040-8
Seth Cameron thinks he's finally made it when he joins the
prestigious firm of Miller and McGrath. But when he's
thrown a hopeless case against a military contractor, he
realizes too late that he's been set up to fall hard. Now Seth
takes on his old firm—and uncovers a conspiracy that may
not only end his career, but his life.

To Order Call: 1-800-788-6262